# PEN NAME
# TRISTAN HUNTER

## PARADISI EXODUS SERIES

Sideris Gate, Book 1

Janua Mutiny, Book 2

## SHORT STORIES

The Fall of Seren

PlanetFall

# PEN NAME
# CHERI LASOTA

## IMMORTAL CODEX SERIES

Petra, Book 1

Leander, Book 2

## STANDALONE NOVELS

Artemis Rising

Echoes in the Glass

# SIDERIS GATE

## PARADISI EXODUS

## BOOK 1

## TRISTAN HUNTER

Ad Astra Press
TristanHunter.com

To book the author for engagements or gain permission for reprints and excerpts, contact: Tristan Hunter at tristan@tristanhunter.com.

ISBN-13: 978-0985146344

# SIC ITUR AD ASTRA

## "Thus, you shall go to the stars"

In the last decades of the twenty-first century, ten founding families seeking to escape an increasingly apocalyptic Earth focused their attention on constructing spaceships that would allow a select few to leave Earth and colonize the planet New Eden in the Paradisi System of Andromeda galaxy.

In 2035, these Founders commissioned Reach Corp to design and build the near-Earth infrastructure required to meet their ambitious goals. Reach Corp agreed with one critical condition: upon the stipulation that they successfully retrofitted the original prototype ship, the Asteria-class SS *Challenge*, they would have full authorization to follow the Founding Families to the Paradisi System and settle peaceably in New Eden.

—*Preface*
*The Interstellar Histories, Volume 1*
*The Paradisi Missions, 2025 to 2094*

# THE BETRAYAL

## Earth, 2094
### Lifter 2, Solix Sky Space Elevator

Today equatorial Earth shone out against the abyss of the cosmos, its blues and greens almost the picture of paradise from this distance. Almost.

As the lifter rose up through the 30,000-kilometer mark toward the Solix Sky Elevator's Docking Station, Solomon Reach's gaze drifted down through the viewing panel beneath his feet for the first time in a long time. It wasn't his custom to think about what was happening down on Earth. He was one of the few living in space who kept his eyes on the stars.

In the last few weeks before launch, almost everyone else, including his Reach Corp crew, focused their attention on what and whom they were leaving behind. Crews gathered to view the planet below, anxious to memorize the shapes of the continents, the vastness of the oceans, and the whorl of storm clouds—signature markings of the only home they'd ever known.

Each vertical kilometer took the elevator's lifter further from Earth and closer toward their final destination: New Eden, Paradisi System, Andromeda galaxy. Earth had been their Eden once. Long before the threat of nuclear war, before the terrorists controlled the world's borders, before the storm of 2093 destroyed much of the food supply. He barely remembered the feel of real earth. It had been years since he had felt blades of grass between his toes. But he no longer cared. Always on his mind was the future he had built and the new world that lay ahead.

One hundred thousand Founders had already left on the ten other Asteria-class spaceships Reach Corp had designed for them. They would have landed on New Eden by now. Thus far there had been no communication from any of them. Of the ten thousand crew and passengers yet to leave on the eleventh and final ship, the SS *Challenge,* most worried that the Founder ships had met with disaster or failed to make it through the Sideris Gate or the wormhole itself. Solomon was not among them. He felt certain now that the Founding Families simply did not care whether the final ship arrived in the Paradisi System at all.

Five thousand of those waiting to take the ship to the Paradisi System were Solomon's Reachers, what he called his Reach Corp crewmembers and their children. When Solomon's father had led Reach Corp, he signed a contract with the Founding Families, the pillars of Earth's elite and the group who had secretly launched the Paradisi Mission back in 2025. Their deal was simple: Reach Corp would build the three space elevators, space stations, and ten ships needed to launch the requisite number of humans to populate the new planet.

Yet, no matter how often his Reachers—highly skilled astrophysicists, engineers, doctors, and biologists the lot of them—had proven their worth during the design, construction, and management phases of the project, the Founder crews had still considered Reachers to be of a lower class. While he tried to minimize this prejudice among his crew whenever possible, he couldn't help but lump the remaining non-Reacher crews on Nautilus-11 Space Station and the SS *Challenge* in with the original Founding Families in his mind. When he called them Founders, it was not a compliment. Solomon smiled grimly. Even the promise of a new beginning on New Eden wouldn't be able to eliminate the human need to segregate. Some things would never change.

Solomon had often wondered what the natives on the new planet would make of these human aliens arriving in droves. He didn't have to wonder if the natives would end up hating the Founders . . . for him, it was an inevitable outcome; humans didn't have what he would call a stellar track record when it came to colonization.

He pressed his hand to the sun-warmed radiation-shielded glass beside him, the black of his skin a sharp contrast to the world's vast oceans below. Pale blue dot, indeed. The rise toward weightlessness was a strange contrast to the gravity of his thoughts. Ignoring the buzz of his crew's conversation around him and the hum and click of the lifter rolling up its carbon nanotube ribbon, Solomon took a final moment to say goodbye to his younger sister, Nisolda.

He figured she had died already, likely by way of disaster, starvation, or bomb. Or maybe the rare mitochondrial disease ravaging her body had finally taken her at last. It was easier to think of her that way. Easier to leave the dead than abandon the living. But the moment his mind flashed back to his last sight of her lying in that sterile sick bed, he had to turn away from Earth—and her.

He glanced instead at the elevation monitor above

him. Just passing 30,100 vertical kilometers. In three days, this bedeviled planet would be a distant memory, a mere speck of light in another galaxy. Even after his fifteen years of hard work on the Paradisi Mission, the thought seemed ludicrous, like the dreams he used to have as a boy, when the constellations came to life and had sword fights across the night sky.

"Sir, can you tell me our ETA?"

Startled, Solomon looked over to see a pale, dark-haired girl who couldn't have been more than seventeen years old. He was surprised she was by herself. Most of the crowd had already left the lounge compartment and headed off to find dinner. He was even more surprised a passenger was aboard the lifter at all. All passengers leaving for New Eden should have been strapped into their cryo beds aboard the SS *Challenge* by now. He glanced down at the UiComm read out at his wrist: May 3, 2094 17:34.

"About two hours or so," Solomon said. "You can see there through the fenestella"—he pointed up through the viewing portal at the massive docking station looming large above them—"that we've just about made it to Solix Sky Station."

"Oh, okay. Thank you."

"I don't think I've seen you before. You're not a Reacher's child, are you?"

"Yes. Well, no." A momentary blush bloomed on her thin cheeks. "He's my uncle, really. Dugal Colgan."

"Ah, Colgan. Of course. He's one of my most brilliant bioengineers. He brought the biome labs online aboard the SS *Challenge* back in '92. His niece, you say? Why aren't you already aboard the ship and in your cryo bed?"

"I'm not going to New Eden. I guess Uncle D called me up to say a final goodbye or something. He didn't tell me the details."

Solomon frowned. He knew her uncle well. He

was an honest, hardworking man. But a Reacher child he'd never heard of traveling out to Nautilus-11 just before launch? Something didn't smell right.

"Do you mind if I see your spacepass?"

The girl seemed wary, and as she held out her wrist so he could check her credentials and ticket, her hand shook.

He scanned her wrist comm device.

FORENAME: NEYVE

SURNAME: COLGAN

CLEARED: SOLIX LIFTPORT, SOLIX SKY
DOCKING STATION, NAUTILUS-11 SPACE STA-
TION

She was certainly related to Colgan, as he had no other Reacher crewmember with that name. And her spacepass looked legitimate. With his thumb, he scrolled down to the most important bit of information.

REASON FOR TRAVEL: 1-DAY BEREAVEMENT
PASS. UNAUTHORIZED FOR TRANSPORT: SS
CHALLENGE.

"Ah, I see," he said, trying to soften his voice. "I understand you've lost a family member."

She seemed confused at first, but then she nodded. "I suppose that's why he'd like me to come up to see him. He's my last relative."

Solomon was surprised she didn't elaborate. But what did he know of teen girls? He supposed he might look a bit intimidating in his red Reacher uniform and aviator cap. He cleared her height by a foot and outweighed her by a hundred pounds. Frankly, he put most men in a state of defense just by entering a room.

"I completely understand." Solomon smiled at her, a poor attempt at putting her at ease. "I'm sure Colgan will be glad to see you one last time. I'm sorry for your loss."

"Thank you," she said, moving off to peer out the opposite window near where Solomon's most loyal crewmembers were discussing the finer points of sex in micro-G.

"It's all about the angle of approach, really," Propulsion Lead Kasen Vokos said, illustrating with his hands in classic Greek fashion. Drive Ops Chief Vida Rosado merely punched him in the arm and laughed. Kasen was always trying to get a rise out of his Argentinian girlfriend. She was so used to him—and all the other brilliant but socially awkward men in the Reacher crew—that, as ever, she remained unfazed.

"You're hopeless. Everyone knows it's all about how well you're strapped into the sex machine," she retorted in a level voice, though her vixen-brown eyes sparkled suggestively.

Flight Engineer Exley Brooker hovered at the edge of their conversation looking decidedly uncomfortable. The man was nearing the edge of acceptable age in the program and had just made the cut. Knowing he'd lucked out, he worked twice as hard as anyone else. He was also still the epitome of a Southern gentleman.

Vida must have noticed Brooker's reaction, because she changed topics almost immediately. "Brooker, what are you going to miss most?"

"About Earth, you mean?"

"Of course," Kasen said, raising his hands up in mock exasperation. "What else?"

"Hmm . . ." Brooker steepled his forefingers at his lips and stared off toward Earth. "I really don't know yet. Too soon to tell."

"If you had to guess?" Kasen pressed.

"I suppose I'll eventually start missing Cross Creek."

"Cross what?" Kasen asked, crinkling his wide

swath of dark brows.

"Oh, it's a little old creek by my granddaddy's place down in Florida. He used to take me fishing out back when I was a kid. Catfish mostly. We'd have fish fries with the whole family every Friday." Brooker licked his lips unconsciously. "And hush puppies," he drawled out in his deep Southern accent.

"Your family make it out in time?" Kasen asked.

"God, no. Hurricane of '76 took them all out."

The smiles and laughter left the group at the sobering reminder of life on the ground.

"We're sorry to hear it," Vida whispered for them all.

"Yeah, well, we all lost somebody in the flooding. I am starting to forget their faces, which is just as well, I suppose. Except granddaddy. He had a face only a momma could love." Brooker's brilliantly white teeth peeked out through his black skin as his mind ambled through some ancient memory.

"What about you, Vida?" Kasen asked. "Though, I think I can guess."

"Yes, I think you probably could. Obvious, really. I'll miss Argentina in general, but my mother especially. Yes, and—oh, the nightclubs in Buenos Aires. I used to dance the tango, you know." Vida shimmied around Brooker with a couple of dance moves, which brought a smile of embarrassment to his face.

Her toothy grin would have made any man pull her into a dance spin, and Kasen took up the call, though a little slowly due to the lessening gravity. She laughed at him as he dropped her into a dip. When he raised her up again, she erupted in a laughing fit that made her straight brown hair wave about beneath her red cloche hat.

"That was back before you turned me into a little Greek girl, Mr. Vokos."

"Oh, you know you love my mother's moussaka."

"Which I haven't had the chance to eat in years." Vida glanced up and saw Solomon eying the conversation. "Come on over, Sol. You haven't told us what you'll miss."

With a half-smile, Solomon stepped over to join them. His thoughts wouldn't settle on any one thing. A multitude of pictures flitted through his mind like a movie. Finally, it stopped on that same image of his sister lying still and silent in her sick bed. He shook his head.

"Can't really say."

"Surely something from back home," Brooker ventured. "Didn't you live in the South at one point too?"

"I lived all over. Mostly up and down the East Coast to whatever schools the authorities wanted me to go to: a quick stint at Berkeley before the quake of '72, and then on to Cambridge, Georgia Tech, and MIT."

"Hadn't realized," Brooker said. "They were grooming you a long time, then? Took your aptitude tests early as well, I'm guessin'."

Solomon nodded. "Seven years old when my father brought me down to the ground and dumped me into the fast-track system. Eventually Mads Graversen found me and the rest is history."

"Come on now. There must be something," Vida pressed Solomon, though her gaze shifted slightly to a spot just beyond him. She must have gotten a Ui message.

They all waited as she read her message via her Ueyes HUD. Her expression changed so suddenly that it twisted her usually stunning brown eyes and easy smile into cold lines.

This didn't bode well at all.

"Report, Vida," Solomon demanded immediately after she shifted her gaze back to him.

She ignored him, glancing at Kasen instead. She whispered to him as she relaxed her expression. He raised an eyebrow, but moved to the lounge's comm unit and pressed in a code.

"Vida?" Solomon said.

She smiled and shook her head while keeping her gaze locked on Kasen. When he glanced back at her and nodded, she turned her attention back to Solomon.

"I've asked Kasen to disable the comms." She glanced around nonchalantly to see if anyone was nearby.

Solomon did the same. The only person close enough was the girl who had approached him earlier, Neyve Colgan, but she seemed sufficiently occupied with her own thoughts.

"What's the news?" Brooker asked.

"Tavian Hunt just sent me an encrypted message."

Definitely didn't bode well. Tav worked as Vida's right-hand man as Drive Ops Specialist in the SS *Challenge*'s Propulsion Sector, and more specifically, the Cavitran Drive that ensured they'd escape this disastrous planet for good. An irreparable problem with the Cav Drive would be catastrophic for the 10,000 souls aboard the ship.

Solomon massaged the pressure points on the back of his neck with both hands. "Is the SS *Challenge*'s Cav Drive down?" he asked her.

Vida gave him a strange look that morphed from worry to triumph in a matter of an instant.

"Well, no, not yet. It will be soon. But that's the good news."

Solomon raised an eyebrow but waited.

"Out with it, Vida," Kasen pressed.

"Just start from the beginning," Solomon said.

"Yes, better to start there." Vida reverted back into her usual serious tones. "Yesterday Tav heard a rumor that Challenge Command has been bringing people up in the Tolux Sky Elevator lifters at a steady clip for about three weeks."

"Did he say who they are? I've heard rumors about increased spacecraft activity between the Tolux Sky Elevator and Nautilus-11 in the last couple of weeks. I assumed it was Founder business. I wondered about it but—" Solomon frowned.

The look on Vida's face told him everything.

"They're planning to sneak those people aboard the *Challenge?*"

"It's worse. Challenge Command is going to kick us off the ship altogether and give our cryo beds— and our ticket to New Eden—to these people. "

"What the actual fuck?" Kasen blurted out, slicing his hand through the air with the severity of a guillotine.

"Tavian has to be mistaken," Solomon said. "Where is he now?"

"Tav's back on the SS *Challenge* at the moment, but he investigated around the space station earlier today and saw them himself. Hidden in the Serica Sector on Nautilus-11. He heard one of the Founder crew call them the Serica group. Solomon . . ."—Vida touched his arm and the look in her eyes said it all—"Tav said he saw thousands of them."

"Damn." Solomon pressed his thumb and forefinger into his eyelids, trying to focus.

What the hell were the Founders thinking? Reach Corp had constructed these ships for them over the course of decades. They had worked far beyond everything they were contractually obligated to do. The Reachers had earned their tickets aboard the last ship to leave Earth. No one had earned it more.

"Solomon, this could be disastrous for the Reachers," Vida said.

He felt his fists tightening involuntarily, but he

crossed his arms instead.

"We'll follow your lead, sir," Brooker said, his gaze steady and clear.

Solomon nodded and swept his gaze over them all. "So the Founders—or at least members of Challenge Command—have betrayed us."

"Or Nautilus Command, even?" Vida said. "They could have jointly planned this coup."

"Does it even matter?" Brooker said. "When all is said and done, Solix Sky and Nautilus-11 command crews will be incorporated into the Challenge Command group once the ship launches."

"We'll mutiny before they get away with this," Kasen spat out as he paced around them.

Solomon shook his head at Kasen and motioned all of them to move away from the girl, Neyve, who now seemed to be hovering nearby. The last thing they needed was to have this news spread. An actual mutiny would get people killed.

"Vida, did Tavian say anything about how they planned to get us off the ship?" Solomon asked.

"Tav didn't say, but they'll have a plan. Most likely a ruse. They know we wouldn't go willingly."

"But I can't imagine they'd kick us all out," Solomon countered. "They need key Reacher crew to run and repair systems. Two thousand Reachers alone have been tagged to work on the watch crews during the gatejump to Paradisi. Unless that was also a lie."

"They're training *Challenge* crew in secret, I suppose?" Brooker said.

"Could be. But that would have taken them months if not years in the planning," Solomon said. "Which would mean the betrayal goes all the way back to our original contract with the Founding Families."

"That's the most critical question," Vida asked. "Did they always plan to boot us off, or is this a new directive from Challenge Command?"

"Or the Joint Command Board of Directors?" Kasen piped in.

"Yes, and maybe they were paid off by these people, whoever they are," Brooker added.

"Possibly," Solomon said. "But with what currency? Earth money will be irrelevant on New Eden."

"Those bastards must have something Command wants," Kasen said.

Solomon ran a hand down his face, thinking. "Well, practically everyone in the world now knows that the Paradisi Project's pretended mission to Mars was a lie. We've already got terrorists circling our elevator liftports looking for a way on, so maybe a collection of rich or powerful people could have made the Founders an offer they couldn't refuse. Which sector did you say they were in, Vida? Northern Light?"

"No, Serica Sector."

"That makes sense. It's the closest to Challenge Sector, giving them easy access for boarding."

"It doesn't matter." Vida touched Kasen's shoulder, as her eyes brightened. "I've got a plan."

Solomon raised an eyebrow. "The drive?"

"Yes. The Cav can be disabled to buy us some time." Solomon frowned. "How?"

"Don't ask. Plausible deniability is a priceless commodity," Vida said, a grim smile darkening her expression. "All you need to know is that I'll have Tavian Hunt take care of it, since he's already aboard the SS *Challenge*. In fact, I'll Ui him now."

She set about multitasking as Solomon raised an eyebrow at that. "Disabling the drive would buy us time," he conceded. "But to what end?"

"So you can come up with a brilliant plan to save us all," she said, not looking up from her UiComm.

"Ah," was all he could muster.

Kasen touched Vida's arm. "Keep in mind, Command will know almost immediately, since they've been monitoring the drive tests for the last couple of days."

"I know, Kasen. But it can't be helped at this point."

Solomon had no idea what to do. If he told his Reacher crew about the betrayal, they would inevitably fight back. In all truth, it's what he wanted to do right now. Or at least punch a wall. But Vida, Kasen, and Brooker were staring at him, waiting for their fearless leader to step up. He glanced at the girl, Neyve, who was eyeing him from her perch near the fenestella. Her wide eyes stared at him without blinking as the setting sun haloed around her shadowed form.

"Tell us what more we can do and we'll do it," Vida said, glancing up, her voice back to its sweeter Argentinian lilt.

It pulled his gaze back to her. "I'll give it some thought," he said. "But ensure that Tavian doesn't even tell you where he hid the part and plans."

"Why?"

"In case you're also . . . detained."

Vida nodded, showing no sign of fear. "And in the meantime, you'll be . . .?"

"Coming up with a brilliant plan to save five thousand of my crew and their children from certain death," Solomon finished.

"No problem," Kasen said with supreme confidence, slapping him on the back.

"Yes," Solomon said, though his voice trailed off as he glanced toward Earth below. "No problem at all."

# THE SABOTAGE

Solomon nudged his boot further under a foothold and pressed his hand against the viewing portal as Lifter 2 rose up the final meters to its Solix Sky Station docking hatch. Beyond the hum and click caused by the lifter's wheels rolling up the ribbon and the voices of the hundreds of crewmembers around him waiting to disembark, Solomon felt the jolt and shudder of connection beneath his hands as the lifter's hatch sealed with the docking module above.

Strange to think this would be his last ride up. Solomon glanced around, taking in his surroundings. This level was the topmost of ten decks on the lifter. Most of the other levels were sleeping quarters for crew and passengers as well as a smaller number of eating establishments, viewing rooms, and engineering/lab compartments. On this last ride, only a small fraction of the usual capacity of 5,000 people was filled. Almost everyone was already aboard the SS *Challenge* or Nautilus-11 Space Station.

Everyone waited to disembark in the famous— or rather infamous—Orbital Lounge, which put most mile-high clubs to shame. The bathrooms and darkened corners of the bar were legendary. Not that he'd know anything about that. He was too high in the food chain to ethically date anyone on his own crew and too low class to turn any Founder women's heads. Besides that, he was just too damn busy to think about it most days. He caught them staring at him from time to time, though. His mixed English and African-American race left him with sharp, ice blue eyes, which seemed to surprise everyone he met.

The lounge was rather quirky, with boxy Earth-viewing drinking rooms, complete with tiny couches sporting footholds and tiny but heavily shielded portholes for those wanting a last long look at Earth while getting righteously sloshed in the process. A beautiful thing, really. The planet-themed décor had fallen into somewhat of a shambles with half the patches featuring the different solar system planets having been ripped off the bar seats by souvenir thieves, and old beer bags littering the air above the bar. Solomon didn't blame the bartenders and janitors. This place would be abandoned in a few days. No point in tidying up.

A message popped up in Solomon's UiComm HUD, which connected contacts in his eyes to a peripheral display of information on both his internal processes and the surgically implanted communications chip behind his left ear. It was an older technology than the top-of-the-line comms that the Founder crews used, but it also helped to keep Reacher internal communications more private.

He scanned quickly.

"OPEN MESSAGE."

The message appeared to be from Mads Graversen. Not good. He scanned it quickly.

3 MAY, 2094 20:23:02

MADS GRAVERSEN, SOLIX LIFTPORT DIRECTOR

I'VE JUST HEARD FROM PROPULSION THERE IS
A PROBLEM WITH THE CAV. CAN YOU CON-
FIRM? HAS REACH CORP PERFORMED UN-
SCHEDULED MAINTENANCE? RESPOND ASAP.
I WILL MEET YOU AT THE DOCKING MODULE.

Damn. Solomon was hoping for a little more time to prepare for the inevitable encounter with his old mentor from MIT. Or was he now Solomon's enemy? He needed to figure out how to squeeze Graversen for information while keeping his mouth shut about everything else.

Turning to his fidgeting crew, Solomon eyed them all in turn. Vida was tucking her floating hair further back into her synthetic leather cap while ignoring the ogling Founder men jostling around her. Brooker took to running a hand repeatedly down his face, compelling Solomon to wonder if he'd had enough coffee today. Kasen, as ever, looked ready for a fight.

"Everyone clear on the plan?" They each gave him a resolute nod. "Let's run it one more time."

Kasen spoke up first. "After arriving on Nautilus, I'll make my way to the Challenge Sector to monitor the docking module. If I see any Reachers attempting to leave the ship, I'll redirect them. I'll regroup and debrief with you on Nautilus unless I hear otherwise from you."

Solomon nodded once and then focused his attention on Vida.

"I'll move straight toward the Serica docking module after we arrive on Nautilus, taking care to remain unnoticed. If questioned, I'll say I've been cooped up on Trafero 2 all night and wanted a stretch. I'll access Maintenance Compartment 5A and work to disable and lock the main entrance to the Serica Sector."

"And if Graversen finds you?"

"I'll let him know I was picking up my favorite tool from my buddy in Serica maintenance so I can start tinkering with the Cav Drive."

"Brooker?" Solomon asked.

"I'll start rumoring an airlock leak on the SS *Challenge*'s Engineering Sector mid-ship so as to cause confusion and distract Command away from our movements."

"One other thing," Solomon added, "and this is critical. I want you to switch on the global Ui tracking system, figure out which Reachers are not aboard the *Challenge*, and via encrypted Ui tell the stragglers to report immediately to . . . Watch Deck 16, I think, since there's no exit on that level. It will be harder for them to round up the Reachers and cart them off the ship from there. Do *not* issue a company-wide message. Too easy for Challenge Security to track that kind of system traffic. And this goes for all of you: send only encrypted messages from here on out, and even then, keep the chatter to a minimum."

Brooker nodded. "Anything else?"

"Yes, message me—no Vida, as I may be detained—the moment you hear the last Reacher is aboard." With that thought, Solomon realized he had an ace up his sleeve that he'd completely forgotten about. He began sifting through the code database in his Ui while they talked. This was definitely going to buy them some more time.

"Will do."

"And you?" Vida said, turning to Solomon.

His smile was grim. "I've just had a Ui from Mads Graversen."

"He went up in Lifter 1 ahead of us, right?" Brooker asked.

"Yes, along with the rest of Challenge Command and the board members," Solomon said. "I plan to question Graversen about what's going on in Serica Sector."

"No, he'll find out what we're up to, Sol," Vida said, her soft voice tinged with sharper notes. "That man is too perceptive."

"Agreed. But we need more information. And they may know already what we're up to. Tavian Hunt's earlier message wasn't encrypted." Solomon found the restricted code he was looking for and changed it to something a bit more memorable. He couldn't seem to wipe the smirk off his face as he glanced up at the sound of Vida's laugh. If he could pull this off, all of his Reachers would be safely aboard the SS *Challenge*.

"Want me to give Mads a little Argentinian charm?" Vida ran a hand down Kasen's arm and winked at him suggestively.

"He does seem to have a thing for you, Vida," Brooker noted.

"He what?" Kasen said, his eyes darting around as if he'd challenge Mads to a duel if he could only find him in the pressing crowd. Vida gave him a disarming smile, distracting Kasen from his sudden bloodlust.

The opening of the lifter's docking hatch in the ceiling above provided another distraction. On Solix Sky, crew took precedence over passengers in the line up, so Solomon and his crew were the first to begin disembarking, which was always a surreal experience. The sight of hundreds of people lifting off the floor and rising up through the docking hatch always reminded Solomon of a flutter of butterflies taking flight.

Today, however, Solomon had no time to marvel at the strangeness of it. He shoved off the deck floor toward the hatch. It was always a bit awkward to return to weightlessness again. The dread of what lay ahead mixed with the lightness of his body, and it all settled uncomfortably in the pit of his queasy stomach.

He had lived on Nautilus-11 Space Station and the SS *Challenge* for years, but they both had artificial gravity generators, so the weightlessness on the Solix Sky Space Elevator was usually a pleasant change. It would take him only minutes to grow accustomed to micro-G again.

They hadn't been on the ground for overlong this time. Just a series of short meetings down at the Solix LiftPort to discuss the elevator's decommissioning and security protocols after the SS *Challenge*'s departure from the solar system. More and more terrorist groups were learning about the Founders' true mission and threatening to overrun Earth's three elevators near the Indonesian, Galapagos, and Maldive island chains.

The window for launch was short.

The majority of the cost involved in running the elevators was in security alone. No other ships had been authorized to leave Earth due to lack of funding for the four critical elements needed for deep space travel: a Cavitran Drive, a thorium reactor, an artificial gravity generator, and cryo capability. Anyone left on Earth had no hope of escape. What they did have was the promise of death, either by natural disaster or man-made weapons.

All of the bigwigs had been at the meetings: the Joint Command Board of Directors, Challenge Command, Janus Corp security personnel, and various other higher ups in the astrophysics and engineering departments aboard Solix Sky and Nautilus. The meetings had been tense, secretive, and to the point. Mads had been distracted and irritable during the meetings, which was unusual. Graversen had a calculating personality, and every issue brought to his attention would be weighed and measured with cold precision. When challenged, Mads would stare down his opponent with stone-grey eyes, demanding subordination through sheer force of will.

Solomon had known him a long time, and he knew the man's tactics. They were equals as far as intelligence and wits were concerned. But Solomon had just one question for his longtime friend: was he involved in this betrayal and, if so, why?

Solomon rose up through the lifter's hatch, and with his boot, he touched off the edge to launch himself through the long docking module, situated similarly to a NASA-style module, with white bulkheads, no viewing windows, and little in the way of the "welcome to space" atmosphere so prevalent elsewhere on Solix Sky.

Yet, the Solix Sky Docking Station itself more than made up for its lackluster first impression. The initial technological breakthrough on the Solix Sky's ribbon had been discovered by Alastair Johns, a genius revered among aerospace engineers and astrophysicists. He had also worked up the original drawings for the Solix Sky Space Elevator, though its final design had gone through many subsequent iterations. The station had retained much of Johns's eclectic design motifs, complete with his clean lines, heavy use of metals in the furnishings, and clever use of paneling to hide the equipment used to run the Solix. The same elements were mirrored in Nautilus's design, which gave it an uncluttered, uber-modern feel.

Yet Solomon saw beyond all this to the dying plants in the pots lining the main concourse bridging the two symmetrical sections of the station. He looked down at the worn synthetic wooden boards beneath him and at the marked up cement-like walls that rose up toward the Skyway Star Portals where he used to watch the constellations wheel by. But none of this really mattered. Solix Sky was just another element of a dying planet. And it was his job to get everyone out of here. Well, everyone but the hidden people in Serica Sector.

With that thought foremost in his mind, the first face Solomon noticed on the other side of the busy docking area's glass enclosure was Mads Graversen. As with all members of the Challenge, Solix and Nautilus Command groups, he wore the standard-issue black synth-leather uniform complete with its white patch signifying his director position. Two Founder guards flanked him. They had the look of serious bar bouncers itching for a face to punch. Mads himself zeroed his gaze—and his dour expression—on Solomon immediately. On the way through security—which for Solomon and his crewmates consisted of being waved through without so much as a ticket check—Solomon noticed a few of his other crewmembers going past.

"Franklin," he called out to the most responsible of the three. "Are there any other Reachers on the Solix currently?"

His swarthy lab tech Jeb Franklin glanced over and nodded. "Yes, sir. A few finishing up with some final materials experiments." Franklin floated over while Ginna and Raro waited in the expansive main throughway of the docking station.

"What can I do for you, sir?"

Solomon floated around so his back was turned to Mads. "I want you to round up anyone on Solix and get them on the next available transporter. Ensure all Reachers aboard Solix and Nautilus make their way to the SS *Challenge* ASAP. This is an order and it's urgent."

Franklin's eyebrows rose up to his hairline, but he nodded without a word and rejoined his companions.

Solomon swung around to face Mads, who looked suspicious of his exchange with Franklin. Couldn't be helped, though he should probably come up with a decent lie if Mads called him on it.

"Mads," Solomon said, lifting his chin once in acknowledgement.

"You got my message?" Mads said, his thick Danish accent slightly thicker with impatience.

"Yes, I had heard from Propulsion that something

was going haywire in the Cav, but I don't have any details."

Mads took a moment to gauge Solomon's response. From experience, Solomon knew he likely wouldn't be able to tell whether Mads thought he was lying. The man had an exceptional poker face.

"The *Challenge* Propulsion crew," Mads began, obviously making a clear distinction between the Reacher crew and the Founder crew in the Propulsion sector, "were running drive tests all day. The Cavitran suddenly halted in the middle of a run. They suspect sabotage." He left the comment open-ended with a subtle lilt at the end that turned it into a question.

Solomon did not break eye contact. "Why do they suspect sabotage?" He kept his voice even but inquisitive.

Mads narrowed his eyes slightly at Solomon, and then he shifted his gaze behind him to Kasen, who was about to head toward the transporter docking bays.

"Why did you disable the comms in the lifter's lounge, Vokos?" he asked Kasen.

"Sir?"

"You heard me the first time." Mads stared pointedly, waiting.

"We heard some unusual beeping sounds coming from the comm unit is all. It was getting annoying, so I disabled it. I plan to let maintenance know on my way over to the Trafero 2 docking bay."

There was a collective breath while they waited to see if Mads would buy this explanation. Mads blinked a few times while staring at Kasen and Solomon in turns. He gave nothing away.

"If it was sabotage, does Propulsion have any leads on a culprit?" Solomon asked Mads.

"Yes, you."

# THE TRAFERO

Mads nodded once to his guards, and they moved toward Solomon immediately.

Solomon never took his eyes off Mads's face. His expression, while unreadable as ever, took on a strange new light. It seemed to Solomon that he might feel a tinge of irritation at such a setback, which would indicate he had been involved in the betrayal. And now Mads suspected Solomon's involvement in the sabotage. Where did that leave their carefully laid plans now?

"Chief?" Vida called back to them when she caught sight of what was happening.

"Vida, it's all right," Solomon said, holding up his hand to her. "I will answer any questions you have, Mads. I have no reason to sabotage my only ticket off this planet!"

"Yes, you *will* answer our questions, Solomon," Mads said, and his hooded eyes betrayed nothing more.

"I'm sure it's just a glitch, sir," Vida started in, touching the bouncer's arm. "The Cav is my baby. No one can keep her purring like I can. I'll check her out when we get to Nautilus."

"Stay back, Ms. Rosado, or you'll find yourself in lockdown." The tone of Mads's voice demanded her obedience, and she immediately floated back away from the bouncer who was glaring at her. She must have realized if she pushed it, she'd end up in custody as well, which would destroy any chance she had to make it to the maintenance compartment to rig Serica Sector's locking system.

"Yes, please check with the Propulsion team when we get to Nautilus, Vida," Solomon said, reassuring her with a smile. "It's probably an easy fix. They could use your expertise."

"Certainly, sir." Vida moved further back and rejoined the others as they headed toward the Trafero 2 docking bay.

Solomon once again faced Mads. "What evidence has Propulsion found? And did they say whether this will likely delay our departure?"

"We'll discuss this with the other members of Challenge Command on the way to Nautilus," Mads said with his usual cold voice, motioning to his guards for them to proceed.

One of the bouncers tapped Solomon on the shoulder, which prompted him to start moving through the main concourse toward the docking bay sector. The crowd thinned out as they continued on. At this late stage, mostly Solix Sky crew and the occasional Founder were decommissioning equipment or handling maintenance tasks. Solomon didn't see a single civilian or Reacher crewmember, which was a good thing. No matter how this went down, he wanted to save as many as he could before it was all over.

As they passed the Arctic Plunge Lounge, Solomon saw absolutely no one, save for the barkeeper attempting to juggle some packaged drinks in his hands. It wasn't going well. One had hit the ceiling and was on its way back down and on target to smack him in the head. The deserted bar made the decor look even more surreal than usual. The lounge had an arctic theme, complete with synthetic polar bear furs, silver and blue bar stools, and a giant bar shaped like an iceberg. Beside it, the Jungle Burger Restaurant, complete with its garish decor and taxidermic tiger, looked similarly empty. Perhaps a mere thousand or so crew were still finishing things up aboard the elevator and space station before they all boarded the SS *Challenge* for the last time. Not long now. One way or the other, this would all be over soon.

He wondered if knowledge about the disabled Cav Drive had made its way out to the SS *Challenge* crews as yet. It was probably just a matter of time. Nothing stayed a secret for long in space.

The bouncers moved Solomon through the station's long concourse at a fair clip. When built, the station had been the cutting edge of design and appointments. Alistair Johns had modeled his breakthrough carbon nanotube design for the elevator's ribbon after a shell shape. He used the same fractal design for the Solix Sky Docking Station, which, when viewed from the outside, resembled two conch-shaped shells laid horizontally end-to-end. The west end housed living quarters, eateries, viewing modules, and laboratories while the east end contained Solix Sky Command offices, engineering, systems, crew quarters, lifter connectors, and transporter and cargo bays.

Mads stopped suddenly, noticing Neyve, Dugal Colgan's niece, as she maneuvered through the crowd in the direction of the docking bays.

"Wait here," Mads demanded, so the bouncers stopped Solomon's forward movement, and they waited while Mads cornered the girl. What he wanted of her Solomon had no idea. She was of no consequence to him. Then again, she had been in the lounge with them while they discussed their plans. Mads could have spotted her on the security cameras. The way he kept cutting off the girl's progress and questioning her didn't bode well. Solomon hoped she wouldn't spill any vital secrets. He had no idea how much she might have overheard.

Mads finally stalked back after he left the girl scurrying away. Solomon hoped she hadn't been traumatized too much. Mads wasn't known for his people skills. He wanted to question Mads about Neyve, but it was too risky. He might give something away; or worse, get the girl in trouble.

"Did you see which way Vida Rosado went?" Mads asked the bouncers when he took up the lead again in their merry party.

"Why?" Solomon blurted, which made him sound immediately suspicious to his own ears. Keep it cool, Reach, or you'll give the game away.

"She and the other two went on ahead toward the docking bays," Bouncer 1 said, shoving Solomon forward.

"When we get there, detain her after she boards," Mads said, not bothering to glance back.

"If you have an issue, Graversen, talk to me. Not my crew," Solomon said, straining to keep his voice as flat and emotionless as Graversen's maddening monotones.

"I am your manager, Solomon. I will talk to whomever I please."

Solomon started to respond with some strongly worded expletives but thought better of it. The more he protested the more Mads would suspect him. But how could he protect Vida while he was in custody? Surely they would just question her and nothing more?

When they approached the vast expanse of the transporter docking bay, Solomon studied the situation dispassionately. Traferos 1 and 2 were currently loading crew. Looks like they'd make the connection to Nautilus. He already knew Mads would choose Trafero 2, as it was the most luxuriously appointed crew transporter. Mads was never one to forego comfort. He had grown up a rich boy in Amsterdam, and his family was old money born out of an expertise in water management systems, hence the reason why he was slotted to manage the elevator's sea-level LiftPort. His arrogance about this fact was legendary on Solix Sky. Now that the elevator was being decommissioned, Mads would switch more fully into his newly appointed position in the Challenge Command group, joining Dickson Edge and Alexandra Justice.

Solomon glanced around, looking for any Reacher stragglers, but he didn't see any. He hoped Franklin, Raro, and Ginna were already aboard. The Trafero class transporters all had the look of a wolf's head to Solomon. Each Trafero was slate gray in color, though the underbelly gleamed nearly white. Two pinnacles rose up like wolf's ears, and the viewing module atop the flight deck resembled the wolf's eyes.

The passenger class transporters could haul 300 people and crew transports were able to comfortably take 500. Given their limited nuclear propulsion capabilities, the Founders only used the Traferos for travel to LEO, MEO, and GEO Earth orbits as well as the 24-hour haul to the Nautilus-11 Space Station at Earth-Moon Lagrange Point 1 or to the lunar elevator even further away. Occasionally, they were used to transport equipment and materials to asteroids orbiting the moon, but usually the larger Transfero-class cargo ships were put to good use in that endeavor.

Mads led them into the lift that would take them down to the loading deck. He said only one thing to Solomon on the short ride down.

"You will tell us what you know, Solomon. One way or the other."

Solomon did not reply. There was no need. He had no intention of revealing anything that would incriminate his crew. Solomon had taken over management of Reach Corp at his father's death in 2084. He had inherited 5,000 Reachers who were now fully under his care and command. Reach Corp's mission had always been clear: design, construct, and maintain the Nautilus-11 Space Station and its accompanying spaceship fleet. Their ultimate goal had always been to earn a ticket to ride to the new planet. And now the man who stood beside him threatened this decades-long objective.

All he really wanted to do was strangle this asshole. Times like these, he really wished he had the fighting blood of Kasen Vokos running through his veins. He practiced clenching his fists instead of looping his fingers around Graversen's neck.

Patience. Wait for the moment.

The lift's heavy doors opened, and the bouncers shoved Solomon toward the stair car. Workers milled about on the loading deck as the line of crew slowly moved toward Trafero 2's open hatch.

Once aboard, Solomon smiled at the attendant checking tickets and glanced around, looking for Vida and the others. The Trafero's interiors were much more in line with classic spacecraft design. Rather than the quirky mix of natural and industrial elements in the Solix Sky, the Trafero 2 was full of gunmetal grey bulkheads and seatbacks. Rows and rows of *Challenge* and Nautilus crewmembers stared at Solomon as they continued on. Chief Engineering Officer Solomon Reach of Reach Corp surrounded by Founder guards wasn't a usual occurrence aboard Solix Sky Station.

Solomon caught sight of his Reachers as he followed Mads toward the fore of the craft. They were already strapped in and awaiting take off. Solomon locked eyes with Vida. He gestured for her silence with his finger across his lips. Vida's resolve was evident in her unwavering gaze. She gave him a single nod even as Mads tilted his head in her direction.

Bouncer 2 immediately stood over her. "You are to come with us for questioning, Ms. Rosado."

With a single movement, Kasen was unbuckled, upright, and facing the bouncer with a glare of murder written in his eyes.

"Don't even think about it," Kasen said, voice raised. Everyone in the compartment turned to watch the exchange.

Vida unbuckled herself and lightly touched her boyfriend's arm, obviously realizing his blood would be coursing double-time through his veins right now. He was liable to do anything at this point. He didn't look at her; instead, he held the bouncer's gaze. Neither of them was backing down.

"Babe, it's nothing," Vida said in her most calming voice. "They just want some info on the Cav, eh? I'll be back before you know it. Isn't that right, Mads?" She leveled her gaze toward him and waited.

Mads raised a single eyebrow while his gaze, the wide plains of his face, and his perfectly stubbled jaw remained utterly motionless. Solomon would love to put this guy in an interrogation chair just to get some kind of emotion out of him. After what seemed like an eon had elapsed, Graversen gave a single nod and smartly didn't elaborate. Everyone knew you didn't rile up mad-dog Vokos without a damn good reason.

To his credit, Kasen attempted not to give the game away by turning away from Mads as he passed by them. But Kasen touched Vida's face and whispered softly to her before she moved into the aisle.

"Love you," Solomon saw her whisper back, and

when she glanced up at Solomon and moved in behind bouncer 2, the look of courage in her eyes made him wince with both fear and pride.

Bouncer 1 shoved Solomon along again. Once they moved into the less-trafficked forward section of the transporter, Mads glanced back at Vida.

"Vida Rosado, I'll speak with you first."

She met Solomon's gaze, lifting her chin in defiance of Mads. If he had been able, he would have told her everything would be all right. But somewhere in the center of his chest, fear was exploding. What if they did more than question her? Surely, they wouldn't go that far. Surely . . .

"It's fine, Vida. Just answer Graversen's questions on what you know about the Cav Drive situation. And remember to include info on drive test 24. That one was glitchy."

Mads merely heaved an irritable sigh and directed her to enter the nearest meeting room. She smiled at Solomon and then she was gone.

"James," Mads said to Bouncer 1, nodding toward the opposite direction. "Lock him in Stateroom 3. At 0600 tomorrow, bring him to Meeting Room Beta. Think it all over, Solomon. We have much to discuss before we arrive on Nautilus."

A bland "I'll see you in the morning" was all Solomon could muster. What he really wanted to do was open the Trafero's hatch and shove him out into the deep, black ocean of space. Solomon sighed instead, turning with Bouncer 1 toward the starboard staterooms. It was going to be a long night. Best he just eat something and get some sleep. He was going to need it tomorrow.

The guard waved him into the stateroom. "You'll be locked in here until approximately 0550, Chief Reach. Have a good night."

Solomon nodded as the guard closed the door in

his face. He thought it odd that the guard didn't take his UiComm, but then he realized it was purposefully done. They *wanted* him to attempt communication with anyone he might be working with. He endeavored not to use it until he could get to a tracking dampener aboard ship at the very least. If he ever made it to the *Challenge* . . . but he'd focus on that later.

First things first. The stateroom was quite tiny and its furnishings were understated but he had always found Trafero accommodations rather comfortable. The first item of business was to unpack the standard-issue sleeping bag and strap it to the wall near the fenestella, so he would drift off to sleep with a clear view of the stars.

Next he rummaged around in the food locker for a packaged dinner. He pulled out an apple juice, a water packet, and fried rice. While he worked to rehydrate the rice by pressing a bit of water into its package, he moved over to the fenestella. He spotted the Cassiopeia constellation immediately. A quick glance down to Earth showed him that night had fallen over much of South America. A massive anvil cloud hovered over Mexico, and lightning occasionally flashed within and around it. He hurriedly finished shaking the food package and settled himself by the portal to watch the storm. Space watching never got old.

When Solomon entered Meeting Room Beta the next morning, the rest of Challenge Command had already arrived. SS *Challenge* Commander Dicson Edge floated near the far bulkhead, arm braced against the window. Executive Officer Alexandra Justice's cold blue gaze locked on Solomon. Her arms were crossed, but he could see that the fingers grasp-ing her arm were turning white. He often saw her doing that. For the first time, it occurred to him that it probably calmed a constant anxiety she could never bear to show her colleagues.

At the sound of Mads clearing his throat, Edge made a glacially slow turn to face Solomon. They glared at each other, and after an interminable silence of staring at his mole-ridden face and acerbic eyes, two things became clear to Solomon: Edge believed he was the saboteur, and he was going to do every-thing in his power to get his own plan of betrayal back on track. Edge didn't have Mads's taciturn features—he was too mercurial to be that calm—and now Solo-mon was kicking himself that he hadn't uncovered this betrayal long before this moment.

"Did you betray us?" Edge asked him, his voice tinged with a strange sort of contempt. It couldn't have been shock, because he himself was guilty of be-trayal. No, it was a kind of twisted irritation at this minor setback. Dickson Edge was about to find out this development wasn't minor after all.

"No, I did not. Where is Vida Rosado?" Solomon directed that pointed question at Mads. He said noth-ing. "She is a member of my crew, and I have an obli-gation to look after her well-being."

"Rosado was belligerent and gave us no informa-tion," Edge said, his voice rising. "You need to teach your *crew* some respect."

"Where is she now?" While the commander's description of Vida didn't sound like her, he silently thanked her for her bravery.

"Back in the main compartment with the rest of your crew," Justice said irritably, though Mads flashed her the briefest frown of disapproval.

Ah, so that was meant to be a secret they'd use to their advantage during the proceedings. Reading between the lines, it sounded to him like Vida was safe—at least for now. Solomon offered nothing in response. He now knew they couldn't use Vida's safety as a trading card.

"Restrain him," Edge said to Bouncer 2.

"I don't need restraining. Ask your questions and I will answer."

Bouncer 2 waited for Edge to respond. When he nodded his assent for the bouncer to proceed, it pissed Solomon off immediately. Getting manhandled by what amounted to Graversen's bodyguards was not particularly high on his list of favorite things. Solomon pushed one of them away, and the guy grabbed hold of the table bolted to the floor before he hit the opposite bulkhead.

"Stop this, Solomon. You say you want to cooperate? Then do it."

Solomon scowled at him, which resulted in the second bouncer punching him in the stomach. Even though the bouncer couldn't pack enough power in it to cause much pain, it pressed Sol up against the closest bulkhead. By that point, the second guy was already restraining his leg with a makeshift set of straps, which appeared to be tied to the bulkhead for just such a situation. Solomon didn't stop. He strained against the straps. No point in it, but he was now at the mercy of everyone in this room, and he could see in his Ui HUD that his pulse rate was out of control.

"Pull that UiComm chip out of his head, O'Neal," Edge snapped at Bouncer 2.

Damn. Losing his comm was going to cause him serious problems later. Maybe when he met up with Vida or Kasen he could use one of theirs. Of course, then he'd be unable to communicate with them.

He winced when O'Neal pressed his head to the bulkhead and jabbed his thumb into the UiComm's locking mechanism. It beeped twice, and Solomon felt the oddly pleasant feeling of the chip ejecting from his surgically implanted jack. His HUD disappeared instantly. He supposed not being able to see his pulse skyrocket while they questioned him would probably be a good thing in the end.

O'Neal tossed it to the other guard, who slipped it into his pocket.

"I'd like to speak with you both outside for a moment," Mads said. Justice and Edge nodded and rose to follow him. One of the guards gave Mads a questioning gaze and he nodded, so they both followed the others out of the compartment as well.

For the moment, that left Solomon alone in the compartment. He glanced out through the window in the door, but one of the bouncers paused there and stared in at Solomon, blocking his view of the stars shimmering through the window on the opposite side of the outer corridor. No matter. He remembered every constellation outside this spacecraft. He'd taken this trip so many times through the years. He realized now that it was likely the last trip to Nautilus-11 he would ever take. As much as he wanted to leave Earth, the thought made him suddenly uncomfortable.

Solomon heard the faint whir of the slider and instinctively jerked against the ties that bound him. Commander Edge blustered back in and slammed his foot in one of the footholds in the floor. Hard to look badass when you're floating in micro-G, but he was giving it an admirable effort. Justice pulled in after him, followed by Graversen. Whatever they discussed out there had left them all in a foul mood. Solomon hoped it wasn't hard evidence about the sabotage.

"The evidence is beyond doubt now, Reach," Dickson said. "One of the Cav Drive parts has been removed, and all the 3D printing software was stolen. You authorized this. Why?"

"You know why you're here, Solomon," Justice began, in a firm but relaxed tone. He wasn't surprised. Despite her tendency toward capitulating to Dickson Edge's every whim, she had a cool head. "Answer our questions and we can get on with this."

Suddenly Solomon didn't give a shit about playing his cards right. "I know exactly why you're all here. Your spaceship is busted, and you're hoping I'll help you leave this waste of a planet—and five thousand of my crew—in two days' time."

Justice squeezed her arm again. "What are you talking about?"

Solomon glared at her, knowing his anger was getting the better of him. "You know exactly what I'm talking about, Alexandra."

"Is this a game to you, Reach?" Edge's scowl etched deep into his aging skin, lending further ugliness to his sunken eyes and thin, misshapen nose. He was chosen for his skill and experience alone through special dispensation. By Paradisi Mission Regulation standards, he was far too old at age 59 for this voyage. So many of the Founders who hadn't made the initial cut had purchased or bartered skills for spots aboard the SS *Challenge*. Edge had had decades of experience as an astronaut with a footlocker full of medals and awards for services rendered, but the psychiatrists had deemed him too "combative" to command any of the other ships. So Joint Command had dumped him on the SS *Challenge* crew, hoping that would shut him up. "Lives are at stake—"

"Yes, they are, Commander Edge," Solomon cut in. "The lives of *my* employees and their families."

"So you'd kill all of us, then?" Mads asked. "To what? Prove a point?"

"A man is nothing but his word." He looked pointedly back at his one-time friend. "Wouldn't you agree, Graversen?"

Mads didn't miss the reference, but he stared back at him anyway. "You'll kill us all, Solomon. I know you well enough to know you don't want that on your conscience."

"And yet, by breaking your binding contract with Reach Corp—" he stared hard at each of them in turn "—you've sentenced thousands of my crew to death. A crew who unwittingly signed a breached contract with Challenge Command and originally with the ten Founding Families that guaranteed their transport off this hellhole."

"You don't know that Earth will die out," Justice countered.

Solomon raised a single eyebrow. "Terrorists wielding 3D-printed weapons own this planet. Global disasters that have plagued us for decades destroyed our climate beyond reparation. What sort of fantasy world do you live in, XO Justice?"

"Tell us where the propulsion breach occurred, Reach," Edge cut in. "Tell us how to fix it. Or you will find yourself—and your crew—on a one-way trip back to the ground tonight. You will no longer have our protection. God save you, then."

"You've already turned me into a walking dead man, Commander. I have nothing to lose."

"We will seek out your family, Reach. We will find them. And we will put a gun to their heads. Tell us where the breach is!"

"I repeat, Commander Edge: I have nothing to lose." And he damn well meant it. An image of Nisolda came to mind, her frail body sleeping, the machines beeping in the background.

"Your crew," Edge stated in a monotone voice, interrupting his thoughts.

"If I do what you want, you still plan to murder five thousand Reacher souls—the people who have essentially made it possible for you to fly to a new planet to escape the destruction of your own."

"It's only three thousand," Justice piped in, as if that would soothe the horror of their imminent deaths. "We would retain two thousand for critical positions on the SS *Challenge* Watch Crews."

"It doesn't matter how many you plan to *retain,* XO Justice." Solomon stared at her. These people astounded him. "I'm not going to bargain for a single life. They built this ship for you. They are saving your lives. They earned this ride."

"We don't have time to debate ethics anymore, Solomon," Graversen said. "You have every single life in this complex in your hands. At least save some of us."

"Do you mean you, Graversen? Since I am apparently going to die, *friend,* my ethics and my honor are all I have left. You saw to that."

"Dammit, Reach, you will tell us what we want to know," Edge said.

"And if I don't tell you?"

"You will find your death more imminent than you had anticipated." His heated voice grew louder with every word. Then he touched the DOT unit behind his left ear and spoke: "O'Neal, bring in the table, the AED, and the surgery kit you prepared for us."

"Do not test us," Graversen said.

He could tell Justice was becoming uncomfortable with this turn of events. This time she tugged absently at her synth-leather uniform hat, smoothing it over her ears with the palms of her hands. Her confidence was wavering.

Solomon needed to think. And fast. He had no doubt that Edge would torture him until he had the answers he wanted.

Commander Edge was right. He had everything to lose: his crew.

His Reachers were good people. When he had cherry-picked them from the elite of the elite in the science, technology, engineering, and mathematics fields, he also made sure they were ethically and psychologically fit. When they arrived on New Eden, they would be some of the most useful and productive of all the settlers as they worked to build a new society among the natives. They deserved to be saved. And he would do what he must to get them to New Eden.

Solomon looked up at the commander, then, as the guard O'Neal carried in the surgical instruments and the AED that would presumably keep him alive long enough to spill his guts. He looked at Justice and Graversen in turn.

"If you kill me, the answer will die with me. You will miss your launch window, and you will be the ones stuck on a planet you helped to destroy. What did they call that back when the workers still went to school? Oh, yes. Poetic justice."

# THE
# INTERROGATION

"I won't need to kill you, Reach," Edge said. "You're about to tell me everything I want to know."

Solomon didn't know how much he could withstand before he caved. Fortune had favored him up to this point, and in micro-G, humans don't even have so much as a backache. But Edge might well be right. He also didn't want to be so crippled that he couldn't get to his Reacher crew aboard the SS *Challenge*. He needed to formulate a plan. If he offered to help Challenge Command, he could buy himself some time.

Commander Edge had a background in tactical aeronautics and apparently had a penchant for inflicting pain, but Justice and Graversen were not professional soldiers. He needed to focus this battle of wits on Edge, but underestimating Graversen would be a mistake. If his old friend could turn against him this easily, there was no telling what he was capable of doing.

Edge detached a particularly sharp-looking scalpel from the medical kit. Then he situated himself next to Solomon, securing himself into a foothold at the base of the bulkhead. He braced an arm on either side of Solomon and leaned in to intimidate.

"We've disabled the comm unit in this compartment, Solomon. There is no one to come to your rescue. This is your last chance. Tell us how to fix the Cavitran Drive."

"Why would you risk a Reacher mutiny for these people?" Solomon asked. "Who are they? What did they offer you?" He stared at Graversen. "Money? Power?"

"You tell me when to stop, Solomon," Commander Edge said in a low growl that gave Solomon the impression of a wolf on the hunt. "Remember that you control what I'm about to do to you."

"No, asshole. You control your own actions. And when my crew mutinies, I hope you remember the history of the SS *Challenge*'s last captain, Commander Edge. Remember it didn't turn out so well for Robert Waterman." That little niggling reminder of the SS *Challenge*'s namesake, the 19th century clipper ship made famous by its cruel captain and mutinous crew, made Edge's scowl turned even darker.

"Ah, but he got away with it in the end," Edge said with a sickening smile, taking a stronger hold of the index finger of Solomon's left hand.

Solomon could feel his heart rate raising with every moment that scalpel got closer. At the last second, Solomon had to look away. The pain as the blade slid beneath his fingernail was exquisite. He bit his lip and dug his nails into his other palm. It didn't help at all when Edge twisted the blade back and forth under his nail bed. Don't scream. Don't scream. Don't scream.

He screamed, until he was sure even the stars of the distant constellations could hear it.

After what felt like an eon, he felt a blob of his own sticky blood smack into his face. He realized then that he had closed his eyes at some point. He opened them to see Commander Edge's sharp-angled face hovering inches from his own. Sweat beads floated off his forehead in smaller droplets around them.

Graversen, his face unreadable, moved over to the med kit and AED, as ready as a nurse at a sick man's bedside. Dammit if he didn't want to punch the living daylights out of that traitor. Or at least smear his blood blobs all over the guy's face. Instead, he focused on his shaky breathing, trying to think about anything but the pain pulsing out of his vulnerable finger.

A glance at Alexandra told him she was really getting uncomfortable now. She was alternating between digging her own fingernails into her palm and pressing her hat down even harder than before. What she wasn't doing was looking at Solomon.

"Torture getting to you, Justice?" Solomon taunted her through heavy breaths. He certainly wasn't going to make it easy for any of them.

She shook her head and turned even further away to look out at the stars.

"Tell me how to fix that drive, or I'll move on to the next one," Commander Edge yelled. "How did you sabotage it?"

Frankly, he wasn't quite sure how it was done, but he certainly knew who did it. They ought to know that only two people could disable the Cav Drive without damaging it. The resident expert was his Drive Ops Chief Vida Rosado. She was the true wizard. But it was her right-hand man, Drive Ops Specialist Tavian Hunt, who did the honors this time around.

And Edge wasn't going to get that useful bit of data out of his mouth, no matter how much blood was floating around this compartment. He spotted Graversen swatting several bubbles of blood away from his face. If his finger wasn't throbbing in agony, he'd have found it amusing.

"There is no sabotage," Solomon said.

"You bastard," Edge yelled. "I'm going to make this one hurt."

Solomon sighed. "Feel free."

That might have been the wrong thing to say. Edge's transformation from smug satisfaction to mild insanity was swift. Up until the point where Edge slammed the scalpel through the center of Solomon's palm. He felt a pounding in his hand, as if Edge were stabbing him over and over, but it was just the waves of pain consuming him.

Somewhere beyond the sound of his own scream echoing around the compartment, Solomon heard a commotion of slamming and shouts.

"Stop!" a new voice burst in. Someone must have entered the compartment. "What you're doing goes against all board protocols—"

"You don't understand what is happening here, Dextra," Justice snapped. "Stay out of it."

"I won't, mother. No matter what is happening, you have no right to harm another human life."

So this woman—he knew her as a member of the Joint Command Procedural Group—was Alexandra Justice's daughter. He had never made the connection before.

"Dextra, leave this compartment immediately," Alexandra said, grabbing her daughter by the arm. "This is not your concern."

"O'Neal," Graversen said, "remove this woman now."

"No. You have to stop whether you want to or not. Nautilus Command has ordered an urgent meeting. We're docking to Nautilus within the hour. You all need to listen to me now."

"What the hell is this all about?" Commander Edge shouted.

"Iranian militants unleashed a bird 90 minutes ago. Israel had no choice but to counterattack when they learned of a second bird aimed at Jerusalem."

Solomon heard it in Dextra's lowering voice, saw it in her frightened dark eyes. It was the truth.

Alexandra gasped and Edge ripped the scalpel out of Solomon's palm, releasing a fresh wave of agony. The blood floated out in a bulbous gush.

"Result," Edge demanded.

"Devastation. Nautilus Command has confirmed that nuclear winter is a mathematical certainty."

Everything the world had feared after decades of waiting out the peace talks. All that he, himself, had feared. No escape now but this one chance. He could just see the hull of the SS *Challenge* coming into view out the window, docked at Nautilus and waiting. Never had that hunk of metal seemed more precious, more beautiful than it did right now. Soon, he'd see the Nautilus-11 Space Station itself, it's giant fractal arm reaching out like a spiral galaxy, reaching toward Andromeda and the promise of life on New Eden.

"A winter is confirmed by the International Consortium?" Graversen asked in his steady, quiet way.

"Yes, I believe so. The board has called an emergency meeting. No exceptions. You must all join them in the Nautilus Command Module without delay."

"Dammit. Dextra, tell them I'll be there after I've extracted the information we need. Nothing is more important than this."

"No exceptions," Dextra repeated. "They wish to talk to you about this . . . About Reach Corp."

That admission right there told Solomon beyond any doubt that the leaders of Challenge Command—Edge, Justice, and Graversen—as well as Nautilus Command and the board itself were in on this Reacher betrayal from the beginning. Not only that, but they were about to execute their plan to get the Reachers off the SS *Challenge*. Well, not on his watch.

Commander Edge suddenly pulled away from

Solomon, obviously realizing that Dextra had given away too much. "I'll be back, Reach, and if you don't release the information we need, I will hurt you and every Reacher you care about in any way I can. Do not doubt me."

He heard voices around him, only catching snippets here and there as he tried to steady his breathing and focus on anything but the pain.

"Stand guard, O'Neal," he thought he heard Mads say.

"Dextra, I don't want you interfering with Challenge business ever again." Alexandra's voice was low but commanding.

"You know I'll have to report this, Mother."

"There's no one to report it to," Alexandra said, her voice sarcastic.

"Go on. I'll come shortly after I've talked with O'Neal."

"I'll be back in a moment, ma'am . . ." was O'Neal's professional reply as his voice trailed off.

Solomon closed his eyes for a moment and listened to the rustling of them all leaving the compartment, his pulsing hand somehow feeling disconnected from the rest of his body, his breathing labored and his body sweating.

But one remained. He could hear her heightened breathing.

"Are you all right?"

It was Dextra Justice.

"Chief Reach?" she ventured again.

He opened his eyes and just gazed at her as his sweat and fear and blood floated surreally around her. The feeling in the muscles of his bleeding hand came back in a rush, which made his fingers twitch and ache. She had an almost Asian or Dutch look to her slanted eyes, and her tiny mouth shimmered with near-black lipstick. Her dark hair was tucked neatly under her Nautilus-issued black leather cloche hat, and her black uniform outlined every sleek muscle in her limbs. He looked for a spark of humanity in her face. Something he could hold on to. It all lay in her eyes.

"It's Solomon," he finally croaked out. He kept his gaze steady on hers, though he ached to see if anyone watched at the door. It was time to make this happen, and he needed every advantage he could get.

"Do you need . . . water?" she asked, though she floated back from him. "Something from the med kit?"

Solomon decided to be straight with her. He knew only one thing would reach a woman whose life and work revolved around procedures and rules: the truth.

"Ms. Justice, I'm going to tell you what's really going on here, and then I will let *you* decide my fate and that of my crew."

# THE EGRESS

Dextra Justice's thin, sculpted eyebrows rose. Her surprise wasn't a shock, but Solomon had surprised himself. He had just put the lives of at least three thousand souls in this woman's hands, and he didn't even know her. As far as he knew, she was just another Founder stooge, always dong as she was told. But again, he saw a flash of something in those coal-lined cat eyes. It was sympathy, if not outright empathy. He had to try.

"Let me stop the bleeding first," she said, deflecting.

Dextra didn't release the ties around his wrists. Rather, she took a foothold and rummaged around in the med kit for a nano-band. She pulled it from its casing and pushed herself nearer to him.

"Relax your hand, Chief Reach," she said, touching his forearm lightly.

Without thinking, he did as she told him. After wrapping the nano-band loosely around his palm, which was bleeding into the air around them quite freely now, they both sat quietly watching the nano-bots slowly tighten the thrombin coagulant at its core around his skin. He flinched when she pressed to secure it.

Dextra shifted her body to face him squarely.

"All right, Chief. Now you can tell me."

Solomon nodded, fiddling with the band and flexing his fingers to test mobility. "Ms. Justice, I've given my life to Reach Corp, to the design and construction of these Asteria ships, to the Founders. In return, they promised me—in a signed contract—that they would guarantee safe passage for those I care for: my employees and their families. It's what we've worked so hard for. It's why we've sacrificed our lives up here. It was all for our joint survival."

"What changed? Did you not—"

"Up until this day, I gave them everything they ever asked of me. But no more."

"Do you mean that you refuse to repair the propulsion system?"

"That is correct, Ms. Justice."

"You would allow the deaths of so many innocents? Why?"

"Challenge Command, including your mother, betrayed us. They have secretly been letting unauthorized people come up via the Tolux Sky Elevator lifters in recent weeks. I just discovered this today. When I questioned Commander Edge about it, he refused to answer.

"He wouldn't tell you what they are doing here?" she asked.

"No."

Dextra shook her head and glanced out the fenestella.

"Don't misunderstand me, Ms. Justice. If I did not play this hand, I surely would be signing the death warrants of innocents; except in that case, it would be the deaths of my loyal crew and their families. The deaths of innocents are on my hands no matter how this ends, Dextra."

His informal use of her first name surprised them both, as he could see from her raised eyebrows and slightly dropped jaw. But even as he said it out loud, he realized merely a glimpse of the gravity of the choice he had made. The people were innocent on both sides of this game for survival. And he was the chess master who had dealt a check to the Founders. Right now, Dextra Justice was his opponent, but their pawns were his employees and their husbands, wives, parents, and children. A dangerous game to play with not only a stranger but a Founder.

"If you were in my place, what would you do?" He hated the way his question sounded, but he was starting to feel a panic rising in his chest along with the pain in his hand.

She pursed her lip, glanced down at his bandaged hand, and finally met his gaze head on. "I'm just thanking the Creator that I am not in your position, Solomon."

It was his turn to raise his eyebrows. Was he getting through to her? But why would she choose his obligations, his employees over her own family and coworkers? But still, she did not answer. He should have started with a lie. Worked her over. Schemed out a way for her to free him from his restraints.

"But if you were . . . Ms. Justice, I want to know."

What he wanted to say was that he *needed* to know. Those working in her procedural group were chosen for their exceptional skills in viewing ethically grey situations dispassionately with an eye toward the regulations aboard ship. When any situation arose requiring their assistance, it was most often their group who would make the final decision and not the station and ship's commanding groups. Given this, he knew she ought to have the right answer, ought to know the right course of action.

He suddenly felt fear pricking at his eyes. But he would not give into that. He had no more time, no more pieces to play but the truth. He had laid it all out before her, and now he would wait.

He watched Dextra's eyes with such an intensity that he started seeing flashes of light like the Cherenkov radiation streaks the old astronauts complained about before NASA invented better shielding. But as he gazed at her, watched the careful deliberation in her eyes, he saw a change come over her that he hadn't truly expected.

She released her foot from its hold, and then slowly, deliberately, began to untie his wrist. Her eyes never wavered from his.

"I've seen you around, Solomon Reach," she said, touching his hurt hand lightly. He studied her unearthly pale skin against his own brown skin. The difference was like a solar eclipse to his eyes. "You're a good man."

Somehow, hearing that from a woman, from a Founder, from the daughter of the woman who had just condoned his torture made him angry. He had no idea why. It was the "in" he needed with her. It was an open door to take advantage. But now he had an overwhelming itch to punch a hole in the wall. He made a fist with his good hand and blew out a breath. Maybe it was because he was mad that he had been put in this impossible situation by posturing politicos in the first place. Damn them all.

"I think we should go to that board meeting and present your case," she said flatly.

"You actually think they'll listen?"

"Maybe not my mother," Dextra said with a faint smile, "but others on the board might."

"I'll talk to them," was all he could muster.

What else could he say? He was about to betray her just as they had betrayed him. He could look at it as an eye for an eye, but in his mind he had no choice. He had an obligation to thousands of people, and if he did not act, he would have their deaths on his hands. Three thousand of his hardworking crew, some who had been with him since the beginning. He would not abandon them to the Founders.

"You will do the right thing, Solomon?" The question in her eyes was one of trust.

He nodded, unable to speak the words.

She finished untying his wrists, then. And for a moment, as she pulled the ties from his ankles, he stretched his smarting hand and curled it up against his chest. A tiny crust of dried blood flecked off from the nano-band to float past the Reach Corp patch on his red leather uniform.

"We need to get you to Nautilus Med Bay first."

"No, bleeding's slowing down, and it doesn't hurt as much." He rather thought that might be true. He kept his eyes on the slider's window. No sign of the guard, O'Neal.

"O'Neal won't be gone long—"

"And he won't be too keen on this particular plan, so we should hurry," Solomon interrupted, putting the cover back on the scalpel and slipping it into his pocket. He had a feeling if he saw Edge again today, that little instrument would come in handy. He would certainly enjoy a bit of payback, anyway.

"Agreed," Dextra said.

She glanced both directions after reaching the short hallway and led the way out of the compartment. Solomon stayed close behind her. He glanced to the left where she was headed. All clear.

"Hey!" Solomon heard O'Neal yell from the far end of the corridor behind him. "Get back in there!" the guard said, his face contorted with anger.

Solomon swung his body around, his adrenaline kicking in. He had just one idea for how to neutralize O'Neal, and he figured he had a 50–50 shot at it. The guy was rushing him fast, and he braced his arm against the slider's edge, his boot firmly secured in a foothold at the base.

Solomon reached out and grabbed the DOT unit on his wrist just as he floated near. Using the guy's momentum, he yanked him around through the slider's opening, and then let him go while ripping the unit off his wrist. O'Neal gave a shout, as did Dextra next to him. The guard flew toward the far bulkhead, and Solomon rushed to pull Dextra away and close the slider before the guard could recover.

The guard rolled to face him and immediately touched off against the bulkhead to come at him again. Solomon nearly had the slider shut. He just needed to lock it with his emergency passcode. Challenge Command gave him way too much access control—a fact they'd be lamenting shortly.

He saw the guy reaching out for the codebox just as the slider fully slid closed. Solomon hoped he had set the manual emergency lock in time. But there was no help for it. At least the room's comm unit was disabled. The guard wouldn't be able to alert anyone until someone walked by.

"Solomon, stop!" Dextra grabbed his arm and tried to pull him away from the codebox. "You can't lock him in there. It's against protocol."

He needed to secure Dextra and fast.

He shoved the guard's comm unit into his pocket and maneuvered upside down while rummaging in his uniform pocket for the scalpel. He kept his eyes on her as he ripped off its cover. Her eyes widened in shock and fear, but he didn't miss the undercurrent of anger in her eyes.

Before she could pull herself away from his grasp, he had her by the arm.

"Let me go. I won't—"

He pulled her back up against his chest and held her as she struggled.

"I didn't want to do this, Dextra," he said, and she froze when the point touched her throat, and his bandaged hand covered her mouth, "but I can't risk going into that meeting and pleading my case to the board. There are too many possibilities for failure. I have an obligation to my people, to honor the promise I made to them years ago. They are counting on me. Everyone who is currently aboard that ship is meant for New Eden; Reacher or Founder makes no matter."

She struggled to talk, but he held firm.

"Those people trying to hitch aboard? They didn't earn this. Let them build new ships using my designs. Let them work for two decades on a new dream to save themselves and their children. This ship is about to set sail, Dextra. Do you want to be on it?"

He turned her, so that he could look her in the eye. His knife was at the ready, and he tried to make it clear with his eyes that he would kill her if she didn't answer.

"Do you want the last seat on that ship, Dextra?" He moved his hand away slightly so that she could speak.

"If I refuse?"

"Why would you? I'm offering you life. A life you were already meant for. One of those cryo beds has your name above it. It's still yours if you want it."

She said nothing but turned her face away.

Solomon frowned at her. He didn't have time for this. Didn't have time to think about his own betrayal of her trust.

"I'll make the decision for you," he said, voice firmer than he meant. She struggled, but he pressed the scalpel harder to her throat.

"You can't do this, Solomon. This isn't—"

"I have to." He slipped a hand over her mouth and used his feet to maneuver. "I have no choice."

With his foot, he touched off the bulkhead and floated them both down the corridor toward the back of the deserted Trafero. Even if she didn't seem to value her own life, Dextra Justice would be a valuable bargaining chip in his bid to save the Reachers. If he must, he would use her against them.

# THE GRAV

Solomon held tightly to Dextra's small waist as he pushed them through the docking module that snaked its way toward the T4, or Transporter Hatch 4, where passengers and crew disembarked from the Trafero 2 and initially entered the Nautilus-11 Space Station.

Just before they rounded the last corner of the long docking module, he stopped and turned Dextra to face him.

"There's a guard stationed around the corner. If I let go of you, are you going to cooperate?"

"You don't keep your word. Why should I?"

"You know there is much more to this than the two of us. Lives are at stake. Lives I must protect. Do you want to help me keep them safe, or do you want me to leave you behind on the Trafero? You have three seconds to decide."

She glared at him but on three, her gaze softened slightly.

"I'll go with you, if only to keep an eye on what you're up to."

Solomon almost smiled. Ah, women. Control freaks, the lot of them.

He nodded. "Stay behind me and give nothing away. Be cordial and say hello. If he asks, we're on our way to the Joint Command meeting but we're running late."

"If I'm cordial, he'll suspect something."

Solomon raised an eyebrow.

"What? Flip is a complete moron who hits on me every time he sees me."

He raised both eyebrows and pursed his lips to keep from smiling at that. He couldn't blame the guy. She was a beautiful woman. "Understood."

The guard in question stood alone just inside the hatch.

"Heya, Flip," Solomon said loudly, startling Flip Hedgely out of his stargazing via the large window across from him. "Heard any news today about the nuclear standoff?"

"Uh, what? Oh, it's just you, Sol. What the heck did you do to your hand, man?"

Solomon glanced at his bandaged palm and shrugged. "Eh, just a maintenance task gone wrong. No news from the ground?"

"I've been holed up here for hours, so I don't know firsthand. But I overheard Command folks saying that it's really happening down there. Dropping nukes left and right, apparently."

Flip started to stare openly at Dextra, and she uncomfortably turned toward the window.

"Good-day, Miss Justice. Saw your mother come through a while back."

"How long ago did they pass by here?" Dextra asked, her voice clipped.

"Oh, not more than fifteen minutes or so."

"Ah, we were, uh, detained longer than I thought," Solomon said, a little more awkwardly than he intended, as he rubbed at the bandage on his palm. "We're running late for the Joint Command meeting, so we've got to get going."

"Yes, you'd best get on, then. No need to mess with your spacepass. Your mother will be asking for you, Miss Justice."

"All right. Thanks for the updates." Solomon glanced back before they continued on. "Hey Flip, if you hear a call to board the ship, don't delay, okay?"

Flip frowned but nodded. "Yeah, sure, man. Will do."

Solomon looked out the fenestella as they passed by. Below them, massive and glorious in its scale, was the main hub of the Nautilus-11 Space Station. When the Founding Families first commissioned his father's company to construct the station back in 2046, its spiral arm was designed to rotate to simulate artificial gravity. Once the artificial gravity generator had been invented and implemented, the Founding Families had charged Reach Corp's engineering and construction teams with the task of retrofitting Nautilus-11 into a stationary space station.

By 2060, Reach Corp had completed the majority of the work on Nautilus-11 and began their work on Sideris Station and eventually the other ships in the Nautilus Fleet. It seemed at the time that his father's work would never end. He grew up on the station, watching year after year as progress was made. His father was a workaholic, and the only topics they ever discussed were about engineering or astrophysics.

Once he was old enough, his father sent him to the ground for more advanced schooling, first at Berkeley and then a year at Cambridge. After that, he did graduate work at Georgia Tech and MIT. Mads had tracked him down at Georgia Tech and continued to follow his grad work at MIT. Graversen wanted to bring him back to the Nautilus-11 to take up his father's work, something he had nearly sworn off after having a falling out with his father. For Solomon, school was a break from the endless schooling his father had given him.

"I need to send some encrypted messages via your DOT unit. Do you mind?"

Dextra looked dubious. "I suppose not." She held out her wrist, and he held onto her synth-leather covered forearm lightly as he navigated through her device's interface to the message center. He tapped out messages to Tavian, Vida, Kasen, and Brooker asking for a status update. Then he deleted the messages to make it harder for them to find.

"Thanks," he said, letting go of her arm. "Let me know if any of them send responses."

"Won't they assume you're still in custody, and I'm attempting to trap them into revealing information?"

"Possibly. They don't know you, but they know your mother. It's a gamble either way. If any do respond, keep me posted."

Next up was passing through the T4 Hatch into Nautilus-11's Gravitational Flux Chamber, which would take them from micro-G to simulated Earth gravity in a matter of minutes. Well, less than a second. The electronics needed to reach a steady-state, which took several minutes longer. A much faster process in the ten more whiz-bang Founder ships that had already left them in the dust. Solomon wished now that he had retrofitted his own ship better than he had theirs. Ungrateful bastards. He heaved a sigh that rippled down to his bones and wiped a hand down his face. That line of thinking was just going to piss him off even more. Besides he had this next hurdle to focus on.

The Grav Chamber was going to be the biggest risk thus far. The chamber was full of cameras. They also had to get by the Nautilus guard stationed at the entrance. As soon as Dextra tucked in behind him, he pulled her along by the hand toward Nautilus Hatch T4. Unfortunately, three *Challenge* crewmembers were loitering around talking with the guard stationed at the Grav. How the devil were they going to neutralize them?

"Wait here," Dextra said. "Let me see what I can do." With that she let go of his hand and moved toward the guard station.

"Dextra, wait!" Solomon whispered, but she was already halfway down the corridor. He ducked back behind a bend in the docking module when the guard glanced toward his direction. Solomon didn't quite know what to make of this woman. She had guts. He had to give her props for that. But he had no idea if she'd get him thrown in lockdown or what. He watched from the corner, taking care to listen for anyone else approaching the area. The last thing he needed was to run into Edge or Graversen.

"Look, guys, I know you're on break, but I'm on urgent Command business. I need to go see Shuttlemaster Valek."

The guard—Solomon thought his name might be John something or other—cleared his throat gruffly, and said, "What's this business to do with?"

"I apologize, Mr. Beecher, but it's confidential."

Ah, yes. John Beecher was his name. Solomon remembered him only as the guy who replaced the last Nautilus guard who was dismissed for peeing in the micro-G module after a drunken night in the Paradise Bar on the SS *Challenge*'s Watch Deck 16. What he didn't remember was whether this new guard— or his chatty buddies—would potentially cause them problems. He'd find out soon enough when the guy responded to Dextra's evasive answer.

"Humpf," was all Beecher could muster, sporting the ridiculous look of a miffed English gentleman from bygone days.

Dextra's smile lit up her face as she tried to assuage the man. Solomon was well aware it would have worked on him. And it seemed to be working on Beecher, who looked rather dumbfounded. "I do apologize, Mr. Beecher," Dextra continued. "I am tasked with relaying a message to Valek, but I am not at liberty to say more."

"Well, John, we'll leave you to your *official business*," one of the other crewmembers said to Beecher as she squeezed his arm and flashed him a toothy grin. "Come by the bar after your shift, eh?"

"Yeah," said the other one, a tall, skinny fellow with a long, horsey face. "Gia wants to tell you all about her latest theory on natural wormholes. Ha ha!"

"Shut up, Felix. It's a solid theory. I even asked the guys in the Astro Lab about it . . ." Solomon couldn't hear anymore as their voices trailed off down the opposite corridor.

Well done, Dextra, Solomon thought. Behind her back, she motioned him to follow her.

Solomon floated down, pulling himself along faster via the bulkhead handholds.

"Hold that grav flux, John. I need to head over to the Shuttle Sector myself," Solomon said, hoping his voice came off sounding good-natured and easy.

Beecher frowned. "And what's your business, Chief Reach?"

"Same reason that Dextra Justice is heading that way, I imagine. Going to see Shuttlemaster Valek on the SS *Challenge* as well, I heard?"

"Yes, I am, actually. We must be on different errands, though."

"I think so. Anyway, you got room for one more, Mr. Beecher?" Solomon asked.

"Certainly, Chief," the guard said. "But we need to hurry. I'll be relieved shortly."

Perfect. That meant he would not be around to answer any questions later about why he let Solomon Reach slip through his grasp. Solomon smiled despite himself. He might make it through this alive. Well, through the Grav Flux Chamber, at least.

"Not a problem, John," Solomon said, hoping his smile wasn't too over the top. He wasn't cut out to be an actor. Frankly, he wasn't cut out for subterfuge and torture either. "We'll be fluxing out of your hair in no time."

"Yes, just say the word, John," Dextra said, flashing that stunning smile again. Damn, she was stunning.

"Just a moment," Beecher said. He coded them in via the panel log. Solomon hoped it wouldn't flag them immediately, but nothing seemed amiss as he waved them through the hatch.

They both nodded to him as they strapped into two of the seats that lined the bulkhead.

"You know the drill," Beecher said, as he programmed the door to shut and stepped out of the Grav.

"Thank you, John. See you next time around," Dextra said, flashing that winning smile again and straightening her cap harder on her head. A tendril of hair had slipped from under her hat and fell across her forehead. He had to stop himself from reaching out to tuck it back in. He took a deep breath and blew it out slowly instead.

Focus, Reach. You've got a job to do.

Solomon kept an eye on the window at the far end of the Grav. The next hurdle stood there, but this time it was one of his own. Security Specialist Aaron Borden had been with his Reacher crew since its inception. Normally, he worked security aboard the

SS *Challenge,* but it looked like they were short-hand-ed at the moment, likely due to the news of nuclear war. He'd need to talk to Borden immediately after fluxing through the Grav. He hoped the man would be on board with his plans.

Solomon closed his eyes while the Grav worked its magic, accumulating gravitational charge within just a few minutes to turn micro-gravity into artifi-cial gravity by means of electromagnetic waves and a whole lot of science Solomon hadn't bothered to concern himself with when he had plenty of other issues to deal with as lead engineer on this project: design, logistics, materials handling, gatejumping, cryo science, and on and on. It was a good thing he paid smart astrophysicists to work those numbers. He didn't have time for that shit.

As the minutes passed, a solution to his predica-ment started to take shape in his mind, and it all re-volved around Nautilus-11 Docking Commander Daniela Marcks's son, Zander. Solomon visualized his plan as a series of steps up a staircase.

First step: get to the Joint Command board meeting on Nautilus and somehow eavesdrop undetected. He needed to uncover the Founders' ultimate endgame as well as track down where the docking commander was going to be for the rest of the day. Life was about to get very unpleasant for her very shortly.

Second step: somehow make it aboard the SS *Chal-lenge.* This would be the most difficult step of all, and he didn't have a clue how he was going to pull it off.

Third step: if Tavian reported in that he had dis-abled the Cav, Solomon would move on with the rest of his plans. If he didn't hear from Tavian, he'd have to go to the Propulsion Sector and somehow disable the drive himself.

Fourth step: attempt to contact Brooker and Kas-en. Brooker held his ace card, and he hoped he'd get him what he needed before it was too late. He knew Brooker had successfully spread the airlock rumor, but no one had heard from him since.

Fifth step: if necessary, locate Tavian in the Propulsion Sector and debrief. If Tavian had completed his task, he'd have him sit tight while he went after Daniela Marcks's son.

Sixth and final step: he had to find Zander. He should probably find him first but without knowing Tavian's status, his plan wouldn't succeed. Hopefully, Marcks was working over in his usual lab station on the SS *Challenge*.

He felt Dextra's touch on his arm and it startled him. He'd been too far gone into his mental calculations to notice the instantaneous switch back to gravity. He shook his head to focus on the here and now. He contracted and relaxed the various muscle groups in his body, trying to get used to the weight of the gravity again. It shouldn't take long, but he might have to move fast once out of the Grav Chamber. Strangely, his hand felt worse. The bandage had helped a bit earlier, but now his hand was throbbing nonstop.

"Your hand hurting you?" Dextra whispered, her eyes crystalline with concern.

"A bit," he acknowledged. "But we've got to get moving."

"Will he let us through?" Dextra asked, nodding toward Aaron.

He was studying Solomon from the edge of the Grav slider, raised eyebrows and all.

Solomon smiled at him as he took Dextra's hand and helped her up on unsteady feet in the sudden gravity well.

"Haven't seen you up at this hatch in a while, Chief. Nice to see you!" Borden said, his Boston accent an oddly comforting reminder of his MIT days.

"Aaron, do you trust me?" Solomon asked, wobbling a bit from the gravity.

Aaron's eyebrows rose even further. "Um, yes, sir. I do. Without a doubt."

"You've got to be certain, because you're about to put yourself in danger on my account."

Aaron frowned, one side of his mouth twitching. "What do you need?"

"I want you block anyone from leaving the *Challenge*. Say you've been instructed to by your superiors, and don't give any further information than that. And I need you to ask Riva to do the same at the Cargo Hatch. Don't lock it down, though. Anyone who wishes to board may do so."

Solomon gave him a few seconds to let that sink in. Aaron's mouth bobbed open like a fish for a moment.

"Am I allowed to ask why, sir?"

Shrewd fellow.

"I'll give you the abbreviated version. Joint Command just fucked the Reachers over and gave three thousand of our people a ticket down the lifters toward certain death."

"Wha—?"

"I couldn't believe it either, Aaron. But there it is. I'm trying to keep those three thousand Reachers onboard the *Challenge* so I can save their lives, and I need your help to do it. I will handle the rest. Will you help me?"

Aaron turned speechless, but bless him, his noggin' was working just fine. He nodded with all the vigor of a woodpecker hammering away at a tree.

"Good man. You just saved three thousand of your coworkers. Not bad for a days' work, eh?"

"Very good, sir. Yes, sir. I'll call up Riva. What else can I do?"

"If you keep your mouth shut, I'll give you a raise."

Aaron smiled. "I do believe I can manage that, Chief."

"Wait, sir," Aaron said, distracted as he apparently read a Ui he'd just received. It gave Solomon a start. If Challenge Command caught sight of them via the Grav cameras, his recent torture session was shortly about to be extended. His hand twitched at the thought.

"I've just received a . . ." Aaron's long forehead rippled into a frown. "Well, it seems Tavian Hunt has a message for you, though the Ui came from Jazeem Rajan."

"Yes? I've been waiting for a message from Rajan actually." Solomon kept his voice sounding monotone and bored. The less information that caught Aaron's attention, the better.

"Jazeem relays that Tavian requires assistance in the Propulsion Sector."

"Ah, as expected. I'll send someone else to assist. Anything else?"

"No, that's it."

"Solomon, we'd better go," Dextra whispered from behind him.

Solomon pulled her aside, out of Aaron's earshot. "Tavian must have been detained by Challenge Command. Doesn't bode well. If Edge gets a hold of him and makes him talk . . ."

"Is he strong-willed? Maybe he could handle—"

"Tavian?" Solomon nearly laughed despite the gravity of the situation. "No, I wouldn't say that would describe him." Now put a beautiful woman within three feet of that ladies' man, and Solomon might have a different opinion. Solomon kept that last thought to himself as he stared at Dextra's black-shimmered lips. Unfortunately, he started to picture Dextra Justice strapped down in a torture room while Edge extracted what he wanted from her.

"Look, I think I better go it alone from here on out," Solomon said. "They are going to look at the cameras eventually and realize you let me go. You should stay hidden somewhere. Maybe even in your cryo bed. No one would think to look for you there."

"You and I both know I'd be useful to you."

"Useful, yes," he conceded, "but safe, no. You're in procedures. Doesn't all this make you . . . uncomfortable?"

"Of course it does." Her sideways smile disarmed him utterly. "But it would make me more uncomfortable if I had to sit and worry over you, not knowing if they've caught and tortured you again. I saw the look in the commander's eyes. He won't stop until he gets what he wants from you."

Solomon bit his lip, thinking. He was starting to like this woman—possibly the result of space-imposed celibacy and the minor fact that she saved his life—and putting her in danger made *him* uncomfortable. But he couldn't deny that she would either be useful in the execution of his plan or as a bargaining chip should it come to that.

"Stay close to me," he said. "We've got a long way to go."

# THE NAUTILUS

Solomon figured they'd make it down to Nauti-lus-11's Main Hub in about 15 minutes, granted there were no delays. The Transporter Hub, where both Trafero- and Transfero-class transporters docked upon arrival, was connected to the massive cylindrical module that connected all the major hubs of the space station. The Systems Hub, where the majority of the systems and engineering sectors resided, was located below Nautilus-11's Main Hub.

"Take care what you say from here on out. And keep your head down. Too many cameras . . ." Solomon let his voice trail off.

Dextra nodded. "Which lift?"

Solomon waved a nonchalant hand toward the sign labeled "Passenger Lift 1." He figured they were less likely to be stopped if they took passenger lifts and entrances instead of crew routes throughout Nautilus-11 and SS *Challenge.* They'd stand out more against the passengers around them in their black and red uniforms, but at least they wouldn't be recognized as easily among their own crewmates.

They made their way through the fairly crowded

hub connector corridor. Solomon counted around thirty Nautilus and *Challenge* crewmembers embarking or disembarking from various docking modules. Most were heading down the crew lifts, but others were stopping by the coffee shops and restaurants located around the inner rim of the circular hub. The corridors and connectors were blessedly free of Reachers. Kasen must be doing his job keeping Reachers aboard the ship down at the Crew Hatch.

They moved at a steady pace through the gunmetal grey interiors of the hub and joined a small group of maintenance and restaurant workers in Lift 1. A quick glance at them made Solomon sigh in relief. No members of Command among them.

"Which stop?" one of the workers, a tall man sporting a ridiculous mustache, asked Solomon.

"Main," he answered.

"Same for me," Dextra said quietly.

"Hold the lift!" a shout came from the corridor.

Solomon sucked in a breath, realizing he'd recognize that voice anywhere.

The tall worker put his hand out to stop the slider from closing, and in walked Alexandra Justice and Commander Edge.

What the hell were they doing on this lift? He glanced at Dextra, and her eyes were about to bug out of her head. Solomon shook his head slightly and tried to reassure her with his eyes.

Just hold on, he wanted to tell her. Say nothing, and maybe we'll get out of here without the entire Founder crew descending on us. He moved them back behind a couple of taller guys toward the far right corner and turned his face to the side toward Dextra.

Edge and Justice stared straight ahead and didn't say a word. Once the doors closed, other quiet conversations erupted around them, but he and Dextra and his torturers remained silent.

Eventually, Edge turned toward Justice, and Solomon strained to listen. "We need to get back up to the transporter soon. We need to question him further."

"We're late for the board meeting. We have to deal with that and this damned airlock issue first. He's not going anywhere."

Solomon tried to exhale, but his breath came out in a ragged lump. He couldn't believe it, but it seemed his plan was still in play. They had no idea he'd escaped, and it seemed as if Brooker's rumor about an airlock leak on the SS *Challenge* was spreading fast. And of course, Challenge Command was going to have a devil of a time pinpointing the leak because it didn't actually exist. That should keep them busy for quite a while. If he and Dextra made it out of this elevator without being detected, they might just pull this off.

The moments ticked by. Solomon felt the sweat beading up on his forehead, remembering the feel of Edge's scalpel driving into his palm. It pulsed again, as much in pain as in the desperate need to sucker punch Dickson Edge right now. Damn that man.

The elevator came to an abrupt halt, knocking Dextra into him, and the door dinged and opened. Solomon took hold of her hand to steady her, but he didn't let go afterward. He held her back as people started to file out, Justice and Edge beginning to lead the way.

"Wait," Edge said, blocking Alexandra from exiting, as the other workers filed out around them.

For a breathless moment, Dextra squeezed the life out of Solomon's hand while they waited for Edge's next move.

"Got a message from Challenge Security." He stared blankly ahead, obviously reading the message via his DOT HUD.

Jesus, Edge. Get on with it already! The suspense

was killing Solomon. He'd rather be arrested than stand right behind his torturer and be unable to act.

"It's nothing," Edge finally said. "They haven't found any leaks as yet."

"All right. Let's get going," Alexandra said, rushing out.

When they had both left, Solomon paused the lift for a moment and just breathed.

"My God," Dextra whispered. "I thought for sure my mother would turn around."

Solomon glanced at her. "Still sure you want to come with me?"

She paused only a beat before responding. "Absolutely."

After checking around the corner for Alexandra and Dickson, Solomon pulled Dextra out of the lift into the bustle of the Nautilus-11's Main Hub. Nautilus crew were everywhere and SS *Challenge* crew dotted the crowd as well. He scanned the expansive area surrounding the inner lifts, but didn't immediately see any Reachers loitering around the restaurants or corridors.

Most of the crew sectors on Nautilus were located in and around its cylindrical core. Shops, eateries, and markets lined the outer perimeters while the long spiral arm leading off into the various ship sectors spun off to their right. And here again was the same odd mixture of natural and modern decor as could be found on the Solix Sky Docking Station. As much as he admired Alastair Johns, he decidedly disliked his sense of style. He led Dextra down the crew passage toward the Nautilus-11 conference compartments. They would be meeting in Compartment 1A, where all Joint Command Board meetings took place, he had no doubt.

"Do you know where any tracking dampeners are located?" she asked. "There must be some on Nautilus or *Challenge*."

"I've got some hidden in a locker on *Challenge.*" He touched his wrist, annoyed at himself for forgetting that Command would start tracking them once they realized he was missing. If he wasn't still smarting from his wounds, he'd cut it out of his wrist. He needed every safeguard he could get. But it was unlikely they'd discover him gone until after the board meeting.

"If we make it there."

"We will. Trust me," Solomon said.

She raised a thin eyebrow, and her dark lips twisted into an incredulous smile.

He grinned back. "Well, try at least."

"No promises."

"Fair enough."

"Hold on while I destroy the guard's chip." Solomon pulled out the DOT he had shoved into his pocket earlier. He pressed the release button on the back of the wrist unit, and with a beep, the chip popped out. He didn't have much strength in his injured hand, but he was able to bend and crack the delicate components. He tossed it into the nearest waste receptacle.

"Okay, let's go," he said, directing her with gentle pressure on her shoulder toward the flow of people in the center aisle.

They cut through a couple of empty compartments in the center of the hub and finally made it to the right corridor, but a guard stood in front of the slider leading to Conference Compartment 1A. He was going to be a big problem.

Dextra held out her arm to stop Solomon. "Wait here," she said confidently. "I'll take care of him."

"Be careful," Solomon hissed as she walked down the corridor at a steady clip, the movement of her hips catching his eye. For a split-second, Solomon worried she'd bust into the meeting and start screaming for help. He waited, ready to bolt.

Dextra must have smiled at the guard, because he grinned at her with a nod. "Ms. Justice."

She spoke to him briefly and the guy nodded.

"Are you sure he wanted me to leave my post?"

Dextra finally spoke loud enough for Solomon to hear. "That's what I heard. Secondhand, of course. I can keep an eye on things here, if you like. That was my intention, anyway."

"Yes. I'll just see what he wants. Be back in a bit."

The guard moved down the opposite corridor, and Solomon released the breath he hadn't realized he'd been holding.

Dextra waved him over.

"Thank you," he said, not knowing what else to say.

She nodded. "Useful, that's me."

"I'd be happy to give you a glowing letter of recommendation."

"I'm touched. Now, I don't know how long that idiot is going to be gone, so all I can say is you better have a good plan for this next bit, Reach."

"Simple: we sneak in there and eavesdrop on their plans. Then we head to the ship before the meeting breaks up."

"So, zero chance of success, then?"

"Where's your vote of confidence now? There's an extra podium and some chairs stacked right by this door, actually. I plan to tuck us in behind them. That should give us an earful of what they're saying and possibly a clear line of sight."

"And what if something goes wrong?"

"You are going to be my bargaining chip."

"What?" She was genuinely concerned at that admission. He hoped it wouldn't come to that. Given what he'd seen of Alexandra, Mads, and Edge today, he wouldn't put it past them to sacrifice Dextra for the "greater good."

"Just follow my lead," Solomon reassured her. "I'll get us through this."

"Why do I not feel overly confident just now?"

"Because the fate of your life is in the hands of a man you barely know."

"Well, you're perceptive. I'll give you that."

"Let's get going. The guard won't be gone for long," Solomon said.

# THE VOTE

Solomon peeked through the slider's window. The meeting table was out of his immediate view, but no one lingered around the area beyond the slider. It looked like they had a real chance of slipping in undetected.

"Use your pass to get us through," Solomon whispered. "Mine might already be flagged."

Dextra waved her wrist in front of the slider's codebox, and it slid open quietly. They ducked down and immediately hid behind the podium and chairs stacked in the far corner of the meeting room. Solomon slowly moved some of the chairs to shield them from anyone exiting or entering the room from this far door. Then they knelt on the floor and listened in to the meeting already in progress, looking through the legs of the chairs to watch as all the bigwigs discussed their fate.

"Is it certain, Giles?" he heard Docking Commander Daniela Marcks ask. Solomon shifted his position so he could find her location. So she was here. Good. Solomon would have to start tracking her whereabouts after this. He was going to need her later.

"Yes. Given the sheer number of nukes both countries let loose, nuclear winter is a mathematical certainty according our own scientists as well as the International Consortium."

Silence took over the group as that sunk in. It wasn't every day you hear about the imminent destruction of the only planet you've ever lived on. And nothing was ever going to be certain about New Eden. Once the Nautilus Fleet had gatejumped through the wormhole, Earth had lost contact with them.

There was no way to know how the Founders had fared through the gatejump other than to assume that the ships he had built for them had made it through safely. He had tried to make sure of that with a layer of nanosilc lining the hulls, buffering each ship from micrometeorites, solar radiation, and space debris.

"Let's go over the details again," he heard Alexandra Justice say. "We need to reduce time to launch by a half-day given what the latest calculations show."

Solomon moved over a couple of inches so he could peer through the chairs to better watch the proceedings.

"What's delaying us is the group in Serica Sector." Flight Director Giles Benson stood and pressed his palms onto the table. "I still say we need to leave them."

Dickson Edge glanced around the room. "You all know why that is not an option."

"If you hadn't started this mess," Benson countered, "we would have left already." He stared coldly at Commander Edge, who seemed to be struggling between wanting to shout in Benson's face or punching him. He stood and opted for shouting, likely since they'd go further.

"Everyone here has a stake in this except you, Benson. I don't think you get a vote on this one. Even if you did, you'd be outnumbered."

"I wouldn't make that assumption lightly," Benson

said, glancing around at each board member, "if I were you, Commander."

"He's right, Giles," Alexandra said.

Benson ignored Alexandra entirely and kept his eyes on Edge. "We've got one chance to leave this station. Ten thousand people cannot be held hostage by these people, no matter how important they are. The needs of the many, remember?"

"You can say that easily since you've outlived everyone who ever gave a damn about you, Benson."

The older man's smile spoke of a grim certainty that Solomon didn't quite understand. "Granted, but that fact also allows me to view this situation with impartiality."

"Enough, gentlemen. Our launch window is short, and we cannot wait to make a decision," the docking commander said. "The Serica group's extra cargo has reduced our surplus fuel tolerances."

"We extracted nothing out of Vida Rosado," Graversen said. "She wouldn't reveal the location of the missing part or tell us where the 3D design is. Even the backup file is missing. It is certainly sabotage. We need to get Solomon Reach talking before we miss that window entirely," he said, steepling his fingers in front of him with maddening calm. "He is the key."

"Agreed," Alexandra said, causing Dextra to drop her jaw in horror at her mother.

"Forgive my ignorance, but who is this Vida Rosado?" Jiva Yarod asked.

"She's the Propulsion Sector Drive Ops Chief," Alexandra said. "She is in charge of the Cav Drive systems."

"Ah, I don't believe I've met her as yet," was Jiva's reply.

"These new people you're bringing on haven't even been quarantined appropriately," Benson protested. "They will almost certainly cause an outbreak of disease aboard ship."

"Benson is correct," Operations Manager James Reece piped in. "They could potentially kill us all. At least the Reachers have already been cleared for travel, Commander. And their skill sets are valuable."

"We've gone over this, Reece," Flight Surgeon Mava Sparks, a short-haired woman in her early forties, piped in. "We'll put those with illnesses in the isolated cryo chamber, and a dedicated tech in Med Bay will be monitoring vitals throughout the journey."

"I'm with Justice on this," Commander Edge said. "We have yet to get Solomon Reach to talk. That's our number one priority. Every other decision related to the launch must come after that."

"Agreed. We need to stop wasting time," Justice said. "Let's get back to our interrogation of Reach."

"Interrogation?" Jiva asked with raised eyebrows.

"Yes, Jiva. Interrogation," Justice said dryly. "Chief Reach is being . . . combative."

"Perhaps he's being combative *because* you're interrogating him, XO Justice."

Solomon instinctively nodded in agreement, which made Dextra smile grimly at him. This guy Jiva—Solomon recalled he was a lead engineer on Nautilus-11 or something like that but not a usual member of the board—was a bit more perceptive than they gave him credit for. He must be standing in for another member, but Solomon couldn't call up the name.

"He's a means to an end, Jiva. He—and his crew—will not be joining us, so it doesn't matter."

"Hmm . . . so you say," was Jiva's reply.

Solomon made a mental note. This Jiva guy might be a potential ally. Same with Reece, who was nodding along with Jiva's comments.

"As I see it, we have two scenarios—well, three actually," Benson said. One: we don't get Reach talking, and in that scenario, we all inevitably die from some nasty means in a nuclear winter if we don't get swept up in a weapons race, gang war, or one of the natural disasters taking place all over the world. I think we'd all agree that scenario is less than appealing.

"Two: we get the ship operational, and the Serica group switches places with the Reacher crew you selected to boot off the ship. Somehow you're going to have to figure out a way to get them to leave without raising suspicions or causing a mutiny. If it comes to a fight and damage is done to the ship, nobody's leaving."

"I already have a plan to get them off the ship," Edge said. "We'll send out an all-staff missive from Reach's account stating that he wants to gather them all in one place on Nautilus-11 to relay some key information regarding their duties during the journey. They won't question—"

"Three," Benson said, cutting him off, "we let the Reachers stay aboard, and we—as I said before—get the hell out of here. I say we put it to a board vote and be done with this."

Everyone at the table glanced at each other, seemingly weighing what the result of such a vote would be and whether it was worth the risk. Solomon could see the cogs in their minds rolling.

"Seconded," Jiva said.

So he was of the democratic variety, Solomon thought. Good, then. Of course, it made sense, since he was not likely to vote in such a proceeding under usual circumstances.

"I see we had the same idea, Chief."

The sound of Vida's whisper behind him made Solomon smile. Excellent. At least he'd find out how things were going on her end.

"Vida!" Solomon whispered though he wanted to shout. He turned and pulled her into a hug. "Did they hurt you? What's your status?" He didn't immediately see any damage, but pain took many forms.

"Don't worry, boss. I'm fine," Vida said, brushing off his concern while glancing warily at Dextra. "Aren't you a Justice?"

Solomon saw Dextra nod out of the corner of his eye.

"She's with us now, Vida. Report."

"Yes, sir. It was mostly just threats and finger wagging. I didn't give them any information. But I was able to disable the Serica locking system. I don't think anyone is aware of it yet."

"No one here has mentioned it, so we're good for now. You've done a damn fine job. When we get out of this, you're going to get a gold star employee of the week award."

"And a vacation on a distant planet?"

"Absolutely. Now hold tight. They are about to take a vote."

Benson had already voted to leave the Serica group behind. As had one other board member from the Nautilus-11 Trust Group who had funded the original retrofitting of the SS *Challenge*. She had been silent until now, but Solomon was happy to see she neither condoned Solomon's further torture nor her fellow board members' attempts to betray their original agreement. Or maybe she just didn't want to risk the potential mutiny once the Reachers discovered the truth. Either way, Solomon would take it. He could use all the would-be allies he could find.

Next up were Graversen, Justice, and Edge.

Alexandra raised her hand up so all eyes would be on her. "I'm in favor of the Serica group."

"I vote in favor of the Serica group as well," Graversen said.

"Shocker," Solomon muttered under his breath.

Why he ever trusted that bastard . . . Well, you

live you learn. Danes, man. Tricky sons of bitches.

"You already know my mind on this," was all Commander Edge would say.

Yeah, next? Solomon thought.

Jiva Yarod considered for a moment, and then finally said, "Given the potential for Reacher mutiny, I say we mitigate risk by allowing them to stay onboard. Remember, there is still the possibility that we will never get the answers we need out of Solomon Reach. He has no reason to give us what we want. He has nothing to lose at this point."

"Except his life."

Solomon broke out in a cold sweat at Commander Edge's coldness.

"I know beyond doubt we can get him to talk," Mads Graversen said, his accent as thick as his head.

Eyebrows went up around the table.

You think? Solomon closed his fist, wishing they were back at MIT's Killian Court where he could bloody him senseless.

"I vote in favor of the Serica group," Flight Surgeon Sparks said after a moment of consideration.

All eyes turned toward the final voter on the board: Daniela Marcks. It seemed the docking commander was about to break the tie. Little did she know how much rested on her vote. If she chose the Serica group, she was about to find the Reachers weren't going to go down without a fight.

He heard Vida's sharp intake of breath behind him. He noticed he was holding his breath too. Marcks was deliberating. He could see the potential scenarios rolling across her pale face. When she had made up her mind, it was written in her eyes before she said the words.

"Send the Reachers to the ground." Marcks's voice cut through a crack-fire succession of his thoughts.

"Vida, we've just lost our vote," Solomon whispered. "We need to get out of here fast and regroup somewhere else."

She nodded, but the board members were already moving away from the table. He heard snippets of their conversation as they began to scatter.

"I'm going to work on contingency backup plans," the trustee said, as she headed out the back door on the opposite side of the room.

"I need to get a full status update from security on the airlock situation," XO Alexandra Justice said. "I'll be in Module D, Compartment Two for the next 15 minutes."

"Page Gregore from the training room. Tell him to report to the Trafero 2 and wait for instructions," Commander Edge said to Graversen. "We'll let the gym rat do the dirty work. I don't have time for it. And Graversen," Edge said grabbing Mads by the shoulder, "do whatever it takes. Find a way to break Solomon Reach. We need that Cavitran Drive working by tomorrow, or we'll all share the same fate as the grounders."

# THE CRYO HATCH

"Someone's coming, Solomon," Dextra said, her voice a harsh whisper.

"Hide. I've got this," Vida said, pushing Solomon back as she stood to face whoever was approaching the slider. This proceeded to shove him into Dextra, who fell backward into the shadows of the podium. His hand shot out instinctively, and he ended up hovering above her, their bodies barely an inch apart, his palm cradling the back of her head.

Her eyes widened, glinting brightly under the lights above them. His heart charged into full race-mode. If they found him hovering over Justice's daughter in the corner of the boardroom, they'd arrest him on the spot, and even Alexandra wouldn't hesitate to break out the scalpels this time.

Solomon begged Dextra with his eyes not to make a move or cry out. He needed her cooperation more than anything else right now. Without it, he was a dead man. Something came into her eyes—a glimmer, a flash. She nodded as if to say, "You have my trust."

It surprised him, and he nearly forgot where he was and what he was doing there with her. He laid

Dextra's head down gently but held his position, palms down on either side of her head, gazing into her eyes because he had nowhere else to look. He should stop kidding himself. He stayed that way because he wanted to memorize her face and think about taking her dark mouth to his own. He was surprised she didn't seem to want to look away either. She met his bold gaze without hesitation, and it made his arms go a bit weak.

Jiva Yarod's voice crashed through his thoughts, and the moment with Dextra passed him by.

"Is there something wrong with the slider?" he asked Vida. Yarod didn't seem to realize who she was; otherwise he would have called for the cavalry immediately. Solomon glanced toward the other side of the room. It looked like the other board members had headed out the back way.

"I've been trying to figure that out myself," Vida said. "I was on an errand and noticed it seemed to have gone faulty. Codebox probably needs a reset."

"Did you only just arrive, or have you been looking at this door for quite a while?" Yarod sounded mildly suspicious.

"Oh no, sir," Vida assured him in her best you're-the-boss tone, "I literally just started taking a look at the codebox the moment you walked up. I was actually looking for Docking Commander Marcks."

"We've just come out of a restricted meeting," Yarod said. "You'll need to come back at a later time. I recommend you contact the docking commander via DOT message, as she will likely be detained by urgent business for some time."

"No problem, sir. It's not critical."

"Certainly. Good day," Yarod said, and Solomon heard his footsteps fading as he made his way down the corridor.

"Are we all clear, Vida?" Solomon whispered.

"All clear."

A moment passed, and Solomon rolled over Dextra to sit beside her.

"Sorry about that," he whispered, holding out his hand to her as he got up. "Are you all right?" With a nod, she took his hand and rose to a sitting position.

"Come," he whispered to Dextra. "Time to get you safely aboard the *Challenge*."

After he lifted her to her feet, she touched his shoulder. "Solomon, what if I messaged my mother and told her I needed to speak with her urgently. That would get her aboard the ship at least, and she'd be none the wiser."

Her steady gaze had a twinge of worry in it. So Dextra didn't agree with her mother, the Executive Bitch, for going along with Edge's unsavory torture methods, but the woman was still her mother, betrayer or not.

Solomon thought for a moment. At first glance, he didn't see a problem with it. Well, as long as they didn't run into Alexandra as they searched for Zander Marcks. "All right. Don't give her any indication of what we're planning, Dextra. It's for her safety as well as ours. If this goes horribly wrong, we could end up with a bloodbath between the Serica group and the Reachers. I don't think either of us want that."

"Agreed."

"Let's go."

Vida glanced beyond them to see whether there was any danger. She nodded. "Hurry."

Solomon and Dextra slipped into an adjoining compartment with Vida following.

"Let's debrief. Vida, have you seen the Nautilus Docking Commander's son recently?"

"You mean that twenty-something lab tech whose been training to be on the Nanosilc Repair Team?"

"Yeah. That's him. And he's already been promoted to that team. What's his name again, Dextra?"

"Zander," Dextra replied, obviously wary of his intentions. "Zander Marcks."

"He's usually in the SS *Challenge*'s Astro Lab, regardless of whether he's on duty, right?" Vida asked. "He's a bit of an over-achiever, eh?"

"That's where I usually see him," Solomon said. "I've come up with a plan that involves him and his mother."

"I know exactly where Zander Marcks is," Dextra said. "He's out spacewalking right now."

Solomon's jaw dropped at that. Who in the blazes authorized him to do that in the middle of all this madness?

"I heard about it from Joany in the Astro Lab yesterday. Somehow he got wind of top-secret information and started asking Command staff some awkward questions. So Commander Edge and his mother sought to distract him with a spacewalk today. He's out practicing a repair on the Northwest Quadrant as we speak."

"Maybe he found the group in Serica Sector," Vida said.

"I don't know the details. I guess the docking commander supposed he couldn't get into trouble if he was spacewalking."

Even as Solomon shook his head, he realized he could use this to his advantage. He now knew where Zander was, he was isolated, and if he headed out there to intercept him, he could maneuver him up right in front of the docking commander's fenestella up on the Nautilus Command Deck. Having his hand on her son's oxygen supply would soften up Daniela's stance on Reachers real quick.

"Where is your cap?" He glanced back at Vida as he said it. "You're going to need it later." Even though it was a requirement, her standard issue women's cap was nowhere in sight, and in its place, she had coiled her hair into a tightly braided bun at the base of her head. That was his Vida. Always breaking the rules just enough to get away with it.

"Why?"

"You're going on a spacewalk."

A sly smile crept into the corners of her mouth. "Well, hot damn. Where and when?"

Solomon smiled despite the situation. Chief Drive Ops Officer Vida Rosado had been with him a long time. No better ally.

"You're going to have to get yourself from Nautilus to the Challenge undetected."

"And taking a walk is the easiest way. Got it."

"But first I want you to get Daniela Marcks to follow you into Conference Compartment 4C. It was empty when we passed through there a while ago. Detain her in whatever way you can. Wait until I contact you. If she won't stay, make her. You can lock her in with the override code of 3056."

Vida nodded. "Consider it done."

"Solomon, you can't—"

"There's no time for protocol now, Dextra. Now is the time for action." She glared at him but didn't argue. "Vida, I need your UiComm chip. Challenge Command took mine. You'll need to communicate with me via Daniela Marcks's DOT."

"All right. Let me get it out of my chip slip." Vida immediately reached back to pull away the hair behind her left ear. Solomon listened for the telltale beep-beep of the UiComm chip releasing from Vida's surgical jack.

"Thanks. But I'm also leaving you in the blind. Be aware that my plan is to find the docking commander's son and use him as a bargaining chip to force Marcks to undock the ship."

"So you did come up with a brilliant plan after all,"

Vida said, a smile of pride flitting across her face.

"Of course. That's what they pay me for, right?" The irony of that question was not lost on any of them. "Keep an eye on the *Challenge.* If you don't make it aboard via one of the hatches, take a walk."

"Got it." Vida's eyes sparkled. She always got a kick out of spacewalking.

"You aren't even going to attempt to use a hatch, are you?"

"Nope."

Solomon smiled. "Figured. Has Tavian contacted you at all, Vida?"

"No, I haven't heard from him. It worries me."

"He got a Ui out to me via relay telling me he needed assistance in propulsion."

Vida's hand immediately went to her mouth. "Something's wrong. Tavian would never do that."

"I know. I don't have any more details, though. So I'm going to head over there myself and see if I can spring him out of there. I have a feeling Command has detained him."

Vida frowned and wrinkled her nose in distaste. "Okay, but you be careful, Chief. That mad bastard Mads has probably got him, and Tav doesn't have enough sense to keep his mouth shut at the best of times. I mean, what if it's a trap?"

Solomon hadn't thought of that. "I'll keep to the backways. Don't worry."

"I always worry about you, boss."

A smile curved up at the corner of his mouth. "Which is why I haven't fired you yet."

"Best boss ever," Vida said, flashing a grin at Dextra.

"What about Kasen or Brooker?" Solomon asked.

"Nothing."

"I need to make contact with Brooker ASAP. He's supposed to contact you first, yes?"

"Yes."

"Good. I have your Ui, so hopefully I'll hear from him soon."

"And what of those left on Nautilus?" Vida asked, turning serious.

"Our focus must be on Reacher safety. If you see any Reachers on Nautilus, tell them Reach orders are to board the ship and muster aft on Watch Deck 16."

"My mother?" Dextra asked, her voice unsure.

Solomon nodded. "Send her that encrypted message we talked about. But tell her to go to the Command Deck. That should keep her out of harm's way."

Dextra immediately turned to the side and began composing the message on her DOT.

Solomon hoped this wouldn't backfire on them, but he wouldn't try to stop her. If it were his own mother, he'd probably do the same.

"And Edge? He is the ship's commander . . .?"

Solomon shook his head. "Don't worry about Challenge Command or the board. They are all good at looking after their own necks. If they can find a way aboard ship, they'll make it," he said, rubbing absently at the bandage on his hand.

Vida nodded toward it. "What happened?"

"Oh, it's nothing," Solomon said.

"It wasn't nothing," Dextra said, anger tingeing her words. "Edge tortured him with Graversen and my mother looking on."

Vida stared at her. "Bastards" was all she would say.

"Don't worry about it, Vida. I'm fine." Solomon hoped his gaze would convince Dextra to drop it.

Vida raised her eyebrow, disbelieving him utterly by the look of it. "I'd like to Taser them all right now, but that won't do anything but get me thrown in lockdown. We've got work that needs doing. The sooner we do it, the sooner I can give Commander Edge a piece of my mind—or my fist if I'm so inclined—when next I see that pompous ass. You two go. They'll be after you soon."

"Take care of yourself. At a certain point, I'll be holding that kid's life in my hands. That's when you need to make a break for the ship. Don't delay."

"Understood."

"Are you ready?" he asked Dextra.

She pressed a few more buttons on her DOT and nodded. "Done."

Peering out the compartment's slider, he found that the corridor was clear.

He glanced back at Vida. "We won't leave you behind. I swear it."

Vida flashed a smile as she nodded.

Solomon hoped she'd succeed in coaxing Marcks to follow her. Every element of his plan depended on it.

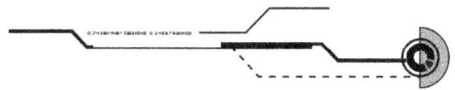

Solomon and Dextra stood nonchalantly near the entrance of the SS *Challenge*'s docking module. He still had no useful plan for boarding the ship undetected. A glance at Dextra told him she didn't either. He knew Founder crew would be guarding the Cryo Hatch, and if they had been notified to keep an eye out for Solomon, it was going to be nearly impossible to board without the whole Founder crew detaining them.

"What if I went up first and talked to them? Distracted them like I've done before . . .?" Dextra asked him.

"Hmm . . . Or we could go together, and if they stop us, you could say Challenge Command requested we report to them."

"That might work. Let's just hope it doesn't come to that. I never professed to be a good actress."

"You're actually quite good at this, you know," Solomon said.

"Don't tell my mother that."

"I'll try to refrain."

Solomon peeked around the corner and got a quick lay of the land. He was surprised to see the girl, Neyve Colgan, again. And her uncle, his best bioengineer Dugal Colgan, walked beside her as they moved down the module toward the hatch. He thought it odd that Dugal would bring her this close to the ship, but they were likely saying a final goodbye. He hoped Dugal would hurry and board. Chaos could easily erupt in the next few minutes, and he didn't want to put either of the Colgans in unnecessary danger.

"All right. There's nothing for it," Solomon said, feeling an anxiety welling in the pit of his stomach as he cradled his spasming palm. "Let's get on with this."

They walked out into the center of the module's long corridor amid mostly *Challenge* and Nautilus crew and the odd passenger here and there. It wasn't overly busy, but Solomon hoped they would blend in a bit even though their uniforms were hard to miss.

"Chief!" he heard a woman call out, and the ball of anxiety in his stomach exploded. He glanced toward the hatch area at the far end and saw Tessra Daleda rushing toward him, smile wide though perplexed. "What the heck are you doing at this hatch?"

Solomon ignored her in favor of checking out the Founder guards' reactions to her outburst. They were looking his way unfortunately, sharing the same perplexed stare. One of them frowned, and Solomon forced himself to smile broadly at Tessra.

Just act the part, Sol. Pretend there's no reason why you shouldn't be here.

"Tessra, how about you? What brings you to this hatch?"

"Oh, I was just eating nearer to this hatch, and thought I'd pop in this way. I know I'm supposed to take the crew hatch. Sorry, boss." She blushed a bit at that, and Solomon took the opportunity to lean close to her ear.

"Tessra, we've got to get aboard the ship no matter what occurs. It's critical. Distract the guards for us?"

Tessra nodded as she smiled for the guards' benefit. "Is it a code 10–36?"

"Yes. Tell no one. And make sure you get aboard as soon as possible. Muster aft on Watch Deck 16."

"Yes, sir."

"Hey, I thought Graversen said he had detained him," Solomon heard the guard with bad teeth say.

Damn.

Solomon tried to focus on Tessra's movements as she strode up to bad-teeth guy. He didn't know either of the guards, which could either be a good thing or a bad thing. He was about to find out.

The dark-eyed guard elbowed bad-teeth guy forward. Tessra stepped right in front of him and started peppering him with questions like a champ. Yet another crew member who was about to get a raise at Reach Corp. Pretty soon they'd bankrupt him, and he was very much okay with that.

Teeth guy wasn't having any of it, trying to push past her to get to Solomon. She cut him off again, and this time, he lost his patience, pulling a stun gun on her.

This was escalating more quickly than Solomon anticipated. He had no idea how to diffuse the situation, but he wasn't going to stand there dumbfounded and lose his only chance to board the ship.

"What are you doing, Georgie?" Tessra protested loudly. "Pulling a gun on me?" she demanded, pushing the gun's barrel away from her. Damn, that woman had guts.

"Here's our chance, Neyve girl," he overheard Dugal say to his niece, who looked petrified. "Let's go!"

It took Solomon a moment to realize what he was saying. He was attempting to sneak Neyve aboard, something he doubted he'd try if he knew his boss was standing right behind him. As it was, Solomon had too much to worry about than a single unauthorized girl.

"Hey, old man," the dark-eyed guard yelled. "I haven't checked you in yet. Wait in the holding area."

"Oh, sir, I have my pass right here," Dugal responded, scrolling through screens on his wrist device.

This might bode well for Solomon and Dextra, as it provided a distraction.

Dugal suddenly shoved Neyve forward toward the hatch.

"What do you mean?" the girl asked Dugal dumbly, her voice high with fear.

On the other side of the docking module, Tessra wrestled with the guard, elbowing his chin as she reached for the stun gun.

Suddenly the gun went off, and gasps went around the module as the impact stream hit Dugal square in the chest. He seemed to convulse and go lax almost immediately, as if he had had a heart attack from the shock of the stun gun. The look on the girl's face as her uncle crumpled to the floor before her was hard to bear. But Solomon knew by the sightlessness of his eyes and the death rattle of his body that he had already passed away. Dugal was a loyal and good man. He didn't deserve such an end.

Solomon immediately wanted to go to him, but the thought of the three thousand Reachers waiting for rescue stopped him. He could either see what could be done for Dugal, or he could callously use this opportunity to reach the SS *Challenge*. Again, he was faced with an impossible but obvious choice. He would have to go on and slip by the guards while they dealt with the Colgans.

"Uncle Dugal! Oh my god. What did you do?" Neyve yelled at the guard.

Both guards stood still with shock as they stared at Dugal.

That was when Solomon grabbed Dextra's hand and skirted around behind the crowd of onlookers beyond the guards' eye line.

"He has a bum heart, you moron!" Neyve shouted, her anger subsiding into a fractured and fragile voice toward the end. "Uncle D, can you hear me?" was the last thing Solomon heard her say as he and Dextra slipped aboard the SS *Challenge*. The echoes of her sobs reminded him of his sister, yet another victim of collateral damage. One soul for three thousand? What gave him the right to make that choice?

# THE PASSAGE

Solomon immediately pulled Dextra into a maintenance compartment right off the Cryo Deck's main esplanade.

"If we're going to make it, we'll need to blend in," he said as he worked to manually lock the slider. "Daughter of the XO and the Reach Corp Chief tend to stick out in a crowd."

"How are we going to manage that?"

Solomon grabbed some maintenance worker uniforms off hooks along the bulkhead. They were loose-fitting, ombre-blue uniforms with separate shirts and pants. They'd keep them from standing out in their own uniforms as well as ensuring—hopefully—anonymity.

"Here, put this on over your uniform." He tossed her one, and she sat on the bench that took up one whole corner of the compartment to pull off her boots.

"What about you?" Dextra mumbled through the fabric she held in her teeth.

"Same. I'll need to strip off the maintenance uniform for my spacewalk later."

"You're really going to do that?" she asked, slipping the uniform over her own and zipping it up.

"It's a lovely day for a walk outside, don't you think?"

Her scowl made him laugh. "Don't joke about it. That boy is innocent."

"From what I hear, he's no innocent boy. And I don't plan to harm him, but Marcks doesn't know that," he said, ripping off his boots and slipping into the too-tight uniform.

"And what if the ship leaves without you?"

If I'm left behind, at least Edge and Graversen will be pleased. That's something, right?"

Dextra punched him in the arm irritably. "I'm not going to let that happen."

"Getting used to having me around, eh?" Solomon asked, the stress of the past few hours making him feel a bit giddy and stupid. They both pulled their boots back on at the same time, and then glanced at each other simultaneously.

"Yes, if you must know." Dextra glanced away, cheeks blooming pink.

Solomon frowned, not sure how to read her. "Well, ah . . ." he tried awkwardly but failed to come up with a brilliant comeback. Yet his curiosity got the best of him. "Why? Why would you want to help me? You're one of them—a Founder."

"Because as hard as it is for you to believe, I have a conscience," she said tartly, as if he had offended her. He started to respond but she waved a hand at him. "And I believe you to be right. I don't think Command should knowingly harm three thousand people who have a right—under contract—to be here."

Solomon shook his head in disbelief. She really did want his plan to succeed.

"My concern is for you right now, Dextra. I don't know what's going to happen when this thing goes down, and I don't want you to get hurt."

"I'll take my chances."

"You should have been a Reacher."

"Oh, really? Prospects aren't exactly looking up for the Reachers at the moment," she observed.

"But we have an excellent benefits package," Solomon protested, attempting not to crack a smile.

She smiled for him. "Where are we going first?" she asked, quite obviously changing the subject.

"Best I don't tell you in case you get caught with me. You'll find out soon enough."

She frowned again. "Not sure that works for me."

Solomon sighed, mildly amused. "We're heading down to the Cargo Sector to a secret passage up through the decks. That much I will tell you. So stick close to me and stay out of sight. The cameras will pick us up, but no one will think anything of it until the alarm is sounded."

"Secret passage?" Dextra glanced sideways at him. "There is no such thing."

"You think that the Chief Aerospace Engineer who designed the state-of-the-art 880-meter spaceship you're standing in wouldn't have included a few hidden compartments?"

"Hmm . . . Why exactly would you need them?"

"I was just betrayed and tortured by my evil overlords. Reason enough?"

"I'm not sure that Challenge Command would—"

"I think we're past considering what they find acceptable professional behavior, yes? Those compartments may save some precious lives when all is said and done—maybe even our own."

"All right. But be aware I find it . . . uncomfortable."

"Not surprising."

Just then her stomach gave a vicious growl, and he couldn't help the laugh that erupted from him. "That making you uncomfortable too?" he asked.

She grinned. "Starving. Got anything to eat?"

"Yes, there should be something in one of these footlockers." He rummaged around and came up with two Aero Energy Bars. He tossed her one and ripped into his, finishing it off in two massive bites. "Should hold us for at least three or four hours."

She ravenously bit into hers and looked around once finished. "Any more for the road?"

"Sorry. That's all I found." He gave her a look-over. "Just one more thing." Solomon pulled a name patch from a drawer full of them and tossing it to her. "Your name is now Greeta Volk."

"And yours"—Dextra rummaged in the drawer and pressed one to his chest—"is Devro Tezer."

"I always knew my parents should have called me Devro."

"No, Solomon fits you," Dextra said, tilting her head. "Do you have any other family on the ground?"

"The Reachers are my family now." He felt a bit uneasy with that line of talk, so he waved her over to the door. "Wait a sec. There are crew just down the corridor. I can hear them." He pressed his ear to the locked slider, straining to hear the voices as they drew nearer.

Suddenly, the alarm he'd been dreading since he escaped nearly made him jump out of his skin. Beyond its initial testing, it was the first time he'd ever heard that alarm go off. He never dreamed he would be the one to trigger it.

"Warning. Warning. Chief Engineering Officer Solomon Reach has gone rogue. If you see him, report him to ship's security immediately."

For a moment, he and Dextra stared at each other. Here was the moment of truth. Would she chicken out at this point? He wouldn't blame her. He ought to make her stay here for her own safety anyway.

"Detain Solomon Reach at all costs," the loud-speaker went on. "Repeat: detain Solomon Reach.

Call in his status and location ASAP."

The alarm bell sounded three more times and fell blessedly silent.

"That's going to make things a bit more difficult," Dextra said, her voice deadpan.

He studied her face, and she flashed him a lop-sided smile. "You don't have to do this, Dextra. You can back out, say I kidnapped you."

"I'm not going to sit around worrying about you while you're out there trying to save the world."

"Not the world. Just my crew. But I'll understand if you want to play it safe. They aren't your people, so I wouldn't blame you."

Dextra looked offended. "I've been working side by side with your crew since the SS *Challenge* launch project started. Even if no one else is willing to honor your sacrifices . . . I will."

Solomon nodded, vowing not to broach the subject again. She was one of them, no matter where she came from.

"While we're still hidden away in here, I'm going to try again to make contact with Tavian."

"You really think Challenge Command is questioning him?"

"I sure as hell hope not."

Solomon spun up Vida's UiComm and reconfigured it a bit to monitor his own vitals.

"New text to Tavian Hunt: Report your status ASAP. Respond to Vida's UI."

Solomon glanced at Dextra who was shoving their hats below a pile of uniforms in a footlocker. He glanced at her shiny black hair as it swung around. It wasn't often he was able to see a woman's free-flowing hair these days. He had to glance away or she was bound to notice him staring.

"All right, we need to go," he said.

"Maintenance caps?"

"Yes, here." He grabbed two from a small bin and gave her one. She clamped it down hard on her head and completed her transformation into janitor. Even in that getup she was beautiful. He pulled his cap on to distract himself.

"You ready?" he asked.

"Yes. Hey, what if we push around this cart? We'd look more official."

Solomon looked over the cart that was filled with various supplies and tools for maintaining the automatic cleaning bots. "That's a good idea. The supplies might also come in handy at some point."

He rummaged around and found just what he was looking for: a hex key set. He slipped it into his pocket. He was going to need that later.

"I'll push it out after you open the door," Dextra said.

"Don't look directly at any cameras and keep a steady walk as we go. Got it?"

They skidded out into the temporarily vacant hallway. Solomon felt at once their vulnerability. He was no criminal or spy. He was an engineer. He was used to commanding respect. But if he wanted to survive this day without dismemberment or worse, he'd have to fake anonymity.

He grabbed Dextra's arm as a group of *Challenge* crew walked by at the end of the corridor.

"We're heading toward that door to the left. It may require a code that could take me some time to override. Pull the cart around so it's between us and them."

Dextra nodded once and pushed the cart to the center of the corridor, which also hid his work on the panel.

Solomon pulled up his Ui HUD to double check the override code he needed.

He felt her touch on his shoulder. "They're coming," Dextra murmured. "Hurry."

Solomon forced himself not to look in the direction of the approaching footsteps. Finally, he found the right code. As he began to input it, he heard them talking.

"Be systematic. Remember he knows every inch of this ship. He has the advantage," a male voice said.

"And we need to figure out where he might be headed and work back from there," a woman responded.

"I suspect he would have disguised himself in some way. It's what I would do. Maintenance crew maybe?"

Awkward silence ensued, and Solomon could feel them staring at the back of his head. He moved to block their view of Dextra's face and motioned her to head into the compartment with the cart. He could see her breathing quicken. He touched her hand briefly as she entered the maintenance compartment to try and calm her down.

"Hey!" one of the *Challenge* employees called out, and Solomon heard their rapid footsteps approaching.

Solomon shut the door immediately and inputted his emergency code to disable further access.

"Did they recognize us?" Dextra asked, breathless.

"I'm not sure. I don't think so, but let's not stick around to find out. Gotta keep moving. Next up, we need to cross another corridor. I don't think you're familiar with this area, are you?"

"No, is this strictly a maintenance sector?"

"Among other things. But service crew only."

"Lead the way."

"A lot of Reacher offices in this area. We should be safe."

"That's comforting," she said, and he didn't miss the sarcasm.

"Well, I'm all about comfort."

"I doubt that."

"Hey, if I had a beach chair and an ice cold beer in front of me right now, you can bet I'd be living it up with the best of them."

She smirked. "Liar."

"Honestly, I can't even recall what a beach looks like. Or the feel of sand or touch of the waves."

"Well, I can drop you down the Solix Sky's ribbon, and you can have a nice little dip in the ocean."

He gave her a lopsided grin. "Thoughtful of you."

"But first, you've got Reachers to save."

"It's always work, work, work with you."

"True enough."

Solomon peeked out the back door that led to another corridor. "All right. Corridor's clear. Let's move."

They rushed down the hall, the cart's wheels squeaking loudly across the floor. The sound caught the attention of a few Reachers, but Solomon ignored them and turned away, hoping they were far enough away not to be recognized.

"Oh my god! Chief? What—"

Jesus. Was he really that recognizable in a janitor's get up?

He sliced a hand through the air and shook his head, hoping whoever it was would get the hint. He squinted and realized it was just Josie. She'd be a good girl and let them pass by. He pressed a finger to his lips. Josie hesitated but nodded.

"Sir, they're looking for you," she whispered as she approached.

"I know. Any Founder crewmember asks . . . tell them you saw me on Watch Deck 18. Tell no Reachers where you saw me. And Josie, do *not* leave this ship for any reason."

"Yes, sir," Josie said.

Solomon nodded his thank you and pressed Dextra into the next compartment.

"Here we are and here is where we leave our trusty cart."

"And where is here exactly?" she asked, peering around the dark, cramped compartment.

"Can't you see we're standing in a broom closet?"

"I have eyes, Solomon."

"Well, look a little more closely, and you'll see what's really here." Though he'd never had a need to use it before, he had always meant to take this route up just to see how it fared in the construction phase. He had built this secret entrance as a route of emergency egress or in case of catastrophe or danger. Little did he know when he had designed it that he'd be using it to aid a saboteur working in his employ. Funny, that. Ridiculous, even. He opened the broom cabinet, pulled the cleaning supplies out, and stacked them neatly. He hit the hidden button on the ceiling, which brought down a succession of stairs, one after the other.

"Wow," was all Dextra could muster. "And what was this built for, really?"

"Emergency, actually. Would you say this qualifies, Ms. Justice?"

"Don't be cheeky, Chief Reach."

"My apologies. After you?"

"Um, no." She eyed the staircase dubiously. "You first."

"Thinking it leads to some sinister lair?"

"I have no idea what to think, but mainly I don't want to run into anyone unpleasant up there."

"This bit here is secret. Won't be anyone here, since only the construction crew that worked on this section and I are aware it's here."

"You're still going first."

Her half-smirk made him weak in the knees. Man, if he wasn't trying to save a bunch of people from death and destruction right now, he'd ask her out.

# THE
# CARGO SECTOR

Solomon ran up the steps with Dextra in tow.

"Hold up. Pit stop." He stopped next to a locker he had built into the wall and rummaged around for the wrist tracker dampeners that would keep Challenge Command from tracking their location. They had probably already started tracking them, which might lead them to the maintenance room below, but he hoped they would assume it was a dead-end.

"Put this on," he said, slipping his over his wrist.

"A dampener?" she asked, turning the flesh-colored, thin band around in her hand. "I've honestly never seen one before. How does it work?"

Solomon switched his on, and then reached for her arm. "Here, let me get it for you." She pressed her fingers together as he stretched the band around her hand and slid it up her wrist. "It basically interferes with your wrist tracker by scrambling the RF signal."

As he pressed a couple of the buttons to turn the dampener on and set it, he was particularly aware that he had a gorgeous woman alone in a deserted corridor at the moment, which made for an excellent time to steal something or other—a kiss?—but also aware he was no James Bond. He really needed to practice this sort of thing more often.

He pulled away slightly, and she fiddled with the band, stretching it here and there. And yet another opportune moment passes . . .

"Let's go," he said gruffly, pulling her along by the elbow.

They moved along the whitewashed corridor until it came out to what looked like a dead-end.

"We're here," Solomon said, pressing his ear to the panel to listen.

"Here being . . .?"

"The cargo hold. Guards are going to be about, so keep an eye out and stay light on your feet."

He heard nothing but the hum of the HVAC systems, so he peeked through the door. All was clear. As long as they didn't run into any guards, they ought to be able to traverse the hold with no issues. He actually recalled where most of the security cameras were, so they could avoid being seen as well.

He led her into the labyrinth of crates and boxes that made up the massive Cargo Sector of the SS *Challenge*. All manner of materials and supplies were stored here—raw materials for the 3D printing devices they were carrying, endless amounts of surplus food, and even priceless artifacts from Earth. They were triple-strapped to sturdy hooks on the ground and netted for when the AGG was turned off for easier cargo loading and unloading or, more importantly, in the event that traveling through the Sideris Cavum turned out to be a less-than-pleasant experience.

"Now we navigate the crate maze and make it over to the crew passage on the other side," Solomon whispered. "I've got another secret door over there for you."

"This is starting to get creepy."

"Glad to amuse."

She punched him in the arm, and it made him grin. A Reacher through and through, this woman.

The cargo hold was quiet, which didn't seem unusual to Solomon since everyone on the ship was probably looking for him, and all of the equipment and supplies needed for the trip had been packed weeks ago. They moved from unit to unit, like walking city blocks back in Boston.

"Guard," Solomon whispered, and he jerked Dextra behind a crate before the guy caught sight of them. He was a *Challenge* guard. The wary eyes and slow walk gave him away. He was most certainly searching for them. Solomon wasn't sure if the guy had heard their approach or not. He hadn't heard the guard's footsteps, so maybe there was a chance. He'd only caught sight of the guy in the fishbowl mirror hanging off one of the crates as he headed down the central aisle.

Solomon and Dextra hid one row to the guard's right. As the man walked down past the crate, he and Dextra soundlessly rounded to the backside of the next crate. They stood there breathing quietly, and Solomon hoped there wasn't another mirror he couldn't see where the guy could catch a glimpse of them.

He heard the guard turn into the aisle just down from the crate they hid behind. They tiptoed to the other side. Solomon only caught the merest glimpse of him. He glanced around wildly. Nothing to hand that he could turn into a makeshift weapon. He'd have to use his fists.

They scooted around toward the center of the aisle as the guard made his way toward their original hiding spot. A squeak of Solomon's shoe sent the man running in their direction.

Ah, hell.

"Make a run for it around the other side, Dextra," he whispered. "Do it now!"

As soon as the guard came around the corner, he'd have to do something to take him down. He didn't think, just grabbed hold of the netting covering the crate above him and swung hard to intercept the guy.

Solomon felt the impact before he heard the thud of his boots against the guy's ribs or his shout of pain. The guard clutched his mid-section and crumpled down on his backside. Solomon reached down to deliver another blow, but the guy was quick. He pressed hard against Solomon's hip with his leg and yanked his ankle out from under him.

It was a hard fall but, once down, Solomon instinctively went for the guy's neck, maneuvering him around to a blood choke knowing it would put him down hard and fast. It took all of four seconds before he went limp in Solomon's arms.

"Solomon, stop!" Dextra hissed. "You killed him!"

Dammit. He'd better check. He pulled out from under the guy and laid his head gently on the floor. While he held his fingers to the guy's pulse, Solomon listened past their collective labored breathing for sounds of any more *Challenge* crew coming their way. He did hear running footsteps.

Solomon finally felt a faint pulse beneath his fingers. "He's okay. Let's move."

"They are behind us," Dextra hissed under her breath. "This way."

She led the way down the center aisle, and they took off at a flat run. Now was the time to gain as much distance as possible. Their pursuers would

come across the fallen guard at any moment and no-
tify Command.

"Straight ahead," Solomon said in a low voice behind her. "You input the code."

"Tell me the numbers," Dextra said, as she approached the slider marked Maintenance 1D.

"Seven-eight-zero-two."

She punched it in just as they heard shouts behind
them.

"It's Reach!"

The two guards were sprinting toward them, closing the gap far too fast.

Solomon shoved Dextra into the compartment
headlong and turned immediately to shut the slider.
He punched in his override code to lock it down. On
the other side of the slider, the guards shouted and
cursed at them.

Dextra had fallen into a spinning chair, and when
it spun around again, he pulled her out by the hand
and yanked her along behind him.

"Wait! I need to catch my breath."

"No time. They'll have an override code of their
own. They are Cargo Sector security guards."

He dragged her down a long corridor and tried to
remember which doors and compartments he needed
to slip through in order to get to the right one. After
confusing the hell out of Dextra to the point where
she just had a look of agitation permanently plastered
on her pale features, he finally made it to his next
stop: compartment 1OH.

"It's here."

"I feel like Alice in Wonderland in here."

"Imagine designing it."

"Well, at least you know where everything is."

He flashed her a half-smile. "Mostly."

This time, his secret passage was through a
hidden door in the panel of one wall in this office

compartment. When he popped it open by pressing against a seemingly non-existent button hidden along one seam of the panel, Dextra raised her eyebrows.

"Impressive."

"I aim to impress."

"Sure, sure. Keep moving, Mr. Reach."

"No, after you. I insist."

She heaved an exaggerated sigh but headed up the stairs first this time around.

"Where does this lead?"

"This staircase bypasses the Shuttle Sector and ends at Engineering."

"Why are we going there, anyway? I thought we were looking for Zander Marcks."

"We have to make sure Tavian hid the Cavitran Drive part. If he failed, we'll do it ourselves."

"Why is hiding the Cav part so important?"

"It's buying me time to get to Zander Marcks, blackmail his mother, and muster my crew onto Watch Deck 16. It's also yet another bargaining chip against Challenge Command."

"Ah, I see. Sounds like you've got it all figured out."

"Hardly. I'm pulling this plan out of my ass."

"I'll refrain from any witty comebacks."

"How professional of you."

They rounded several more corners and headed up the spiral staircase. Solomon pressed his back against the bulkhead for a moment to catch his breath. Dextra did the same, pressing her hands to her knees, and they stood side by side for a few moments, just breathing.

"Hell of a day, huh? Despite how it may seem, I can assure you that I never thought I'd be running for my life today. Or attempting to save the lives of three thousand people."

"This is why the Reachers love you so much. I've seen it. I've seen how they talk about you. They see you as a father figure. Not just a boss paying the bills. And there was a time that my mother felt the same about you. She's been twisted into thinking she needs to go along with Edge's plans. But no matter what, we're going to make it. We're going to survive. It's what humans are built for. We don't know any other way."

"I'm no savior of the world, Dextra. Just took over a job I wasn't prepared for and did the best I could with it."

"But you've been saving all of us for years. With every Asteria ship you built, you were guaranteeing the continuation of the human race. What does it feel like to have that kind of responsibility?" Her teasing tone belied a serious subtext to her question.

"It feels . . . uncomfortable."

She nodded. "I figured as much."

"Well, it'll feel all right if I actually succeed in getting the SS *Challenge* out of the solar system."

"Just all right?"

"Maybe a better word is miraculous. I can't really think about the consequences, the repercussions if I don't pull this off. If I stop to think about it too much, the fear of failure will paralyze me."

She stood and faced him, the look in her eyes so intense he glanced away. But she placed both hands on his cheeks and forced him to look at her.

"You are going to succeed. One way or the other. And I'm going to do everything in my power to help you save them."

The look in her eyes told him that she meant it.

"Why are you helping me?" He hadn't meant to ask her again, but he still couldn't reconcile her motivations with his own.

"I told you before. You are in the right. Even if

Command can no longer see what's right and wrong. I see it. And that is enough."

She leaned forward to kiss his cheek, and it was such a simple gesture of solidarity. It had been years since a woman had even touched him in such a way. Aerospace Engineering 144,000 kilometers from Earth didn't lend itself so well to traditional relationships. He reached up to cover her hand with his own, just to feel her skin beneath his.

At times this idea of saving the Reachers was this high ideal that didn't seem to have a sense of reality for him. He had no family of his own. Living in space and perpetual schooling had left him with a rather sterile and lonely life. He might be respected but he was not loved. Yet, being this close to a woman, feeling her breath on his face . . . It reminded him that there was more to humanity than just the beat of a pulse and air in the lungs.

He knew there were a great many reasons why he shouldn't, but he couldn't remember a single one. So he closed his eyes and kissed her. Just once and then he pulled back in case she needed more room to slap him. But her hands had not moved, so he opened his eyes to look at her.

Dextra had the smallest hint of a smile tugging at the corners of her mouth, but it was the intensity of her gaze that blew his mind. Her lips were still parted, her eyelids lowered, her expression fierce with emotion.

Then she pushed him back and kissed him hard. Solomon met her intensity with his own, reaching to pull her closer, pressing her hips into his. Her forehead reached his chin, and it was altogether delicious to bend to her and feel her rise on her toes to meet his mouth. He pressed his tongue gently to hers, and he rather thought he might be getting the hang of it.

The last time he'd locked lips with a woman had

been at Georgia Tech. The voluptuous Poly Sci major kept her eyes wide open the whole time, whispering "those baby blues of yours," as she had his backside in a firm grip while inhaling his mouth with considerable skill. Dextra was staring at his baby blue eyes right now.

They finally pulled away from each other, breathless. Of course, he was a socially awkward engineer at heart, so the first words out of his mouth made him want to punch himself in the face.

"Well, that was unexpected."

Her laugh was breathtaking. Then she shrugged lightly. "Intense circumstances—the end of the world and all that."

"Oh, right. Not that I'm complaining."

"I should hope not."

He smirked, dipping down for another kiss. "Most definitely not."

She glanced at the door. "Should we do this?"

"Now or never and all that."

"Well, we've got the clichés down. Suppose we better see if we can save the world and add another one to the pile."

"Follow my lead."

By now, the guards would have informed Challenge Command that they had been spotted in the Cargo Hull. Security would do a thorough sweep of the entire sector, which would take them some time. But they were also aware that he and Dextra had entered the office area to the side. He very much doubted any of the Reacher construction crew would be consulted, so it was unlikely they would ever find out about the secret stairwells. So he'd bought them some time at least. But Command would have guards stationed around the Propulsion Sector. At the least, they would have *Challenge* staff coordinating with

Reacher crew in there in order to troubleshoot the sabotaged Cavitran Drive.

Solomon really didn't have a plan for how he would get to Tavian. He'd have to wing it. His plan to blend in didn't seem to be working. He guessed his black skin and blue eyes were more recognizable than he had hoped. The uniforms were better than nothing, though. He knew he'd have to find the switch to open the secret panel out into the corridor. And, of course, try to avoid anyone who might want to take them into custody.

"Got it." Solomon gave her a warning look while he held the latch in his hand. "Once I open this panel, we could run into any sort of trouble. Stay alert."

She nodded and he pulled the panel slightly ajar. Nothing down the right side of the corridor. He listened for any noise or approaching footsteps. Silence.

"I think we're clear. Come on." He opened the panel wide, and they both stepped out into the corridor. He replaced the panel, and they made their way down the corridor, moving aft toward the center of the ship, where the Cav Drive was located. They would come up into the Cav Compartment from below. In his mind, it was the scenario least likely to get them killed or sent to lockdown.

"*Challenge* crew are going to be crawling all over the place once we get near the Propulsion Sector. Keep your eyes and ears open."

"What if we get caught?" she asked.

"Simple, really. You'll get soundly chastised by your mother on your way to the Sideris Gate. And I will likely be floated out for a very long spacewalk after Challenge Command has uncomfortably extracted what they want out of me."

# THE RABBIT HOLE

"Hope you don't have claustrophobia," Solomon whispered, glancing at Dextra as they walked down another long, deserted corridor.

She merely glanced sideways at him.

"We're heading to propulsion but we're going to get there the back way so we can avoid as many people as possible. We'll be coming up from below and between decks through cramped maintenance and systems compartments and corridors, so it may get uncomfortable at times."

"I'm good," she replied.

"Here we go." He stopped at Maintenance Compartment 3K.

"What is this?"

"Nothing of consequence. Just an office. But it's got an access panel we need. Wait by the slider and keep an eye out. Anyone comes, hit five-five-two-zero on the panel."

He pulled the hex key out of his pocket and went to work unscrewing the quarter-turn fasteners on all four sides of the large access panel located along the back bulkhead.

"We're going in there?"

"Yes, this sector of the ship was remodeled a year ago, but this shaft, what is essentially an older crawl space to access the central maintenance chute, was abandoned and likely forgotten about by the Founders. I only remember it because my Reachers had a devil of a time repairing portions of it due to an accident involving a wrench that I won't get into."

"Ah," Dextra said, clearly uninterested in the details. "Well, as long as you know where we're going."

"Long story short, it will eventually connect us to the central maintenance corridor that will take us one step closer to the Cav Compartment. I'm going to try contacting Tavian again. Hold on."

> "UI, NEW MESSAGE TO TAVIAN HUNT:
> WHAT'S YOUR STATUS AND LOCATION?"

He finished with the panel and removed it, tucking his hex key back into his pocket for later use.

"Actually go ahead and lock us in with that code, Dextra. I won't be able to close up this access panel from the inside. Hopefully, no one will try to get in here within the next hour."

"All right."

Solomon saw a message pop up in his HUD. "Hang on. Tavian finally responded."

"Did they detain him?" Dextra asked.

"Ui, check messages." Solomon's muscles tensed as he read with Dextra looking on.

> IN CAV ROOM. 5 FOUNDERS TAKING A SHORT
> BREAK FROM ROUGHING ME UP. IF YOU DON'T
> WANT THIS PERFECT FACE LOOKING LIKE
> ROADKILL, YOU BETTER SPRING ME OUTTA
> HERE.

"Damn," Solomon whispered under his breath, his

hand twitching again. "They've detained him, but he's still in the Cav Room."

> "UI REPLY: DISTRACT COMMAND AND GET THEM OUT OF CAV WITHIN THE HOUR. ON MY WAY."

Tavian replied immediately.

> YOU FUCKING KIDDING ME?

> "UI REPLY: IF YOU WANT TO LIVE, I RECOMMEND IT."

> SURE, PLAY THE "IF YOU WANT TO LIVE" CARD. TYPICAL BOSS.

> "UI REPLY: SMIRK."

"This Tavian Hunt is rather a charming fellow," Dextra said in a posh English accent, her smile distracting him from the fact that he was about to face five Founder crew before the hour was up.

"He better be as smart as I'm paying him to be," Solomon muttered.

"Well, you hired him."

"Actually, Vida did."

"Maybe you should mention that the fate of the world is on his shoulders."

"Tavian's the type who does better when he's relaxed . . . or amused."

"And what type are you, Solomon?"

"Hmm . . . a workaholic."

She wrinkled her nose and smiled. "I noticed."

"I suspect you are as well."

"Touché."

"All right, next leg of the journey is down the rabbit hole."

"Flashlight?" she asked.

"Ah, yes. We'll need it through this abandoned section here." He thought for a moment and eventually found a small one after rummaging around in the desk's bottom drawer. "Keep in mind that most of these shafts—but not all—are built to hold the weight of a man for repair purposes. So follow my lead and go where I go. But just to be on the safe side, stay at least five feet behind me to distribute the weight more evenly. The last thing we need is to bust something in here."

"Comforting," Dextra said, pulling out her best deadpan.

He slipped the flashlight into his mouth and dove headlong into the tubular maintenance shaft, mumbling to her to follow quietly. As they moved through the cool tube filled with various lines of electrical conduit, he flipped through the engineering drawings for this sector in his mind, trying to keep his bearings straight. He eventually found access hatch FH3, which he knew would lead out into the Central Deck 7 Corridor, which was essentially one long gangway down the center of the Engineering Sector for the sole purpose of providing maintenance access for his workers. Once there, they'd head a bit further aft and down toward the maintenance compartment just below the Cav.

The opening lay just ahead. He could see the gaping hole and the corridor beyond. He came out into the gangway and straightened to a standing position. No one in either direction. Good. No hassle. Exactly what he was hoping for.

"I had no idea this was all back here," Dextra said, as he took her hand and helped her to rise out of the shaft.

"We've come to the central maintenance corridor," he said, pointing to the larger rows of conduit as they ran along the corridor's bulkheads. "It branches off into various other compartments."

"You know where we're going?"

"Let's hope so." He smiled.

"Yes, let's."

They walked for several minutes in silence, as he led her further into the bowels of the ship. Eventually, he turned them toward a starboard branch where they crawled through another shaft that led to the corridor he was looking for.

"Once we're out, head straight for the compartment directly across the corridor. Code is six-four-nine-five. Don't forget. And if someone comes, just act normally. Remember, no one is looking for you."

"So you say."

"Well, at least you're not as valuable."

She raised her eyebrows and mock-scowled. "Oh, really?"

Solomon bit his lip. "That might have come out wrong."

"Uh huh."

"Mea culpa. Would it help if I saved your life today?"

"It might. But don't count on it."

"Hmm . . ."

She was playing hardball. He liked it. And he felt like kissing her again.

"Listening one more time." He pressed his ear to the panel. Still nothing.

"We're good. Now go."

He popped the panel out, and it clattered to the ground. Dextra scowled at him, but he shook his head to forbid her to talk and motioned her across the corridor, which was, thankfully, empty.

She rushed to the other side of the corridor to punch in the numbers on the compartment's code-box. Voices forward of their position were faint but approaching fast. He moved quickly to key in the top left fastener. He couldn't leave it open. It would look too suspicious.

"Solomon!" Dextra whispered harshly.

"Keep the slider open," he whispered back as he kept on with the hex key. The people were getting closer. They'd turn the corner at any moment. He just needed the one fastener in to keep it flush with the wall. Damn. He got it to the point where it would stay up, but the fastener was sticking out quite a ways. He'd have to risk it. They were too close.

He brushed past the panel but the hex key hit one of the grills of the panel and fell out of his hand. The people were turning the corner just as he slipped into the compartment. He didn't know if they saw him or not. But it was so fast, they could hardly have identified him. He was certain they were Founders as he saw a flash of their blue uniforms.

He disabled the slider with his override code and then pressed his ear to it to try and pick up any of their talk.

"What's that?" a woman asked.

"Looks like a hex key," a man replied.

"What do you make of this? Looks like someone was repairing this panel."

"And they just left right in the middle of it?"

"Probably just got called away when the alarm sounded about Solomon Reach."

The voices began to fade away aft.

"Where do you think Reach is?"

"Since I don't know what he's after or what his plan is, it's hard to tell."

"Simple: he wants to kill the Founders. Nothing else makes sense . . ."

Solomon couldn't hear anymore. So it seemed that word of the disabled Cav Drive hadn't spread far. He supposed that was a good thing. He didn't want his Reacher crew to catch wind of Challenge Command's betrayal. If they did, they might do something rash, like rising up in mutiny, as Command had originally feared. He wouldn't put it past his crew. They were a loyal bunch, and they valued their lives as much as the next guys. As Dextra would say, it was in their nature after all.

He tried not to be disturbed by the fact that Founders aboard this ship would immediately think he'd want them dead. But then again, they wanted him dead, so they would likely assume he was just as cold-blooded.

"They're gone."

"Where to now?" she asked.

"Now we hitch a ride through another shaft that will lead us directly to the compartment underneath the Cav."

"Do you still need the key?"

"Yes, but I'd need to get it anyway, so we can cover our tracks."

He disabled the door after checking for anyone in the corridor. When he reached out to grab the hex key, the slider next to the maintenance compartment where they were hiding opened suddenly.

"Ha ha!" said a man who was entering the corridor. "You've got nothing on me—wait, what?"

Solomon looked up to see two of his Reacher crewmen staring at him, eyes wide. Looked to be Jonesy and Baern, both engineers in the Operations Sector.

"Hey guys."

"Boss." Jones touched his aviator cap out of amused respect and nodded, even though his eyebrows were still raised.

Baern stared warily at him. "Sir, I suspect you're well aware Command put out a call for you. How should we—"

"Respond?" Solomon answered, starting in on re-securing the panel.

Baern nodded.

"I'll give you the short version, and then you can decide."

He explained the gist of it in approximately 60 seconds.

"How can we help?" was Baern's immediate reply.

"Can you find out whether there are any Founders in the Cav Compartment currently? If there are, can you call them away, saying that Challenge Command wanted to get a status on the Cav Drive as well as an ETA of when it will be fixed? That should alleviate any suspicions on their part as well as reduce the number of people we have to deal with."

"Yeah, sure, boss," Jones said.

"We're heading that way and will be there shortly," Solomon said.

"Via the port or starboard corridor? We'll lead them in the opposite direction," Baern asked.

"It's best I don't tell you in case you are questioned. Once you complete this task, I want you to muster with the rest of the Reachers on Watch Deck 16."

"Got it. We'll get going." Baern slapped Jonesy on the back and the two headed off.

"Hey boss," Jones said, glancing over his shoulder.

"Yeah?"

"Good luck."

"Thanks." Solomon half-smiled. "I'll need it."

"Your crew is incredibly loyal considering they received a direct order from their superiors to turn you in."

"Well, now, *superior* is a subjective word, don't you agree?"

"Yes, agreed."

"All right. Panel's closed up."

Once prepped, they were on their way again, traversing corridors and sectors he knew by heart. He stopped at Maintenance Compartment 3J and got them in. This compartment was little more than a

broom closet, but it would get them where they needed to go.

Once they made it through the panel, it wasn't long
before they came to a junction around which a twenty-
foot drop lay in wait. It was a tight fit in this section, so
he maneuvered around so his feet were facing first. It
was starting to get unbearably hot, and he wiped the
sweat off his forehead.

"This is going to be the most difficult bit here,"
Solomon said. "We're about to drop down twenty feet
through this shaft so we can come out in the compartment just underneath the Cav. So you're going to need
to shimmy your way down. But bear in mind, this shaft
wasn't designed to take our weight, so be careful, eh?"

"Well, I don't know. You look pretty heavy."

"There are a lot of things I could say at this moment, but intelligence dictates that I keep my mouth
shut."

"Good man. You're smarter than you look."

"A backhanded complimented. I should always be
so lucky."

"You first, Chief."

"Don't mind if I do."

Solomon took his time, testing the shaft's sturdi-
ness as he braced his hands and feet against it. Once
down, he shined the flashlight up at Dextra.

"This doesn't look overly easy," she said.

"Just keep a steady pace and push with your legs.
We need to keep the noise down as much as possible.
The sound will carry. And don't jump down at the end
here. You'll dent the metal."

"Heaven forbid."

"You're standing in a work of art, I'll have you
know, woman. A precision piece of ventilation."

"Well, if you had designed it properly, you would
have cooled the place down and left room for a
woman's bust."

"Ah. I'll give that some thought in my next redesign."

She thumped into the shaft just behind Solomon, ending up nose to nose with him.

"Is it wrong to point out that from this vantage point I have an excellent view of the proceedings?" Solomon asked, failing utterly in his attempt not to peer down at her cleavage, which was spilling out from her partially unzipped uniform.

"Yes, I do believe it is."

"Ah, well. I probably should read up on the Nautilus Code of Conduct."

"You're such an engineer."

"Guilty."

"I think it likely we both need to brush up on protocol before my mother gets on to us," she said, eyes mischievous in the flashlight's glare. "Something tells me she would not approve of this particular excursion."

"We'll turn ourselves in for protocol violations after we save the world," Solomon magnanimously offered.

"Good plan."

"Just a few feet more, and we'll be in the maintenance compartment just under the Cav."

Solomon shimmied backward a few more feet, gave Dextra the flashlight and started working on the fasteners.

"Sounds loud up there," Dextra said.

"Yes, that will work in our favor. Should mask any noises we make as we come up through the floor of the Cav Compartment."

He pushed the panel in and lifted himself out into the blinding light of the maintenance compartment directly below the Cav Room. He turned to take Dextra by the hand and pulled her out too.

"You all right? None the worse for wear?"

"Yes, I survived your rabbit hole after all, Chief Reach."

"Take a look up there." Solomon pointed toward the panel above a block of machines that made up part of the ship's power systems.

"That's where we're headed? Ever hear of a door? How do you propose we reach it?"

Solomon glanced around the compartment at what was to hand. "Hold tight and I'll have an answer for you." He pulled over a supply cart and flipped the stopper to lock it in place.

"Ready to save the day?"

"Right."

"Have no fear. I'm a professional."

"You know, I'm pretty sure this wasn't in my job description."

"I'm pretty sure saving the world wasn't in mine."

She raised an eyebrow. "Actually, it was, Solomon."

He snorted at that. "Not really. When I took over Reach Corp back when my father passed away, I had one objective: make a lot of money in the aerospace industry so I could go on spacewalks."

Dextra actually laughed at that. "Are you serious?"

"Yes. It all started with a dream. Vida's not the only one who likes a good jaunt out in the great black vacuum."

"I suppose that's the first dream for anyone who studies enough to get top marks in their astrophysics classes."

"Well, I was an anomaly. I just had a gift for astronomy and engineering. My father kept placing me in special programs. And then Mads Graversen found me and dragged me back up to space."

"What?" By the look on her face, she was genuinely shocked. "What do you mean? I thought you met him on the Solix Sky."

"Oh, no. It was back at MIT."

"That asshole was your classmate?"

Solomon's smile was grim. "He was my professor."

"Wow."

"Yeah, he got me into this mess in more ways than one."

"I saw him when Edge was torturing you," Dextra said, her voice suddenly soft.

Solomon's hand smarted at the memory of it, but he was thankful the majority of his pain had subsided with the healing thrombin bandage.

"He didn't have the look of a mentor to me."

"Yes, well . . . Mads was always a complicated man. And yes, an asshole."

She tilted her head and studied him, then. "I—"

Solomon stopped her with a touch on her arm. Voices resounded overhead. He motioned for her to stand back.

"You'd best stay down here unless you have considerable skill in hand-to-hand combat," he said in a low voice.

"Not usually a useful skill in space," she said, and her wary glance at the ceiling was a sobering reminder to him that she was under his protection too.

"Definitely stay here, then. Likely this will be over quickly."

"Mr. Hunt, I'm not going to ask you again," a muffled voice said from above, "where is Solomon Reach?"

"As I mentioned the previous fifty times your underlings asked me," Tavian responded, "he's not here, and I don't know where he is."

Dextra heard too. She gave Solomon a "now what?" look.

Frankly, he had no idea. He wondered where Jonesy and Baern were. Had they come and gone? He wished he could see what was happening. It would help to know how many people were in the compartment and where they were located in relation to the panel.

No matter what, he was going to have to get in that compartment, so he didn't delay further.

Solomon glanced at Dextra. "No matter what you hear, if you find yourself in danger, just head out the slider door and find the first Founder you see. No sense in you getting hurt."

Dextra nodded, but he could tell his sensible advice was falling on deaf ears. Admirable and maddening woman!

Solomon hoisted himself up on the cart and then rolled onto the whirring systems machines. As he settled onto his back to key the fasteners, he listened to the quiet sounds of pacing and the occasional throat clearing or murmuring of the others in the compartment above. He figured that there might be as many as four people in there. Tavian, the interrogator, and maybe two others. Those other two voices seemed further away from where he lay.

He knew that just to the right the gigantic Cavitran Drive stood on its sturdy pedestal. And lining every bulkhead around it were monitoring systems and computers used not only for the Cavitran but for various other power systems.

"Don't just sit there, Hunt. Get this drive back together again."

"What do you expect me to do? It's missing a critical part, and I don't know where it is. I can't even 3D print a new part, because the designs are missing. Vida Rosado is the expert on this ship. She can fix it when she gets here."

"Where is she, Hunt? You work closely with her, yes?"

The voice sounded vaguely familiar to Solomon,

but he couldn't place it. The whir of the machines masked the nuances of the guy's voice too much. If he hadn't mentioned Tavian by name, he wouldn't have been able to tell it was him either.

"Like I told you, no one can find her."

"Contact Rosado on her UiComm now," the interrogator demanded.

"We may be Reachers, but we're not completely devoid of intelligence," Tavian said, his voice dripping with sardonic irritation. *That* Solomon had no trouble hearing. "Her Ui is no longer responding."

At that, Solomon heard the dull thud of a fist hitting flesh. Tavian grunted loudly. "Dammit. I told you what you wanted to know," he said, his voice even more muddled, as if he had blood in his mouth. Solomon balled up his fist, feeling a particular need to punch someone . . . Well, he'd get his chance soon enough.

"I talked to her myself," the interrogator said. "She said she would report to the Cav as soon as she arrived onboard."

When he said that, Solomon's heart sped up double time, and he dropped the hex key onto his chest. Dextra stared at him, eyes wide. Solomon blew out a shaky breath. She gave him a "what the hell?" look.

"It's Mads Graversen," Solomon whispered to her.

"What? What is he doing all the way back in the Cav?" Dextra said, her voice rising as she said it.

Solomon shook his head, willing her to quiet down. He needed to hurry. But even when he got the panel free, what the hell was he going to do? He couldn't take on three people at once, and Mads wasn't just someone he could put down. Mads was the same size as he was, and he knew the guy could handle himself. He figured Tavian might be able to fend off one. But that left one of them free to grab Dextra if she were spotted. And they'd realize she was either his captive or had fallen into league with him.

"Sir, Nautilus Command requested a status update on the Cavitran Drive repair."

Ah, Jonesy and Baern had finally made an appearance.

"Who sent you?" Graversen asked.

"The crewman sent to tell you was called away on an urgent task, and we were available. We were heading this way to see if Tavian needed assistance anyway."

"I repeat: who sent you?"

"I'm sorry, sir," Baern said. "But I can't recall him telling me his name, and he didn't have a badge on. He had on a blue uniform, of course, and he had brown hair. Do you recall any further details, Jones?"

"No, our apologies, sir."

"But why were you sent here?" Graversen wasn't buying it. "Why didn't they just message me?"

"I don't know, sir."

"Never mind. Win, go report our status using my office comm unit. And Yamoto, go put out a ship-wide call for Drive Ops Chief Vida Rosado. She's up to something, and we need to figure out what it is. Tell Command I suspect she aided Reach in sabotaging the Cav, so she needs to be found ASAP."

"Yes, sir."

Solomon heard the Cav Compartment's slider open and close. All right. That left just Tavian, Baern, and Jonesy plus Graversen. They could take him easily.

Solomon couldn't message his crewmen to warn them, so he thought it best to wait for the moment when hopefully Mads would be close enough to the panel that he could surprise him. Solomon had no idea if he had a weapon, but he'd have to risk it.

It only took five minutes more of tense conversation and awkward silences to get Mads in the right position. He could tell when he had stepped on the side of the panel, as Graversen's weight made the loose panel creak.

Solomon gave Dextra a look to let her know he was going in. She nodded and tensed up immediately.

Moment of truth: either he'd be the conquering hero of all mankind or shortly find himself back in a torture room. He was two seconds from finding out.

# THE CAVITRAN

Solomon shoved against the panel hard with the heel of his palms and felt Mads Graversen's heavy weight shift off the plate as he fell.

Solomon immediately popped up through the hole and shouted, "Somebody grab Mads!"

The room was utter chaos for a moment. Graversen had fallen back against Baern who was butted up against the base of the colossal Cavitran Drive rising up through the center of the compartment, the metal plates of the giant magnetron at the top gleaming in the room's harsh light. Jones was obviously struggling to make sense of what was happening as he got into position to hold Mads down, albeit with a sense of shock that he was restraining a man who had the authority to kick him off the SS *Challenge* permanently.

Graversen was built like a tank, all shoulder and chest. Solomon was a bit taller, had a longer reach, and hopefully was more fit overall. Between the three of them, Solomon was sure they could take him down.

"Grab his other arm," Solomon yelled at Tavian.

While Tavian jumped up to take hold of Graversen's arm, Solomon saw Dextra struggling to pull herself up into the compartment out of the corner of his eye.

"Get out of here, Dextra!" Solomon shouted. She scowled at him and started to respond, but Graversen was struggling to break free. It looked like it took the full strength of all three men to keep him down

Mads yelled out in Danish, and Solomon assumed by his tone it was something like, "Get off me, you bastards."

He was trying to reach behind his head to his DOT, likely to try sending an emergency call to Dickson Edge. While the three Reachers held him down, Solomon punched Mads solidly in the nose. He felt the cartilage crunch beneath his knuckle and the spray of blood scattered over all of them. He had to admit, it felt damn good. He'd been wanting to do that all day. While Graversen's head lolled back, he reached behind his ear and yanked off his DOT device, tossing it into his pocket.

Mads shook his head in an attempt to clear his mind, flinching when wrinkling his broken nose clearly caused him considerable pain. "You're going down for this, Reach. You're going to get us all killed."

"I'm trying to save three thousand Reachers. And I will succeed—with or without Challenge Command's permission."

"You sabotaged the drive, didn't you?"

"No, I didn't." Well, it *was* actually the truth.

"Help!" Mads called out, trying to get the attention of anyone outside the compartment.

Solomon glanced toward the door, and realized Dextra had completely ignored him and was standing in the corner of the room.

"Disable the door," Solomon said.

"Code?" was all she said.

"Five-nine-three-eight."

While she coded that into the panel, Solomon glanced at Tavian. "Have you got anything we can tie him up with?"

Graversen struggled hard against their grip when he heard that, probably because he knew that he'd never get free to warn the other members of Command if they restrained him more permanently.

"Hold him down, guys. We've got one shot at this."

"We got him," Jones said. "He's not going anywhere."

"So you say," Mads spit out. "You do only have one chance. And you've already blown it."

"I've got some cords in the maintenance box," Tavian said.

"Get them now."

Tavian rummaged around in a utility drawer at the far corner of the compartment. "Who is she?" he asked, not turning around.

"I'm XO Alexandra Justice's daughter," Dextra said, lifting her chin at them all, daring them to say a word against her.

"Keep your mouth shut, Justice," Solomon demanded, hoping he could convince Mads she wasn't involved in the coup. He tried not to look at her. If he did, he'd give the game away, as Mads was watching them closely. He hoped she understood what he was trying to do.

Tavian tossed Solomon the cords and held down Graversen's legs while Solomon tied his ankles and restrained his wrists behind his back. He put up a valiant and loud fight in the process.

"Have you got anything to shut him up?" Solomon asked Tavian, unable to keep from smirking at Mads. Nothing like one-upping your old mentor.

"You're talking to a member of Challenge Command and your former professor Solomon Reach. Have some fucking respect."

"I wasn't talking to you, Graversen," Solomon replied, his patience wearing thin. He squeezed his fist and almost reveled in the pain. Quite soon, he was certain that fist was going to make contact with the esteemed Professor Graversen again.

Tavian wrinkled his nose and lifted up a greasy piece of cloth. "A dirty work rag?"

Graversen scowled. "Someone's going to find me in here, Reach. And I'm going to make sure Command sends you out on a very long spacewalk."

"Is that before or after you torture me to death?" Solomon retorted, holding up his bandaged hand.

Baern glanced at Tavian. "Stuff him."

Afterward, they proceeded to work quickly through a hail of muffled Danish swear words from Mads, who they deposited in the far corner of the compartment and hooked securely to a lockout/tagout box at the base of a row of systems panels.

Once Mads was secured, the Reachers gathered on the opposite side of the Cav Drive out of Graversen's earshot and eye line. For good measure, Solomon glared at Dextra.

"You stay back in the corner. I'll deal with you in a minute."

She turned her back to Mads and flashed Solomon a quick smile before anyone else could see. Thank goodness, she was quick-witted. She was becoming more of an asset with every passing moment.

"Okay, here's the deal. Baern and Jonesy, I need you babysit the Cav and Mads while Tav, Dextra, and I go on a little errand."

"Yeah, but—" Baern started.

"Will you be missed by your supervisors?" Solomon asked.

"Doubt it, but even so, I don't think they'll put out

a call for us. We should be good," Jonesy said.

"All right, once we're out of this compartment, disable the door again. Override code is five-nine-three-eight. Baern, you're good with numbers. Remember that code. It's critical that no one is allowed in here—not even Reacher crew."

"Five-nine-three-eight. Got it."

"This mission is confidential. Tell no one what we are doing here. Only open this door for Tavian or Vida or me. And don't tell anyone where we are going."

"Um, boss, we don't know where you're going."

"Yes, well, keep it that way."

"Yes, sir." Baern touched his fingers to his cap out of deferential habit.

"Tavian, you all right?" Solomon asked. Hunt was looking roughed up, with a cut above his eye and blood coming from his nose and mouth. Still a handsome devil for all that.

"Yeah, but have you heard from Vida?" Tavian asked, as he rubbed his bloodied face.

"I debriefed her on Nautilus. She's waiting for my call."

"Where has she been? I've been trying to call her."

"She won't be back in time to help you reassemble the Cav. Can you do it on your own?" Solomon asked.

"I ought to be able to," Tavian said, glancing at the Cav, "I'm the one who pulled the damned thing apart."

Solomon nodded and waved Dextra over. "Do you want to stay here with them?"

"She's a Founder, Chief." Tavian stared at her. "Are you sure . . .?"

Solomon softened his gaze as he settled his eyes on Dextra. "She's one of us now."

She gave him an off-kilter smile, and he grinned back.

"I am going with you," she whispered. "I could be useful, and my mother is going to disown me when she learns what I've done anyway."

"Done what?" Tavian asked, one eyebrow cocked toward Dextra.

"Never mind, Tavian. We need to get going." Solomon started to walk around the Cav toward the door.

"It's my wife, Solomon," he heard Mads say in heavily garbled speech.

Solomon walked around the Cav Drive pedestal to find Mads had partially spit out the rag. His face had turned a deep shade of red as he gagged. Was it anger or fear he saw in his old mentor's face? He honestly couldn't tell.

"What are you talking about? You aren't even married."

"I am," he said, though Solomon could barely understand him.

"Take that rag out of his mouth, Tavian."

Tavian strode over and yanked the rag from Graversen's mouth. He proceeded to curl his lips in contempt, spitting out the taste of the grease and dirt.

Once he had recovered somewhat, the look he gave Solomon stopped him in his tracks. "I've been married for more than a decade to Jessia Mardan. She's an American. I met her at MIT. We kept it secret, as my father said she was holding back my career."

"I never saw this woman. You never mentioned her."

"Why would I tell you—one of my students?"

Solomon thought back to those days. He had never seen Mads with any woman, not even at the events or parties they both attended. But the look in Mads's eyes was one he had never seen before. Desperation? Fear? It was so unlike him, Solomon almost believed it must be true.

"It is the truth, Solomon."

"If it is, why are you bringing her up now? What does she matter to me?" Solomon said, his frustration mounting.

"She was denied, Solomon. She had markers for leukemia. But she's still clean. No cancer yet." Mads's voice was breaking, his short, thickly accented words muffled as if he still had the rag in his mouth.

Solomon had a horrible feeling he knew what Mads was about to say.

"Sol, my wife is in Serica Sector. Waiting to board. She should have been granted passage. She deserves a chance to live, just like the rest of us."

Solomon looked up at the ceiling and blew out a long breath, trying to avoid the awful memory that was spilling into his brain, but he couldn't stop it.

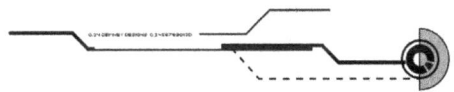

"You can't save her but you can save thousands upon thousands of others," Mads had said. Somehow he had found Solomon at the hospital on the day he finally discovered his sister's whereabouts.

"How did you know I was here, Professor? I told no one where I was going."

Professor Graversen ignored his question, refusing to even look in through the inner window at his sister as she lay utterly still in her hospital bed, ravaged by what her doctor had called a rare form of mitochondrial disease.

"Don't turn away from your chance to save humanity from extinction. One girl versus the lives of so many others. Is it even a choice? She doesn't even know you. Her mind is dead even though her body goes on living. The doctors . . . what did they tell you about her future?"

"They said she has no chance for a normal life at all," Solomon mumbled under his breath.

That realization cut him through. He'd spent so many years searching for her, hoping—no knowing—that he was meant to save her and care for her, and now that purpose had been taken from him. He felt the loss of her as if she had already died. Without her as his guiding compass, did he even know what direction he wanted to go in life anymore? He knew which direction Professor Graversen wanted him to go: up. One hundred and forty-four thousand kilometers into geosynchronous orbit to be exact.

But wasn't that what he had always wanted? To spacewalk, to live among the stars? To take over the company his father had built? It was a dream that didn't exist for billions of others. How did he get to be so lucky? He had been born with a brilliant mind and every opportunity possible while his sister had drawn the short straw. He knew he didn't deserve it. But if he had a chance to save so many others, shouldn't he take it? Would that make this moment easier to bear?

He knew the right answer was simple. Of course, he must take over Reach Corp now that his father had passed away. The furthering of the human species versus the loss of one life, even that of his sister? He must go. He had no choice at all.

"How did you know I was here?" Solomon asked again.

"Your father told me to watch over you. I've kept an eye on you this past year. Just before he died, your father told me you would someday try to find your sister. He told me to accompany you on that day."

"He wanted me to abandon her?" Solomon stared at the professor's inscrutable face. "Or was it you?"

The professor never answered his question.

"Tell me the truth, Mads," Solomon said, kneeling to face him squarely. "Was it my father who wanted me to abandon my sister all those years ago?"

Mads stared back at him. "My answer to that question was irrelevant. You knew you had to do this. For all of humanity."

"Or for your wife?" Solomon said, his anger digging so hard into Mads that he flinched.

"Yes," Mads suddenly shouted. "Is that what you want to hear? I did this all for her. You have no idea what it's like. You never even knew your sister. She was a stranger, and both of your parents were gone. You had nothing left to keep you here."

"It was never your choice to make."

"You would have made the same decision no matter the circumstances, Solomon." Mads's voice was tight with anger. "Don't put this on me. In the face of the annihilation of all life on Earth, there is no other choice."

"I know that, Mads. I know it. And yet, you again tried to make the choice for me. Tried to march my Reachers toward their deaths, just as you did Nisolda all those years ago. You don't have that right. Reach Corp is under contract with the Founding Families, and you cannot change that. We earned this ride."

"And you would knowingly condemn my wife, a healthy woman of proper age, to death?"

Solomon stood and fixed an unwavering stare on his one-time mentor.

"I don't have a choice. The greater good, remember? One life for three thousand. That's no choice at all."

"You bastard," Graversen said.

And that was all it took. Solomon wheeled back,

squeezed his fist, and unloaded a punch to Graversen's jaw that rocked him back against the panels with a thunderous thud. His eyes rolled back in his head and he slumped forward.

His adrenaline kicking in, Solomon moved back in immediately, readying to kick Graversen in the stomach.

"Boss, boss!" Tavian grabbed his arm and pulled him back while Jonesy took up his other one.

He strained against them like a caged animal, shouting, "Get your hands off me!"

"He's out cold, Chief. Leave him be," Solomon heard Tav say through the rush of bloodlust that pulsed through his body.

"Solomon, stop!" Dextra said, her commanding voice cutting through to him.

He stopped, then, at the sound of her voice. He stood over Mads, breathing heavily, attempting to get a handle on his rage.

"I'm all right," he growled at Tavian who let go after a single look from Solomon. Jonesey followed suit. Solomon rolled his shoulders back and moved toward the door, avoiding Dextra's gaze.

"All right. Let's go."

"Yeah, uh . . . okay, boss," Tavian said, and Solomon caught them all exchanging glances that looked like a mix of awe and concern.

"Solomon," Dextra's soft voice sounded near his ear. "May I speak with you a moment?" And she was immediately pulling him to the opposite corner from Mads. He had trouble focusing on her, wanting to see if Mads would wake up so he could punch his lights out again.

"Solomon, look at me," she whispered, taking his face in her hands. "Look at me."

When he finally did, he saw tears in her dark eyes, and he struggled to hold it together as unbidden images of Nisolda came at him from every direction.

"What happened with your sister . . . It wasn't your fault. She was too far gone. They never would have let her up here. You know that."

"Just like his wife? Wasn't good enough to make the cut, right? Who has the right to judge who lives and who dies? I don't know how much more of this god complex I can take today—"

"You don't have a complex, Solomon."

"These aren't just three thousand people in a world of billions. I'm choosing the last three thousand humans of all time. No one will survive the destruction of Earth. Do you see it now? I'm playing god with the last of the human race."

"You *have* been tasked with this decision, Solomon. And you cannot turn away from us now. You still have to save the three thousand people you did choose. As much as you hate him right now, Mads is right. You couldn't save her, but you can save them. Duty. Honor. That's the choice before you now. And you know as well as I that you'll make that same choice over and over again, no matter the consequence."

Solomon made a fist with his good hand, feeling a kind of giddy insanity lacing every inch of his skin, images of his Reachers' smiling faces flashing before him in mug-shot succession. "I've made my choice, then. And I won't fail them. I can't."

The beep of a Ui message popped up in his HUD. It was Brooker messaging Vida at last.

"Check messages."

> AIRLOCK RUMOR SPREAD. ALL REACHERS AC-
> COUNTED FOR AND ABOARD SHIP, CEPT YOU
> AND KASEN. AWAITING INSTRUCTIONS.

Some luck at last. Solomon ran a hand down his face, feeling suddenly tired.

"MESSAGE REPLY: BROOKER, IT'S SOLOMON.
VIDA AND KASEN WILL FIND THEIR OWN WAY
ABOARD. INPUT THIS CODE INTO ONE OF THE
THREE MAIN HATCH CODEBOXES TO PUT THE
ENTIRE SHIP INTO EMERGENCY LOCKDOWN:
40592159. LAY LOW AND WAIT FOR FURTHER
INSTRUCTIONS."

"You're locking down the SS *Challenge*, boss?" Tavian Hunt asked, his eyebrows rising.

"Doing much more than that. We're about to blackmail the docking commander and screw over Challenge Command."

"Can we sneak some food out of the hydroponics lab first? I'm starving." Tavian's stomach gave a vicious growl to reiterate, and something about the ridiculous look on Tav's face made Solomon laugh. That got everyone else laughing, maybe a bit maniacally at first, in an attempt to blow off the stress of the last 24 hours. Dextra touched his arm and her quiet laugh made him pull her to him. He kissed her, drawing raised eyebrows from the guys and a blush from her cheeks.

"All right, all right." Solomon brushed away Tavian's hand as he punched his arm good-naturedly. "Enough of this. Let's go find you some food."

He pulled away from a still-blushing Dextra Justice and marched toward the door. He glanced at Tavian, Baern, and Jonesy who all gave him a nod.

With one last look at Mads Graversen's slumped form, he slipped out the door.

# THE FENESTELLA

## Nautilus-11 Space Station
### Earth-Moon Lagrange Point 1

"We can't wait in here all day for the world to end." Daniela Marcks glared at Vida, straining against the restraints holding her to the conference room chair.

Drive Ops Chief Vida Rosado rubbed at the stress building in her neck muscles. "Considering how soon that's about to happen, I'd say we can." She pressed the stun gun against the docking commander's throat to drive the point home. "It's all quite simple, Marcks. We wait. We watch. And we listen for my boss's call. That's it."

Vida circled back around the table, and glanced out of the fenestella. The glimpse of Earth still took Vida's breath away, even at this far distance of over 300,000 kilometers, this no-man's land where the Nautilus-11 Space Station orbited between the Earth and the Moon. From the station's location at Earth-Moon Lagrange Point 1, her home planet looked twice the size of the Moon when viewed from Earth.

For an instant, she wanted to pretend all was well, that this wasn't a true good-bye, that someday she'd make it back to Argentina, and her whole family would be there to greet her.

But she knew this time was real. This time was forever. Most of her family was long gone now, swept away amid the gang wars and quakes and eruptions down on the surface. And now, she supposed, the nuclear winter would take the rest of them. Even her beloved grandmother would soon be gone.

She had never gotten used to the guilt. She felt it even now as she tried to breathe through the tightness in her chest and the pain in the back of her throat. The Reach Corp crew called it the Paradisi Penitence; the psychologists called it something else. Even the most hardened astronauts among them experienced it. But the doctors had no magic pill to drown out the voices of the soon-to-be dead.

This was unlike anything humans had ever experienced before. The passengers and crew of the SS *Challenge,* the eleventh and final spaceship to leave, were not only escaping the Solar System, they were abandoning eleven billion souls to certain death.

Vida's thoughts turned again to her grandmother while she waited for word from her boss, Reach Corp Chief Solomon Reach, to move ahead with their plan. Vida ran the cross she wore at her neck along its chain as she remembered the last time she had spoken with her beloved abue. In their last communication, she weaseled out of the feisty old woman that she was still quite ill from the spread of a super bug ravaging Vida's old childhood home in Villa Epecuén, Argentina. As far as Vida knew, her grandmother was still alive and daring death to take her.

The cross was the last gift she ever received before her family scattered to terrorist-infested cities, seeking safety where none could be found. She could have been one of them. But her father had been indulgent. He noticed her keen interest in all things mechanical when she was a little girl, and so he let her help him fix old cars in his shop back in Argentina. She had defied her overly protective mother when she took a scholarship at Georgia Tech, where she majored in Electrical and Aeronautical Engineering.

Even there, the universe was looking after her. If she hadn't been switched into the advanced aeronautics class, she never would have met and subsequently had an inconsolable crush on Solomon Reach. And there again, he never would have sought her out for the Paradisi Mission years later if she hadn't asked him out on a date, which he summarily refused, citing a busy schedule. Of course, if he had accepted the date, he wouldn't have been allowed to offer her the job.

But accepting the position of drive ops chief aboard the SS *Challenge* did mean she had to leave her entire family behind. She had gone with their blessing, of course, but it didn't matter. The Paradisi Penitence visited her every night anyway.

"Challenge Command is going to throw you in lockdown if you don't let me out of here." The irritated voice behind her jolted Vida back to the present.

"Oh, I'm sure they'll do worse than that. But it'll be worth it." With a grim smile, she glanced back at Docking Commander Daniela Marcks. The woman's riot of red curly hair stood out in sharp contrast to her pale face and navy blue uniform.

Vida scanned the data on the wall screen wirelessly displaying Marcks's HUD from her wrist comm unit. No new messages. They'd been waiting two hours for word from Chief Reach. Once he made contact, she was to ensure Docking Commander Marcks made it back to her station on the Nautilus-11 Command Bridge so she could start the SS *Challenge*'s undocking procedure at Solomon's command.

"Dammit, Vida. I don't have time for this. I have to go through the protocol checks. Or is your purpose in keeping me here to force us to miss our *very* tight launch window?"

"Wasn't my fault you Founders wasted your precious launch time stowing away illegals from Earth on this station."

Marcks hesitated at that, since it was the first time Vida had openly admitted she was aware of the thousands of people Challenge Command had hidden in Nautilus-11's Serica Sector, people they had hoped to replace the Reacher crew with before her boss had caught wind of their plans.

Hours ago, Vida had tried to keep her curiosity at bay as she worked to disable the Serica Sector's locking system and trap the Serica group in. She was keenly aware that if Marcks and the rest of Challenge Command crew had their way, the majority of the Reachers would be kicked off the ship and replaced with the Serica group. But as she had worked on the code panel far above the expansive main compartment, she opened a small access panel and peered down below.

Thousands upon thousands of them milled about, some napping on cots along the walls, others talking in small groups. Some children cried in their parents' arms while others played quietly with tiny, lightweight toys. She even saw a baby no older than six months old being nursed by its mother. To bring babies aboard a ship with cryo beds meant only for adults—it was sheer madness.

One old woman reminded Vida of her grandmother. She had the same beautiful bronzed skin, the same frizzy grey-white hair. She thought back to her grandmother's final words before she shipped out the final time for the long journey ahead to the Andromeda galaxy.

"I told your mother to call you Vida because I knew you would carry all our lives with you to the stars. I knew it before they did. You were always my little estrella girl." She had nodded her head vehemently, as if Vida had disagreed with her.

"I know, Abue. I know."

Vida had begun wiping the old woman's face with a fresh, cool cloth to try to calm her, but her grandmother leaned up on an elbow and grabbed her arm.

"Vida, listen to me. When you go up there, I want you to take this with you." Her frail fingers grasped the tiny cross sitting on the bedside table and pressed it into her palm. It wasn't until Vida curled her own fingers around the cross that her grandmother leaned her grey-haired head against the pillow and relaxed.

"When you're in space, I will close my eyes and picture myself floating beside you, free of this mad Earth and its unholy wars. I'll be with you among the stars and God."

Vida wished her old abuelita could be with her now. She looked out at Earth again. Rarely did she take the time to look back anymore. There was always more work in the queue, more launch prep to do before they made their way toward the wormhole and on to the planet New Eden. And everything depended on today. She would either be on her way to the Paradisi System with her crewmates aboard the SS *Challenge,* or she'd be left behind—something her grandmother would heartily disapprove of.

Vida had bitten her lip and tried to steel herself against her instinct to save the people in Serica. They weren't her responsibility. She had to do whatever it took to protect her fellow Reachers from getting kicked off the ship and sent back down to Earth. It was their right, under contract, and she would help her boss to force the Founders to honor their agreement. She had every confidence he would save his crew. He had never once failed them, and he wasn't about to start now.

She hadn't told Solomon what she had seen in Serica Sector. How could she? It would only have made his decision to choose between his Reacher crew and the Serica group even harder. No, it was better he never knew who he was leaving behind. While she loved her partner Kasen Vokos with every breath in her body, she knew beyond a doubt Solomon Reach was the most honorable man she had ever met. And if he knew there were children and infants in Serica Sector . . . He would still do as honor dictated, but he would forever feel responsible for their innocent deaths.

"The Serica group . . . They are Founder family members, aren't they?" Vida asked Marcks quietly. "Those too young and diseased to make the cut?"

Marcks glared at her but didn't respond. Vida saw the answer in the way the woman swallowed. The painful truth was stuck like a rock in a pipe in the woman's throat.

"I was there, Daniela, when your deciding vote in that super secret joint board meeting sold the Reachers out."

"What? How did you get into the board room?" Marcks's tone rose to a louder pitch with every word, her expression of shock turning to anger.

Vida shimmied up onto the table next to her, and leaned down to whisper in her ear. "Who's in there for you, Daniela? A husband? A lover? Three illegitimate children you had stashed away in Bavaria?"

Marcks winced. She wouldn't look at Vida. Instead, she stared hard out of the fenestella, which looked down on the disk-shaped Serica and Challenge Sectors. These were joined to Nautilus's Main Hub by long, thin modules. Beyond that, the massive SS *Challenge*, the last of the eleven Asteria-class ships Reach Corp had built, remained connected via a sizable docking module.

"Come on, Daniela. You had to have some legitimate reason to sell out three thousand people—no, let's call it what it is: condemning us to death in a nuclear winter."

Daniela locked eyes with her, then, a challenge giving depth to her stare. And then she began to talk. "There's no one for me in Serica. My son, Zander, is all I have left." She strained against the straps holding her arms to the chair, as if she wanted to gesture with her hands. "No, this was all for them, those cowards in Challenge Command. Wives, children, aunts— they've even got grandmothers and babies in there!"

Vida was surprised to hear irritation in the docking commander's voice. Apparently, the woman wasn't always an advocate of Challenge Command's insane plan.

"You know when the Reachers get wind of this they'll mutiny." Vida kept her tone even. Anyone who knew her well would be aware this was a clear indication of the rising level of her anger.

"I know it," Marcks spit out.

"And still you made the dishonorable choice?"

"There are children in there, Vida."

"And the Reachers—the ones who earned this ride—don't have children worth saving?"

"You don't know—"

"I do. I know what kind of woman you are now."

"Don't preach to me, Vida. This is the end of the world."

"Yes, and we take our honor with us when we pass out of this galaxy." She swiped a hand through the air with Argentinian emphasis, but the docking commander glanced away toward the SS *Challenge*, her lips pursed into a rigid line. Perhaps she was longing to be out there and long gone from this station, but Vida wanted to drive the point home. She jumped down from the table and leaned over her, so she could not look away.

"Know this, Daniela, and do not doubt me. The Founders will never be rid of the Reachers. I swear it."

Marcks's DOT finally buzzed with a message notification. Vida glanced up and read it.

> Vida, you are a go. Head to the bridge
> and await further instructions.

The message came from her UiComm, so she could only assume it was Solomon and not some Founder trying to trick her. She figured she'd double check to be sure.

Vida grabbed hold of Marcks's arm because she started muttering obscenities under her breath while simultaneously attempting to wriggle out of the straps Vida had bound tightly around her limbs.

She flipped through the screens and typed out a question only Solomon would know the answer to.

> Security question: What did I ask you
> after aeronautics class that one time?

After a pause, he messaged back.

> You asked me out, and I should have
> said yes.

Vida smiled.

> Indeed. Headed there now.

# THE TREK

Solomon, Tavian, and Dextra piled up next to the SS Challenge's Cavitran Drive Compartment's slider. Solomon listened, his ear pressed to the metal. He couldn't hear anything.

No help for it, though. They had to traverse the length of the ship's Lab Sector in order to make it to the Astro Lab in time to nab the docking commander's kid before he came in from his spacewalk. Oh, and they had to do all of that without getting caught by any of the Founders looking for him.

"No problem," Solomon mumbled to himself.

"So, boss, since I took a righteous beating from Mads Graversen . . . I'm getting a raise for this, right?" Cavitran Drive Ops Specialist Tavian Hunt scrubbed at his bloodied face with a dirty rag as he glanced back at Solomon Reach.

Solomon flashed him a wide grin. "If you don't die first."

"No worries there," Tavian said with a wink

1

toward Dextra Justice, who was now pressing her synth-leather black cloche hat more firmly over her near-black bobbed hair. "I'm a professional at not dying."

"That may be your only professional designation," Solomon retorted, glancing back to address his other two crew members. "Baern and Jonesy, double check Mads's restraints. We don't want our dear Director Graversen getting loose and wagging his tongue."

"Dude is a total robot. I can't picture him wagging anything at anyone," Baern said, though he was already halfway across the room to check on him. He'd been blessedly unconscious since Solomon had knocked him out only minutes ago.

"He's Danish, Baern." Jonesy's voice was as deadpan as his raised eyebrow.

"Same difference," Baern protested.

"Oh, he'll wave his credentials at anyone who'll listen," Solomon muttered, immediately receiving a reproving glance from Dextra. Oddly, it immediately made him want to kiss her again. "Oh, you know it's true."

"Yes, but you've been breaking protocol for two days now. Challenge Command isn't going to let that slide. Especially Graversen when he wakes up."

Solomon shrugged. "I don't doubt it. But it can't be helped. My crew needs me. And if I have to take a bullet for them, I will."

"Uh, boss? Pretty sure guns aren't allowed in space. They'd just make you take a nice long walk among the constellations."

Solomon chuckled. "Right you are. Well, I always did like a good EVA."

"I'm serious, Solomon." Dextra reached up to put her hands on his shoulders and implored him with her eyes. "We need to be careful out there."

"And we will be. Do you think I'd let any harm

come to you?" he said, touching her cheek briefly. And he meant what he said. He hadn't had a woman in years. He wasn't going to screw this up.

"I don't know, Solomon. But the lives of thousands are at stake. We need to—"

"Excuse the interruption, Miss Justice, but I can re-assure you of one thing: my boss won't stop until everyone is safely aboard and accounted for. He doesn't know how to fail."

Solomon opened his mouth to speak, but Tavian's admission made him speechless. It seemed Dextra had lost her voice as well. A pregnant pause ensued until Tavian finally spoke up again.

"On that awkward note, we'd best get going."

Dextra and Solomon nodded in unison, not know-ing what else to say. He could see the color in Dextra's cheeks had risen, and he could feel his own warming.

Solomon cleared his throat. "Ahem. All right, Jonesy." Solomon held up his hand to signal for quiet and to recover his equanimity. "Remember, no one enters the Cavitran Drive Room except Vida or Tavian. Got it? Hold tight until you hear the alarm sound. We've only got a few hours before Zander comes in from his spacewalk, so I've got to intercept him before that."

"No problem."

Solomon nodded at Tavian, who punched in the code for them, and the heavy door slid open.

"Wait," Solomon whispered. He heard voices down the hall and barred anyone from leaving with an outstretched arm. He listened a few moments longer and realized the people were heading away toward the starboard side of the ship.

"Thanks guys, and good luck," Solomon said to Jonesy and Baern.

"Good luck, boss." Jonesy clapped him on the back. "I think you're gonna need it."

Solomon grinned and turned to Tavian. "All right. Let's move."

"We heading toward Eden now?" Tavian asked, referring to the Reacher crew's nickname for the Lab Sector's lush, green vivaria.

"You tell us. Where is this elusive part for the drive?" Tavian had thus far refused to divulge the location of the part he had removed from the Cavitran Drive, the ship's engine. The SS *Challenge* would be dead in the water until he replaced it.

Tavian smirked. "You'll find out when we get there."

Solomon scowled at him.

"If I told you"—Tavian flashed him a wide grin— "I'd have to kill you and all that. Very messy. And my boss wouldn't appreciate blood smearing the hallways of his pretty spaceship."

"Remind me why I hired you again?"

"My considerable charm with the ladies, of course." Tavian's lascivious smile was directed solely at Dextra.

"Ah, yes," Solomon said, clapping him on the back and steering him away from Dextra, "always an invaluable skill set when escaping an apocalyptic Earth in search of a new planet to colonize."

"Oh, I agree." Tavian laughed a little too loudly, but he stopped abruptly when Dextra put a finger to her lips to shush him.

"You guys should have had a comedy routine back in old Las Vegas," Dextra whispered.

Tavian scratched his chin. "Considering Las Vegas is a pile of rubble thanks to said apocalypse on Earth, I'll settle for a comedy duo on New Eden."

"If we ever get there," Dextra murmured.

"It's only the next galaxy over. Piece of cake," Solomon said, trying to reassure her with a smile. It only took a moment for her to smile back, though it didn't reach her stunning brown eyes, which immediately looked away.

It was obvious she was nervous about what lay ahead. Frankly, so was he. They were bound to run into more Founders and JCorp security guards along the way. His plan was incredibly risky, but they'd come this far.

"This way to Eden." Tavian gave them both one of those obnoxious smiles people reserve for couples in love.

Solomon scowled again but followed his overly confident employee down the corridor.

"Why do the Reachers call it Eden?" Dextra asked him.

"It's what the Reachers have always called the Lab Sector. A bit of home up here among the stars is all we mean."

"It's housing as much of Earth's flora and fauna we can fit in, right?"

"Exactly. Earth was the original Eden after all—"

"Before we fucked it up, that is," Tavian said. "What do you plan to do after we get to the Astro Lab, boss?"

"I plan to take a spacewalk to intercept Docking Commander Daniela Marcks's son and use him as leverage to make her undock us from the space station."

"Zander Marcks? You want to force the docking commander to undock the SS *Challenge* from the Nautilus-11 Space Station? And you expect to accomplish this how?"

"With luck."

Tavian eyed him. "Are you insane?" He looked sideways at Dextra. She merely shrugged.

"Probably."

"Why would you need an EVA for that?" Tavian asked.

Solomon nodded at Dextra. "Credible sources tell

me he is doing nanosilc panel repairs out on the forward hull."

"Yes, it's true," Dextra interjected. "But I still say this plan is risky—and not just for the boy."

"It'll be fine," Solomon assured her.

He hoped he wouldn't have to do anything to the kid. He had no intention of putting him in any real danger, but he had to make it look that way. Zander's mother had to believe he would kill him.

"Solomon, you aren't going to hurt him . . .?" Dextra asked.

"I wouldn't willingly do that."

"Not the answer I was looking for."

"It's up to Docking Commander Marcks. She will decide how far I have to take this."

"That's where you're wrong. You'll be the one with that boy's life in your hands. Remember you're better than Director Graversen and Commander Edge."

"Better than your mother too?" Solomon immediately regretted his words.

Dextra visibly flinched. Her mother, Alexandra Justice, had condoned Commander Edge's methods of torture when he had put the squeeze on Solomon for valuable intel on his plans to prevent their betrayal. Solomon absently fingered the bandage where Edge had stabbed him with a scalpel. The wound still throbbed, but it was healing well as the hours passed by.

"I'm sorry." Solomon stopped and gently took hold of her upper arms and tried to apologize with his eyes. "I don't know why I said that."

Dextra gave him a stony look and pulled away, saying nothing.

Solomon wanted to say more but not with Tavian standing there. It was too personal, he knew, and Dextra wouldn't want to discuss her mother's questionable ethics in front of a near-stranger.

He decided to switch tacks as they turned down another deserted corridor. "Tav, after you get the Cavitran repaired—"

"What do you need?" Tavian interrupted.

"Lay low. You're going to be of little interest to Challenge Command once this thing goes all to hell. I'll be completely exposed when I take my spacewalk. Anything could potentially happen at that point. The ship could leave without me."

"Not going to happen," Dextra said, and he could see in her eyes that she had forgiven him. Whether it was because of the thought of him dying or the remembrance that her mother was not the most moral of individuals, he didn't know.

As much as he loved spacewalking, he couldn't help but admit to himself—and only himself—that his greatest physical fear was being untethered during a spacewalk. The idea of floating free in the vacuum of space was terrifying. Back when he was in EVA training, he used to have frequent nightmares of floating off into the darkness. The loss of light was the worst part, and he would usually wake up in a cold sweat, breathing hard.

Most of his life he had felt so cut off from humanity. With no remaining family ties and only the Reachers to care for, he'd led a singular life. And to be cut off completely with no ability to defend against a black void of endless space, waiting as the minutes ticked by until his oxygen ran out . . .

He shook off that line of thinking. He had to focus on the mission. Save the Reachers. Everything else that came after that would be what was required. He had to face it no matter the cost.

"Mizz Justice is right. We're not going to let that happen."

"Call me Dextra, Tavian."

"Don't mind if I do." Tavian gave her a lopsided grin.

Solomon scowled him. "Focus on the Cav. If anything goes wrong with the drive, none of us are getting out of here."

"You got it, boss." Tavian offered up a salute, touching his forehead and dipping his head.

Solomon brushed off the deference. "Oh, and I forgot to tell you. I am wearing Vida Rosado's UiComm chip, so if you want to call me, you'll need to contact me via her—"

Dextra held out her hand and stopped them. Solomon glanced at her as she nodded toward the far corridor. She put a finger to her lips. Footsteps coming their way fast.

Solomon and Tavian glanced around for a good hiding spot. They were passing a major communications hub in the Engineering Sector. It was the Comms Station where all Ui and DOT data was stored and processed. He probably should have taken them on a more circumspect route, but he knew they needed to get a move on before the Marcks kid came in from his spacewalk—and before Challenge Command got wind of what they were up to.

"Hurry," Dextra whispered.

"Here," Solomon said, tapping in a code for a compartment across the way marked maintenance. He mentally shuffled through engineering drawings for this deck. Only essential areas and sectors were affected by the lockdown sequence. Maintenance compartments were necessarily left unaffected for emergency staff to easily access. Thankfully, he knew the codes for almost everything else he needed. A near-photographic memory was useful like that.

He barely remembered this particular room, but he did remember it was way too small for three people. Couldn't be helped. Whoever was coming was about to make it around the bend in the corridor. He shoved Tavian in after the slider opened and pulled Dextra after him. They dropped a mop, and it clattered on the floor out in the hall.

Solomon swore under his breath and picked it up. Tavian ended up sitting on a bucket at the back while Solomon and Dextra were parted by the mop handle he held between them. Pitch-black darkness descended once the slider closed behind them.

"This slider has no lock from the inside, does it?" Tavian whispered.

"Most people don't want to lock themselves into a closet, do they?"

Tavian grunted. "Damn engineers. You're wishing you had now, huh?"

"Perhaps," was all Solomon would say.

He felt Dextra's breath on his face, and it made him remember her kiss and the feel of her hands on his skin. He reached down and took her hand in his. It made her breath come quick, which rather pleased him. She gripped his hand harder and tried to steady her breathing. And then he realized he could get caught in the next few moments, and he'd better take advantage of this opportune moment. He blindly reached up to touch her cheek, and then pressed lips to hers. He didn't move, didn't breathe. Just kept his mouth on hers, willing himself to remember the feel of her, the taste of her.

The sound of keys rattling and the voices growing louder made Solomon pull away, but still he kept her hand in his.

How would they even know when the hall was clear again? Solomon was currently regretting how soundproof he designed these doors. He'd have to re-think that in his next Asteria-class spaceship design. He almost laughed out loud. What next design? This was the last ship out of the galaxy. And even if he survived this day, Challenge Command would probably float him off this ship or lock him away forever.

He didn't have the luxury to beat around what ifs. He needed to give the Reachers a fighting chance. Challenge Command was attempting to replace three thousand of his Reach Corp employees with three thousand of their own family members—and God knew who else. But the Reachers had a contractual right to be there, to hitch a ride to the Paradisi Planetary System in Andromeda galaxy. It was the ten Founding Families themselves who signed the original contract. Failure was not something Solomon could even consider. Too many lives at stake. Too many hopes resting on this one chance.

"You're going to save the Reachers, Solomon. I know it," Dextra whispered in his ear, as if in answer to his unspoken fears.

"She's right, boss. This is going to work."

Because it has to, Solomon thought. He was going to crack a joke to lighten the mood, but the seriousness of this task hit him like a punch in the gut. His words came out in a whisper.

"I hope you're right."

Unfortunately, the door slid open, making him rethink his efforts at hoping for the best. The bright light was a shock to Solomon's system. He blinked rapidly to get a sense of who they were dealing with. Damn. It was Challenge Security. Two of them. The people coming around the corridor must have tipped them off, so they came to investigate.

"Solomon Reach." The guard, his eyes narrowed and his mouth drawn into a smug line, pointed a Taser at him. "You are to release Dextra Justice and surrender yourself. Challenge Command would like to speak with you immediately."

From behind, Tavian tapped Solomon's leg with something metal. Solomon handed Dextra the mop handle and gave the impression he would give himself up. He then took hold of what Tavian handed him, which felt like a heavy drill. Well, he could knock out one of them with it but not likely before they let loose with the Taser gun. He'd have to risk it in order to block their access to Dextra.

"Dextra, stay back," Solomon said. "Let me handle this."

"No, she will come out first," the second guard commanded from behind the other.

"Not while you have a Taser aimed right at us. I don't think COO Justice would appreciate hearing you've stunned her daughter."

"I'm in complete control of my weapon—"

Solomon knocked the Taser gun out of his grasp with a hammerfist strike while simultaneously whipping the drill up to slam the guy across the side of the head. He dropped unconscious to the floor, his belt clattering loudly. The first guard immediately jumped Solomon, and they struggled with the drill high up in the air.

Dextra shoved Solomon and the second guard out further into the hall, and they hit the far bulkhead hard with their shoulders. Tavian came up from behind, and before Solomon could react, the loud rat-tat-tat-tat of the Taser went off and stuck into the second guard's chest and Solomon's arm before Tavian pulled it away. The guard shouted out in pain.

Solomon knew he got less of it than the guard, but he was surprised at the intensity of the pain. His muscles instantly contracted as the shockwave traveled through his body. The second guard wasn't struggling or fighting him anymore, so Solomon assumed he was experiencing the same thing.

It wasn't until Dextra asked him if he was all right that he realized she was holding him up. Tavian was shoving the other guy up against the bulkhead.

"I've got to put you all into the maintenance closet right now," Tavian whispered to Solomon. "I hear someone else coming."

"What?" Solomon stuttered, though somewhere through the haze of pain he knew Tavian was right. He heard more voices.

"Give me a few minutes, boss." Tavian pushed them both into the claustrophobic closet. Smelled like sweat and fear in there now. Solomon ended up in the back sitting on the bucket while the other two where lumped against each other, one or both of them moaning quietly. Solomon doubted they could see anything but the whites of his eyes, since his skin was so dark.

"Sorry, boss. At least I got the other guy too."

"You're fired," Solomon attempted to say, but nothing came out but a groan of pain.

"Here, boss." Tavian handed him the drill and Taser. "Hold these to the side of their heads."

"Sounds messy," Solomon said, barely able to grip them, his hand muscles were so weak.

"Mission necessity."

"You hear that?" Solomon asked the second guard, pressing the drill hard against the guy's head. He kept his tone flippant but allowed a tinge of anger to come through. "Mission necessity, he says. I'm sure you understand."

"Fuck you," came the reply, accompanied by a look that could cure the devil of his evil ways.

The last thing Solomon saw was Dextra's crinkled brow of concern and Tavian's mile-wide grin, and then instant darkness when the slider closed.

Bastard.

Solomon was left with guard two's onion breath, the chemical smell of whatever nasty substance was left in the bucket, and the after-waves of pain. And on top of it all, his stomach let out a loud growl of hunger making the second guard grunt in irritation. He wasn't going to ask himself if this day could get any worse. He was smarter than that.

Deprived of his sight, his hearing perked up, and he listened for sounds out in the hall.

"Dextra? Is that you?" Solomon heard a woman say. "I heard Command was looking for you."

"No, it's all sorted. Just a misunderstanding." Dextra's voice was cool and breezy, but Solomon detected a tinge of strain at the ends of her words.

"Are you all right? What happened?" The woman's voice rose a notch.

"Sorry, Joya, not at liberty to talk about it per Challenge Command protocols."

"Geez, Dextra. How long have we been friends? You gotta tell me everything, girl."

"When this is all over, I promise I will."

"That's all I get? Gah! So are you going to introduce me or what?"

"Oh, this is . . . uh . . ."

"Tavian Hunt at your service, ma'am."

Solomon pictured Tavian winking and kissing the woman's hand. He must have done because the next words out of her mouth weren't words at all.

"Oh, uh, hmm . . ." the woman stuttered.

"Go on, Joya. I'll talk with you later. Besides, I know you've got loads of comms work to do getting everything ready for the launch. So get to it."

"Yes, mother." Joya laughed, and it nearly woke the unconscious guy, who twitched a bit against Solomon's side.

"Damn it," mumbled the stunned guard, as he shifted to a more comfortable position.

"Your fault for bringing the Taser," Solomon whispered unapologetically. "Those things are obnoxious."

"Only when you're the one getting zapped."

# THE LACUNA

After a few moments of silence, during which Solomon wondered if he was getting high off chemical fumes emanating from the cabinet beside them, the slider opened to reveal the smirking faces of Dextra and Tavian.

"If I didn't know you needed your anonymity today, Boss, I'd take a picture and post it ship-wide."

Behind him, Dextra covered her mouth to stifle a snicker.

"Get these guys off me *now*, Tavian," Solomon said, attempting to bring a little gravity to the situation, though he didn't doubt the three of them stuffed into the closet looked utterly ridiculous. He was still feeling the effects of the Taser and amusement was not in his current bag of tricks.

"All right, all right." With a grunt, Tavian extricated the unconscious guard from the closet and propped him up against the bulkhead. That left Solomon sitting on the bucket with the drill pressed firmly against the stunned guard's temple.

Solomon locked eyes with him. "Keep your mouth shut and slowly move back toward the slider.

1

Are we clear?"

The guard took a moment to consider the alternatives and nodded once, his stare turning more heated as the moments ticked by.

"You want them back in there, Boss?" Tavian asked, grabbing the stunned guard from behind and pulling him out into the corridor while Solomon kept the Taser suctioned to his head.

"Yes."

When Solomon passed the other guard, the man breathed multiple obscenities under his breath.

"No hard feelings." Solomon offered the guy a faint smile of apology.

"Someone will find you eventually," Tavian said to the stunned guard without a hint of remorse, as he clumsily shoved the unconscious guy back into the closet.

"And when they do find us, you can bet I'll be relaying this incident to Challenge Command, Reach," the guard said as he stepped back into the closet.

"Say hi for me," Solomon said cheerfully as he zapped him with the Taser again, tossed the weapon in with him, and shut the slider in the guy's face.

"What'd you do that for, Boss?" Tavian looked longingly at the slider. "We could have used that Taser."

"The last thing we need is to draw attention. Last I checked our uniforms don't leave much room for a Taser holster."

"All right, but I think you're just nervous I'll stun you again."

"Damn straight, I am," he retorted.

"Solomon, are you all right?" Dextra asked, touching his recently zapped arm.

"I'm fine." He rolled his shoulder a bit, contracting and releasing his muscles. He felt much better despite some residual pain. "But we've got to go.

These delays are killing our time table. I'd say the kid is going to be spacewalking for another two hours at most."

"Lab Sector next?" Dextra asked, as they headed up the stairs toward the Lab Sector two decks above.

"Yes, we'll keep a steady pace in there."

"I don't get down to the Lab Sector often." Dextra touched Solomon's arm. "What do I do if we get separated?"

"We're heading up to Lab Deck 10 first thing, and we'll access it aft and head forward through the hydroponics labs and vivaria to the port side labs. If we get separated along the way, we'll meet outside the slider of the Deck 11 Astro Lab where they keep the empty animal cages. Agreed?"

Tavian and Dextra nodded.

"And what if one of us gets detained?" Tavian asked.

Solomon thought a moment. "To be honest, I hope that doesn't happen because I haven't come up with a Plan B."

Tavian waved a hand at Solomon. "You're the only one who can't get caught, boss. We're not being hunted . . . as much."

"Let's move." Solomon motioned them on. "I'll explain all this as we go, Dextra. First up, we'll pass through hydroponics where we'll pick up some food."

"And then take the lower walkway past the Lacuna and Aura Labs?" Tavian asked.

Solomon nodded. "Actually, it's better to take the upper gangway over the filtration pools on the first leg. Less likely to be seen by the lab techs up there."

Tavian nodded. "Got it, boss."

When they finally made it up to Deck 10, sweating and panting from the exertion, Solomon glanced through the window of the Lab Sector's main slider. On the other side lay an interim room designed as a safety measure in case anything in the Lab Sector escaped its confines, whether it be contaminated air, water, or even animals or insects from the vivaria further forward.

Directly on the other side of the inner sliding door lay the central walkway traversing the length of the Lab Sector. Without the life-sustaining labs and processes on this deck working in harmony, they would all die, most likely by suffocation first. The Lab Sector was so vital that it was strictly off-limits to the majority of personnel in order to prevent contamination. If the Founders did eventually kill him today or sometime soon, Solomon was glad he'd have a chance to see Eden one last time.

It was the first area to be built out, and he used to watch the technicians and scientists as they constructed the filtration systems and populated the vivaria housing the various ecosystems they planned to study on the voyage to the Paradisi Planetary System. Eden was truly a wonder. And he had missed it while he'd been so focused on managing the passenger and cargo bay loading, dealing with Challenge Command politics, testing the thorium reactors, checking and rechecking all engineering systems were a go, and on and on.

After decades of planning, it was maddening to realize the entire mission was now threatened by the greed of his management, the ten Founding Families who had started the secret Paradisi Project way back in 2025. And now he was left to wonder when the Founders had turned against his Reachers. The Founding Families had already saved over 100,000 of their own people and delivered them to the Paradisi System in the Andromeda galaxy. It shouldn't surprise him now that the Reachers were dead weight to the remaining Founders, garbage to be cast aside in their attempt to make it out of an apocalyptic Earth alive.

He only wished he had uncovered their plans earlier.

If he were a religious man, he might have surmised the greedy Founders were getting their just due, like the Pharaoh's men swallowed by the Red Sea. It was people like his half-sister, Nisolda, who likely still lay in a hospital bed, her body ravaged by a rare mitochondrial disease, who were caught in the crossfire between greed and fear. In the end, he didn't have time to contemplate the meaning of it all with philosophical debate. He had one single goal: he had to save his crew from getting kicked off the SS *Challenge* or die in the attempt.

Then again, he had seen the wonders of the stars and planets wheeling in their orbits far above the petty greed and political borders of men. Something happened to the mind at the mere glimpse of planet Earth from space, a profoundly altered understanding of life, even without the benefit of science. As they made their way into the beginnings of Eden, Solomon vowed to make the most of it if this was to be the last time he'd pass through the Lab Sector. At the very least, he knew he'd lose his freedom if they caught him. They'd either stick him in lockdown—the irony not lost on him that he would have designed his own prison in that scenario—or they'd put him into cryo sleep for the duration of the journey to ensure he wouldn't cause them any more trouble. Or maybe they'd just float him and be done with it.

"Wait. Lab techs are passing by the inner slider." Tavian stood off to the side, peering through the window again.

Solomon had designed this level with windowed doors, as he knew it would be useful to the lab techs to keep an eye on their experiments at all times, even if they didn't have time to go into a particular lab, or especially if a lab had gone into lockdown for any reason. Little did he know how useful he'd find it for avoiding those same people.

"Okay to go," Tavian whispered.

Solomon keyed in the code. The moment the door slid open, a wave of scents and sounds assaulted their senses. Whereas the rest of the ship smelled of plastic and chemicals and sounded perpetually like the dull whir of machines, here the green of growing things surrounded them and the sound of water had a calming effect. Solomon breathed in deeply, catching the pungent scents of rosemary and oregano mingled with the freshness of greens and berries.

"Welcome back to Eden," Solomon whispered to Dextra, unable to keep the smile from his face. Even a man who lived much of his life in space still found the sensual feast of growing things to be a pleasure. He was human after all.

"Smells like heaven in here," Dextra whispered. "Wish I came here more often."

"Me too," Solomon said, as they all glanced around for any movement across the Lab Sector's main floor and the gangways above them.

To his right lay circular pools stacked atop each other, each holding various kinds of fish in the water below and water plants floating in plant trays above. Several lab technicians were closing the powered plant tray coverings to prevent water spillage during transit.

Further ahead to portside were massive counters of endless starter plant rows. Below the counters, in pristine white cabinets, canisters of myriad seed varieties were stored. When the Paradisi Project first began, the Founding Families had no idea what kind of flora and fauna to expect on the new planet, so they took painstaking care to bottle up every variety of animal and plant they could get their hands on, either to cryo freeze them or extract their DNA or seeds for safekeeping. All of these were kept under lock and key to protect against contamination or sabotage.

Along the starboard bulkhead stood rows of slowly turning rotary hydroponic systems complete with light bulbs at their centers. In the central sections of the floor, Rows of smaller plants to Solomon's left rose up into the cavernous hydroponics chambers in double helix-shaped supports that eventually connected to the overhead bulkheads. Just ahead, long rows of strawberries and other varieties of berries hung overhead. He and his crew designed Eden to make use of every inch of available space; considering how many mouths they had to feed over the course of the journey, it was a requirement.

Tavian and Dextra pulled down handfuls of strawberries and blueberries, and Dextra passed some to Solomon.

"Eat as much as you can," Solomon said as he tossed them into his mouth, momentarily savoring their sweet juices before gathering more. He wasn't optimistic that fruit and vegetables would be sufficient nutrition, but he hoped adrenaline would kick in if needed to see them all through the rest of the day.

"To port?" Tavian whispered. "I don't see any techs over there." He pointed toward the area housing the lettuces and greens.

"Yes, and let's keep an eye on the gangways above," Solomon said.

Hurrying along the aft bulkhead of the Hydroponics Lab behind the lettuce pods, they passed rows of zucchini and cucumber plants strung up vertically reaching toward an upper gangway running perpendicular to port and starboard.

A technician was checking over a water systems panel on the far port bulkhead, but she was turned away from them. Solomon grabbed a handful of kale and shoved it into his mouth while Tavian broke a zucchini in thirds and gave Solomon and Dextra a piece as they traversed the length of the Hydroponics Lab.

Solomon punched in the override code for the Aura Lab, otherwise known as the $CO_2$ Scrub Room. As they traversed Aura, with its machines lining every inch of the lab's bulkheads, he briefly wondered if it would be the last time he'd see the scrubbers at their work.

The process was simple: the $CO_2$ the passengers expelled was converted into breathable oxygen via photosynthesis. A beautiful symbiosis of human, plant, and machine—perfect in its simplicity. The machines had a quiet, almost musical hum and whoosh, which always soothed Solomon's mind when he'd come here to relax during the construction phases of the Paradisi Mission.

He wished he could drop everything and hide out here forever. And again came the thought he might not accomplish his goal. So many things could go wrong. Challenge Command might have even found a way to disable the ship's hatches and were off-loading his crew right now. That thought spurred him into action, and he picked up his pace.

After they had passed through the first half of the scrub room, they moved toward the Lacuna Lab via the main walkway overlooking all areas of the central Lab Sector: the filtration pools, the farming sectors, and eventually the vivaria. Tavian paused at the slider to the Lacuna Lab, listening. Solomon heard only the fall of rushing water into the filtration pools.

Water was such a precious commodity in space, so to hear that sound of all sounds was a miracle in itself. Even if he hadn't designed this ship, he'd still be in awe of this mechanism. And certainly he'd had expert help from Reach Corp's top minds in its design and construction, including the gravity controls and inertia negation required to keep the water in the pools when the ship was on its way. But this lab of all of them was a beauty. Or maybe it was because it had been his favorite thing on the ground.

He loved the feel of water. Much of his early childhood was spent studying in the Baker Library at Harvard Business School while waiting for his mother to finish teaching her finance students. Each night they would walk the Anderson Bridge crossing the Charles River toward home. Solomon would watch the light-play of the sun on its surface for hours and never tire of it. He remembered those as the happiest days of his life. That was before October 15, 2064.

It had started out as any other day in the library. There were parts of it he could not recall while others were burned into his memory like a brand. The acrid odor of gunpowder mixing with the milder scent of the rare books—that he would never forget. Blood pouring from his mother's mouth as she struggled to scream his name. In his nightmares, he still saw the fear in her eyes as she slumped against the bookshelves. The last thing he recalled was the scar running down the side of the terrorist's face. And when the man grinned at him, the scar looked exactly like a snake.

Solomon still had no idea how he made it out of that library alive. And he never saw his mother again. He remembered nothing until the day of her funeral, when his father finally came to fetch him. Tears were streaming down his face as he took Solomon gruffly by the shoulders and looked him in the eyes.

"I'm taking you to the stars, Solomon. It's where you belong. It's where we all belong."

"Solomon," Dextra said, "someone's coming. Hide!"

Her voice snapped Solomon out of his thoughts of the past. He saw a flash of movement a few yards up ahead and felt the reverberation on the gangway underfoot. The three of them tip-toed up the stairs onto the next gangway above, which overlooked the Lacuna Lab, it's air cool and fresh compared to the humidity of the Aura Lab. Streams of water spaced widely apart amid endless varieties of water plants originated from giant pipes in the lab's bulkheads and splashed down via waterfalls, which all fed into a collection basin farther aft.

"There's another tech." Tavian pointed toward the far left quadrant of the lab where the tall man was monitoring a bank of computer terminals. "Follow me."

Solomon and Dextra ducked their heads down. If the tech turned around for any reason, they'd be discovered.

Solomon kept an eye on the tech as they moved quietly above the pools. His engineers had designed them to be aesthetically pleasing, knowing people would come here for solace as well as science. And they were that. They had a natural, unstudied look to them. Otherworldly, almost.

The slider whooshed open far aft. A blue-uni-formed Founder lab assistant came in a mere hundred feet behind them, calling out to the technician in the corner, who finally turned around. The guy made eye contact with Solomon, and he knew their cover was blown.

"Run to the exit ahead!" Solomon shouted at Dextra.

"It's Solomon Reach!" The tech's voice carried loudly across the water.

"Warn Challenge Command," the lab assistant yelled back and immediately rushed at Solomon, his boots clanging loudly on the gangway.

"I'll get the tech, boss." Tavian was already sprinting toward the technician, who was ringing up

Challenge Command on his wrist DOT while preparing for Tavian's onslaught.

"Head toward the vivarium, Dextra. I'll try to buy
us some time."

"Be careful," she shouted to Solomon, as she took
off for the Lacuna Lab's exit toward the Olympia
Vivarium.

Solomon turned back toward the lab assistant, focusing all his attention on the fight ahead. By the look
of him, this guy wasn't going to be an easy takedown.
When was it ever? He took in a heavy breath and felt
the adrenaline rising in his chest. He welcomed it.
Solomon balled up his fist and waited.

# THE AURA

Two hundred pounds of muscle rushed at Solomon. Challenge glinted in the lab assistant's eyes. No shortage of confidence with this guy. The moment the man's fist was about to make contact with his face, Solomon ducked and punched him in the kidney as he swung down. The assistant hit the railing with a loud thwack but recovered quickly, spinning around to come at Solomon again. He got a solid punch into Solomon's gut, and the shock of it reverberated through his body, nearly bringing up his last meal of berries and zucchini.

Solomon jumped back to give himself a moment to recover. The guy missed again, his arc going wide. The gangway shuddered as Solomon rushed him, shoving him down onto his back. He landed a square punch to the guy's nose, which killed his injured hand. It started smarting something fierce, so he moved to punch the guy with his right hand. The guy grabbed his fist and thrust him backward. The move lifted them both to their feet as he shoved at Solomon's stomach with his boot.

Solomon bent him over backward against the rail.

1

He squeezed the assistant's neck and lifted him with his other arm over the top rail. The man grunted and struggled against him, arms flailing. Solomon didn't want to kill him, but he had a feeling he was crushing his windpipe all the same.

The lab assistant's hand slipped, and Solomon was able to push him over the rail entirely. With a shout, the guy fell several meters down to the lower stream. Solomon, breathing hard, glanced down to see if his head would resurface. When it did, the lab assistant fixed him with a glare and shouted, "Command is going to walk you for this."

Solomon didn't disagree as he turned away. He just hoped he'd be able to save his crew before Challenge Command sent him packing into the void. The mere thought of it made him shudder, and he tried to shake the sudden fear out of his shoulders and aching hands.

He glanced over at Tavian, who had the tall, skinny technician on his stomach, hands behind his back. The guy was screaming obscenities and squirming like a toddler throwing a tantrum.

"Can it before I punch you out," Solomon said, the racket instantly making his headache.

It didn't stop the guy, but he lowered his volume at least.

"What do you want to do with him?" Tavian asked, kneeing the technician in the back to get him to lie still.

"Did he get a call out to Command?"

Tavian grimaced. "Yes, unfortunately."

"Then we need to neutralize him the best we can, so we can get out of here."

"What's your name, technician?" Solomon asked the guy.

"Marley Penniman, asshole. Let me go."

"All right, Marley Penniman. You've got two choices: either you tell us what we can tie you up with or we punch you out cold. You have three seconds to decide."

While Marley gave that proposition some serious thought, Tavian scowled. "I say we punch him out, boss. We don't have time for this."

"Marley? Time's up."

"Agh! I can't think of anything."

"All right. We'll try to go easy on you. Tavian, lift him up."

"Stop! You can't do this. It's against—"

Solomon didn't hesitate. The moment Tavian brought Marley's head up, he put all the power he could behind his weaker left punch, connecting with the side of Marley's chin. His body fell against Tavian, his head snapping back as he instantly fell into unconsciousness.

"Damn, boss. Remind me not to piss you off."

Solomon shook off the tension in his hand and felt for the guy's pulse. "He's still alive. Let's go."

"I'll follow you anywhere."

"Since Challenge Command is likely going to float me or throw me in lockdown, I wouldn't be too keen on that." Solomon took off at a run toward the slider leading out into the corridor between the upper deck of the Lacuna Lab and the Olympia vivarium. They ran right into Dextra, who stood off to the side of the slider.

"I saw the whole thing. How are you both still alive?" Dextra gave them both a once over, presumably to check for injuries.

"Noble cause and desperation?" Tavian offered while Dextra checked the bandage on Solomon's hand.

"Or dumb luck?" Dextra replied, taking down their egos a notch.

"All of the above," Solomon added. "We have to go. Security is going to be crawling all over this sector soon."

"Why?" Dextra asked.

"Damn tech put out the emergency call for the cavalry."

"Oh, you mean the defenseless man you punched the living daylights out of?"

Solomon held a finger up, considering several defensive responses but thought better of it. Desperation wasn't a good enough reason for this woman. He lowered his hand and gave her a sheepish smile.

"That's what I thought."

Tavian walked between them to peer through the slider's window. "Challenge Command will automatically assume we'd head toward Olympia, since it's the nearest sector to Lacuna. We could take a more diagonal route through Tibet."

"No." Dextra shook her head. "That's alpine tundra. Not enough cover."

Solomon looked through the slider toward Olympia. "I think we could probably lose them in Olympia. Far more trees, and there's some decent-sized bushes as well."

Tavian nodded. "Hmm . . . true."

"Do your codes actually work on these doors?" Dextra asked Solomon.

"Yes, they do. I just can't disable them from the inside. Safety measure."

"For the record, I disagree with your level of due diligence in the safety measures aboard this ship," Tavian stated.

"Noted."

"We can't stay here any longer." Dextra waved her hand in impatience.

"We'll take the Olympia route." Solomon keyed in the code. "Stay close. If we get separated, remember to head to the Astro Lab."

"Got it."

The moment he walked through the slider to Olympia, the scents of the trees and fresh, crisp air filled his lungs. There was nothing like these vivaria in the universe, save the regions on Earth for which they were named. Even then, the vivarias' namesake biomes on the planet had long since been decimated by drought, volcanic disasters, floods, and the waste borne of human greed. Each of these labs, including Olympia, a replica of the Pacific Northwest rainforests of the old Olympic National Park, were priceless. Almost, it seemed to Solomon, more priceless than their human cargo. They were bringing with them a nearly impossible-to-encapsulate world in the hope that these little pieces of their home would not be lost or forgotten.

The original hope was that the ships would remain in orbit above New Eden and be used as living museums of Earth life among other more practical scientific pursuits. And, of course, they had no guarantee these fragile flora and fauna would even survive the gatejump or the long months across the Paradisi Planetary System to New Eden. Yet when the construction budget was discussed among the Founding Families and the Joint Command Board, there was never any question of approving Solomon's proposals for the Lab Sector. Even the most greedy and selfish among them all knew how important preserving Earth's life forms would be when arriving on an alien planet. If nothing else, a little bit of home in a foreign land was life sustaining in and of itself.

Solomon reveled in New Olympia's teeming life as they moved quickly into the forest: the mushrooms and lichens dotting a fallen cedar tree eaten through by insects; the trickle of a stream feeding life to the young spruce, cedar, and hemlock trees; the calls of the thrushes, wrens, and kingfishers ringing through the breezy air. A few wildflowers were scattered among the meadow grasses along the edge of the forest where they entered.

It was always easy to know the season in each of these ecosystems. He noted it on the screen above the code panel: spring. May, to be exact. They monitored temperatures constantly, relying on centuries of Farmer's Almanac data to fluctuate seasonal temperatures to simulate Earth-like conditions. They even used thermo-control systems to regulate lighting, heating, and humidity. It was the most advanced ecosystem humans had ever created. And it was mind-blowing to be surrounded by all the beauty of the Earth while being thousands of kilometers above it.

"Let's take the northwest path," Tavian said in a low voice, taking Dextra's hand as they all vaulted over the downed cedar. Oddly, it bothered Solomon, which was foolish given the circumstances. He barely knew the woman. Then he thought back to the kiss she had given him back in the Cavitran Room, when he had knocked out his boss, Mads Graversen. And he remembered again when she had saved him from further torture from Commander Edge. She must feel something for him, despite the short time they'd known each other. Or maybe he was just hard up for a woman.

"Toward that grove of trees?" Dextra asked, pointing to a dense grove of young spruce trees.

Tavian nodded.

"And it will provide us cover if someone takes this path," Solomon added.

"Exactly," Tavian said a bit too loudly.

"Shh," Dextra whispered, "I hear footsteps."

Solomon froze, listening. The crackle of boots plodding on leaf litter and wood mulch was faint but clear. "Hurry. We've got to get to those trees, or things are going to get messy fast."

They moved as quietly as possible through the bushes and trees, along a moss-covered path that followed the meanderings of the stream running throughout the vivarium. At least the rush of water masked their footfalls.

They heard voices from time to time, voices that were getting closer.

"Hurry." Solomon picked up his speed.

Eventually they rounded a grove of trees and came out into a clearing featuring Home Lake, which was more along the lines of a pond in size, but named for an actual lake in the original Olympic National Park. They pressed on until they reached its edge.

Solomon gestured to the right. "Let's circle around to the back, and then hide in the underbrush beneath the trees."

They took pains to hide their tracks as they rounded Home Lake, swiping away footprints with branches. Solomon never had much call to know how to hide his tracks, but he was starting to get damn good at it lately. Maybe he missed his calling.

"Here?" Tavian veered off the path and trudged through the undergrowth toward a stand of bushes.

"I can't tell which way they went." Dextra crouched down behind a particularly thick bush.

"Still likely behind us but hard to tell if they are still on the path. Keep your eyes out for movement." Solomon took a knee beside her.

"What's the plan here?" Tavian asked. "Stay put and hope they think we passed on to Tibet or even the Everglade?"

"Well, they don't know our end game—"

"At least we've got that working for us," Tavian interrupted.

"Yes, let's hope they pass us by. We're running low on time."

For a few tense moments, they heard nothing. This alarmed Solomon more than hearing their approach. It meant either that they had left Olympia, perhaps in search of a computer to track heat signatures in the vivarium to pinpoint their location or, more likely, that their pursuers had figured out where they were hiding and were preparing to ambush them. The thought made Solomon glance behind him. He suddenly imagined dozens of Tasers and stun guns coming down on them from all sides. He'd had quite enough of that already.

He caught a movement out of the corner of his eye, heightening his attention, but it was only a doe and her fawn coming to drink from the lake. He looked at Dextra who gazed at the deer with a faint smile.

"Beautiful, aren't they?" she whispered to him.

"Yes, and hopefully they'll hear the guards approaching before we do." He'd barely finished saying the words, when the doe whipped her head up, listening intently. She swung her head around and looked right at Solomon, and then she and her fawn bolted away.

# THE VIVARIUM

A shout erupted behind Solomon, and several guards jumped from a hedge of bushes from their left and rear.

The main question on Solomon's mind was whether their pursuers were Challenge Security Guards or if some JCorpers were in the mix. Some of the Janus Security Corporation guards had superior fighting skills and weapons. Sure, he might spar every once in a while with a boxing partner, but he was no match for JCorp elites. He'd have to assume they were all skilled fighters, even if they weren't.

He wasn't even sure if JCorpers would deem him an enemy. As they had with Reachers, the Founders had always viewed Janus crew as a step below themselves. Maybe he could leverage that somehow.

The key was not to get snared in one of their Lewies, a nunchuck-style nightstick that expanded into polymer handcuffs that tightened on impact. They also shocked those unfortunate enough to get caught with a fairly significant electrical pulse. They were perfect for belligerent

1

drunks stumbling out of the Paradise Bar, but he didn't fancy a go at this particular moment. He had a schedule to keep.

In seconds, Solomon had assessed the situation. Outnumbered: four to three. Two JCorpers, one rushing him with a Lewie at the ready. Two Challenge Security guards heading for Tavian, also holding a Lewie. Dextra was nowhere to be found.

The tall JCorper with the blond crew cut and cold eyes immediately whipped his Lewie forward and caught one of Solomon's wrists. Luckily, he'd had his other up in defense. Solomon was ready for the forthcoming shock, so he grabbed hold of the guy and let the uncomfortable jolt rock through him as well.

The other guard, a stocky, muscled dude who actually appeared mildly amused Solomon had had the foresight to zap the other guy, too, stood well away. Maybe they didn't like each other.

"Lay off the button, Jenks," the stocky guard finally shouted, and Solomon was blessedly released from the electrical charge hitting his wrist. With that, he didn't hesitate to throw a punch into Jenks's undefended abdomen when he'd recovered.

"We've got you surrounded, Reach. You're under arrest—"

Solomon didn't wait for him to finish his BS. He spun around and used his momentum to whip the Lewie toward Mr. Smiley. It hit him square across the jaw. His shout of pain startled a group of birds, which scattered noisily above them. Winging the stick up into his hand, Solomon wielded it golf-swing style and got the guy right in the balls.

Eyes-wide, he fell to his knees, clutching his crotch. Solomon immediately spun around to finish off Jenks who had recovered from the Lewie's shock. But he got a solid punch into Solomon's kidney before he could fully turn.

Solomon instinctively shied away to recover and regroup. He felt like he was in a drunken bar brawl in the Old West. Much higher stakes this time. He faced his opponent with a grim smile.

As they circled each other, Solomon desperately wanted to sneak a peek at how Tavian was making out. He heard some grunts of pain toward his left behind a stand of trees. Sounded like they were still going at it. He didn't hear Dextra at all. He hoped she had made a beeline straight for the far exit.

He and the JCorper threw out some feints, gauging each other's skills and reflexes. Solomon quickly assessed he'd be no match for this man. Brute force was his only chance to take him down, since he was pulling some kind of martial arts moves. Solomon wasn't up on any of those fighting styles. He was more of a slugger than a true boxer anyway.

Jenks leaned in and got a jab into his abdomen. Dude was quick. And his move was surprisingly effective. Solomon circled again, waiting for an opening, but the guy had some solid defense moves, which was smart because, despite his height, Solomon's reach was longer.

"Sol, I could use your help over here, yeah?" Tavian shouted. Out of the corner of his eye, he saw one of the guards had already tackled Tavian to the ground with a Lewie around his wrists.

Damn. There went his backup. He was also running out of time. A glance in the other direction showed him the muscly JCorper was recovering from his groin hit and had nearly made it to a standing position.

Those distractions resulted in Jenks punching Solomon in the same spot. And again, he sucked in a breath, the pain a little more intense. Solomon shrugged off the pain and rushed the guy, whose eyes widened in surprise. He shouldered into him while pressing the end of the Lewie into his throat. The guard fell back, taking Solomon down with him. Solomon jerked up and landed a solid right punch to the guy's windpipe, which he hoped would give him some time to handle the other guard. While Jenks struggled to breath, Solomon yanked his hand up and pressed his forefinger to the Lewie's finger-print locking mechanism. It beeped and released Solomon's wrist.

While he was messing with the lock, the second guard circled behind Solomon and pulled him by the forearm into a vice-like arm lock move. The pain ripped a shout from Solomon, as the man shifted to finish the move with a headlock.

Solomon wasn't having any of that. He grabbed the Lewie stick and whacked the guy upside the head. Then he pushed back and away, knocking him off-balance, as they both fell to the ground. Solomon slid his hips off him, and with as much strength as he could muster, he hammerfisted the guy's groin, which elicited a strangely satisfying gasp from him, leaving Solomon free to turn around and slug the guard into unconsciousness. He whipped back around and did the same to the winded JCorper who was still sprawled out, clutching at his throat.

Solomon glanced around at his handiwork, and felt oddly pleased with himself. Apparently sloppy brute force got the job done too. With those two taken care of, Solomon took off toward the direction of Tavian's expletive-ridden shouts.

The stand of trees blocked his immediate view, and he kept out of sight until he could see how to assist. From the flashes of movement between the tree trunks, it looked like the guards still had Tavian by the Lewie and were attempting to hold him still while he kicked at them.

Solomon moved around behind the three and

quietly approached. How he was going to handle the situation he didn't immediately know, but he'd just taken down two Janus security guards, so that was something.

Positioning himself, so he could rush them, he took a deep breath and went for it. He was in the middle of a high kick to the first guy's left kidney when he looked up in time to see something that made him gasp in surprise. It was Dextra, looking for all the world like a ninja as she leapt down from the branch of a large tree onto the shoulders of the other guard.

It stunned Solomon to the point where his kick went a little sideways, as his guy let go of Tavian, who face-planted into a batch of moss on the ground. The guard whipped around to face Solomon.

Hesitation was not an option. Solomon landed what he hoped would be a KO to the guy's jaw. The man's head whipped sideways and up, and he fell to the ground with a thud. A quick glance told him the guy wasn't unconscious but wouldn't be getting up any time soon.

At this point, the other guard, who had the look of a pale-faced, broad-nosed Viking, had pulled Dextra down off his shoulders and had her pressed up against his chest, a Lewie barred across her neck.

The image of her in danger—and that look of fear in her eyes—made Solomon see red. He took a breath and tried to think clearly. Tavian was struggling to get up, and Solomon circled around the guard and Dextra to position Tavian behind them.

"Look," he started in, trying to keep his voice steady, "you've seen me neutralize three guards. Do you really want to risk your life for this?"

"You are under arrest, Solomon Reach." The guard's accent was thick. Ah, Solomon thought, so he's Russian. He wasn't familiar with any of these guards, mostly because he rarely needed to deal with security issues. He let his Reach Corp security team interface with Janus Security Corporation and Challenge Security crews most of the time.

"Do you even know who this woman is? She is the daughter of XO Alexandra Justice. I'm sure she's watching you on the lab cameras right now. Do you want to jeopardize your ticket to New Eden by threatening the XO's daughter? Let her go, and we'll walk out of here without further incident."

This gave the guard pause. After an uncomfortable silence, he finally spoke. "I can't let you walk out of here, Reach."

By some miracle, Tavian had made it to a standing position just steps behind the guard. Solomon kept his eyes on the guard, who was still hesitating.

"At least let the XO's daughter go. She isn't who Challenge Command wants. I am."

While the guard was busy giving him a mistrustful glare, the look in Dextra's eyes caught Solomon's attention. It said all he needed to know. She was about to try something, and he needed to be ready to act. He gave an imperceptible nod, knowing it would be impossible for him to convince her not to put herself in further danger. Out of his peripheral, he saw Tavian—awkwardly with his hands restrained behind him—preparing to rush the guard.

In one smooth move, Dextra elbowed the guy hard in the stomach and slipped down through his arms. She stumbled forward and fell into Solomon. He pulled her behind him as the guard shouted and flailed around haphazardly with some MMA-style moves, likely realizing he was in a bit of a bind being surrounded closely by three of his adversaries.

Solomon head-butted the guard at the same time Tavian kicked at the back of his knee. After he fell, Solomon finished him off with a slug to the temple.

"Dang, boss. Four guys down? You're a cyborg."

"I wish," was the only response Solomon could muster before he turned his attention to Dextra.

"Are you all right?" He gently touched her chin as he noticed a faint bruise forming on her otherwise flawless cheek.

"I'm fine. He hit me with his elbow when I jumped him."

"Jesus, you sure did." Solomon was unable to hide his smile of admiration. "And the elbow to the gut? An inspired choice."

"Damn right." Tavian whistled and let loose a grin the size of the Nautilus. "Impressive. I wasn't sure how I was going to get you out of that. But you didn't need my help at all."

Dextra laughed. "Think I'll get hazard pay for it?" Solomon's wry half-smile made her punch him playfully in the arm. "Maybe I'll switch to the Reacher crew if you can guarantee me a raise."

"Now you're talking." Solomon desperately wanted to pull her to him and kiss her until she forgot where she was or even who she was, but this was no picnic in the park, and the cameras along the bulkheads above them recorded their every move. They needed to get moving.

He was starting to feel the effects of the fight in his limbs. He touched at what he knew was going to be a bruise on his forehead, but he didn't think he had any broken bones or sprains.

Dextra's smile fell and her expression turned serious. "And you? Are you injured?" she asked, moving closer to inspect his face. She gently touched his forehead and smoothed her cool fingers down his temple to his cheek.

"Nothing serious." He reassured her with a smile, and then turned to Tavian. "How about you?" Solomon glanced over at his employee. "All your pieces and parts working?"

"Does it look like it?" Tavian twisted around to show Solomon his restrained wrists.

"All right. The last thing we need is this guy waking up. So sit down next to him, and I'll try to get you unlocked."

With a great deal of awkwardness, Solomon managed to get the unconscious man's forefinger up to unlock the Lewie around Tavian's wrists.

"Please tell me you have more excitement planned ahead." Tavian immediately jumped up and rubbed at his reddening forearms.

Dextra rolled her eyes. "A man of drama, are you, Mr. Hunt?"

"Of course. This type of situation happens every day of the week for me," he said, affecting a British spy accent while brushing the dirt and moss from his shoulder.

It was Solomon who rolled his eyes this time. "Sure, it does. And don't you worry, Tavian. I'm sure we're just getting started."

# THE DOG

They all took a moment to catch their breath, having run through the grassy and hot Serengeti vivarium without further incident. The silver lining was, of course, that Solomon wouldn't have to hit the gym compartment later. He'd had quite enough exercise for one day, thank you very much.

Now they stood in the deserted main passageway connecting the massive central vivaria and hydroponics labs with the outer labs along the port side of Deck 10. They were heading to the Astrophysics Lab, which was where the majority of the critical experiments took place. The Astro Lab's various compartments spanned two decks and curved along 20 meters of the outer bulkhead of the SS *Challenge*'s hull.

"So I'm thinking we'll head in the back way through compartment 10M," Solomon said.

"Don't worry about it, Boss. I've got an 'in.'"

"A what?" Solomon raised an eyebrow.

Dextra glanced sideways at Solomon. "Should I be worried when he says something like that?"

Solomon tilted his head and studied Tavian. "Normally, yes, but I do believe he's got something useful up his sleeve this time around."

"Damn right I do." Tavian turned to Dextra. "Now, how do I look?"

"Um . . ." She glanced at Solomon, obviously not sure what Tavian was up to. "Why do you ask?"

"Like, do I look like somebody you'd want to sleep with?"

Solomon glared at him. "Tavian, you do realize Dextra and I . . ." he couldn't quite finish the statement or even look Dextra in the eye, because he didn't actually quite know what to say. What was between them was entirely too new to label.

Tavian laughed. "No, boss, I mean, do I have any blood still on my face? I need to look, well, hot before I head in there."

Solomon was still entirely too baffled to respond, but Dextra seemed to understand finally. She nodded her head, stuck her forefinger into her mouth to wet it, and began to scrub at the crusted blood spatters still in evidence on his temple and near his lip. She then ran her hands through his longish hair while Solomon grew more uncomfortable by the minute.

"There. Now you're good enough to sleep with. Some women like the disheveled look." She smiled at Tavian, who flashed her a megawatt grin.

"Excellent. Now follow my lead." And with that, Tavian typed a code into the code panel and walked straight into Lab 10E like he owned the joint. To Solomon's surprise, it was nearly deserted. This lab was mostly filled with low-temp experiment storage containers. However, a lab tech sat at a desk, inputting data into a wall of computers.

They all ducked down behind a workstation, and Tavian peered up over the table to reconnoiter the situation. He leaned back down with the most obnoxious smile on his face. "You stay here. I've got this."

Without another word, he stood up and started

walking right toward the lab tech's desk. Solomon tried to grab at Tavian's arm, but Dextra shook her head and stayed his hand.

"What the hell is he doing? Only credentialed scientists are allowed in this area of the Astro Lab."

"Trust me," Dextra smiled knowingly, "he'll be able to handle this one."

"Reina!" Tavian called out loudly.

They heard a squeal turning into a gasp and a thump, as if she whacked him a good one.

"Dammit, Tavian. You scared me."

"My deepest apologies, Miss McKennet," he drawled in his best Rhett Butler rendition. "I merely came to visit my little lady."

"Not now, Tavian. I have too much work to do."

"Aww, come on. I've been stuck down there in engineering for days on end tinkering with that old Cavitran clunker, the memory of my two favorite ladies the only thing to keep me company. Can you blame me?"

Dextra laughed softly. Solomon frowned back at her. What the hell was Tavian up to? That bastard better have a good plan because they were wasting precious time.

"Tav, you are nothing but trouble. I told you the last time you wandered in here during that staff meeting."

"And the time before that and the time before that. It's an established fact by now, wouldn't you say?"

"Yes, I do say. Now go away. I'm right in the middle of logging experiment data."

"Not experimenting on my little girl, surely?"

"No, it's George, the turtle. He's on a new med."

"Maybe I'll join you. You know how I love to watch you work."

"You're ridiculous, you know that? Go on back there. You can see her for a few minutes. Don't let her disturb any of the other specimens in there, or I'll get you spacewalked."

"Who me? Never."

Solomon peeked around the corner and caught Tavian's eye, who nodded them toward the slider of Lab 10F.

"I won't be long, darlin'," Tavian cooed to Reina, who gave him a frowning smirk.

"Oh, go see about Frankie, you idiot. I'm sure she'd love to cuddle you. She's been anxious all day."

Dextra took up Solomon's hand. "We're in," she whispered. They crawled along the floor, hiding behind counters and cabinets and tables as they followed Tavian through to the next lab.

Once inside the soundproof lab, Tavian flashed Dextra a smug smile. "As you can see, the ladies can't resist."

"Yeah, uh huh. Get on with it." Dextra shoved him forward. "We're on a tight schedule."

"Pushy, pushy." Tavian was obviously enjoying his inexplicable ability to garner female attention. "You'll have to wait your turn."

Solomon shook his head. "So where is this long lost part, Tavian?" His voice was more stern than he intended. "And who is this woman you keep talking about?"

"Tsk, tsk. Wait for it. You're about to realize my schnauzer saved us all."

"Your what?" Solomon looked thoroughly perplexed. Dextra smiled at his ignorance, and he had to admit he suddenly felt like a complete moron. Tavian exchanging a smirk with Dextra didn't help the situation.

The squeal of a dog echoed loudly through the lab, shrill and sharp. They rounded the cage of an iguana, and finally glimpsed a fluffy, bearded salt-and-pepper miniature schnauzer wagging her little backside in sheer ecstasy at seeing her master.

"Ah," Solomon said, his smile crooked. "This must be the elusive Miss Frankie."

"Well, of course she is. Aren't you, baby?" Tavian said in a mock-motherly voice. He had completely transformed from the debonair womanizer to a proud papa absolutely ecstatic at seeing his dog again. It was a disconcerting switch from the usual tattooed grease monkey Solomon was used to seeing hanging around the Cav Chamber, elbow deep in complex machinery.

"How's my little pumpkinhead?" Tavian lifted her out of the cage and kissed her flopping ear and nuzzled her neck.

Frankie squealed in delight as she wiggled in Tavian's arms and licked his face. The smile on Dextra's face was worth it to Solomon as she tried to pet the wriggling, bearded head. He had to admit, the scruffy looking dog was making him grin a bit too.

"This is what you brought us all the way over here to see?" Solomon finally said. "Where's the part?"

Tavian frowned good-naturedly. "Well, he's no fun, is he, pumpkin? Five more minutes in your presence, and he'll be eating out of your paw. Just you wait, Frankie." He kissed her, and then let her run wild throughout the lab, terrorizing the other caged animals.

"All right, all right. I'm a genius, really. The part is in . . . er . . . Well, I take it back. I probably should have put it where it wouldn't get dog poop on it."

"What?" Solomon pushed Tavian out of the way so he could see. And he wished he could unsee it. As Tavian lifted it out of the cage, he saw smeared dog feces covered one side of the part they needed to get the Cav up and running again.

"Damn," Solomon muttered. "You're going to get that cleaned off, yeah?"

"Not in here." Tavian covered it with some plastic

sheathing he found in a drawer, and set it on a counter while he rummaged around for a bag to put it in. "Here's hoping nobody asks about the smell on my way back to the Engineering Sector."

"If they know you, they won't think anything of it," Solomon said.

"Is this thing even going to work again?" Dextra asked.

Tavian studied the level of poo on the part and nodded. "Yeah, it's doable. Give me half an hour back in the chamber, and I'll have your Cav Drive right as rain."

"All right. Get it done. The Cav's got to be working perfectly by the time I'm finished with the kid."

"Got it, boss." Tavian clucked his tongue at Frankie, who had ceased torturing the rabbit in the far corner and came racing back to her master, short tail wagging.

"Isn't she a sweetheart?" Tavian asked Dextra.

She started to nod before Solomon interrupted.

"Yeah, yeah. She's a cute dog. Put her back in her cage so we can get going."

"He's no fun, is he, honey? Pay him no mind. You'll get extra treats from Miss Reina today. I'll make sure of it, pumpkin." Tavian kissed Frankie's ears, ruffled her beard, and placed her inside her cage again, which made her growl good-naturedly and lick her chops. Apparently, the word treat was amenable to the little rascal.

"I'll need to go back through Lab 10E again," Tavian said.

"So you can say goodbye to your sweetheart, Reina?" Dextra said, getting her digs in.

"Among other things . . ." Tavian suppressed a laugh and playfully nudged Dextra's shoulder. "Don't worry, Miss Justice, my heart belongs to you."

"Bet you say that to all the girls."

"Taking the fifth on that one."

"Smart fellow."

Without realizing it, Solomon had butted in between them and walked over toward the lab's slider. Frankly, he didn't quite like watching this woman flirting with anyone, much less his most notoriously womanizing employee.

"If the tech seems like she wants to come back in here for any reason, detain her, Tavian. We need to figure out a good time to make our escape. I don't want her to even get a hint we were here. This lab is far too close to the Astro Lab. If they suspect we're in this area, they'll do a thorough search, and I need a fair amount of time to suit up."

"Got it. Want me to really distract her? Give me three minutes, and she'll be oblivious to any other creature on Earth or above it."

Dextra glared at him, and he flashed her a lopsided grin.

"Get to it," Solomon said gruffly.

"Just remember, I took one for the team today," Tavian said. "Well, my schnauzer did, anyway."

"Something tells me this won't be an overly taxing burden. I'll give you a pay raise. How about that?"

"There are so many things wrong with this conversation, I don't even know where to begin." Dextra shook her head and gave Frankie one final pet through the cage bars.

"Normally we Reachers do play by the rules." Solomon lifted his bandaged hand up to remind her of his recent torture session. "But not today."

Dextra begrudgingly nodded.

"Well, milady Dextra, it was a pleasure meeting you. Hope we meet again under less trying circumstances."

"Indeed," Dextra said.

Tavian headed through the lab's slider door with

the Cav part but glanced back. "Bye-bye, pumpkin-face. Love you, honey."

He actually blew his dog a kiss and slipped out the slider. If someone had told Solomon this morning he'd be pulling a priceless propulsion system part out of the poop-caked cage of a schnauzer owned by a womanizing Cavitran Drive engineer who was about to make out with a lab technician in order to save the Reachers from an apocalyptic Earth, he would have had a good laugh. But there it was.

He glanced over at Dextra.

"How on earth did that guy make the cut during your hiring process?" she asked.

Solomon smiled. "I didn't say the Reachers weren't eccentric. They're all basically a bunch of misfits with giant brains. When you think outside the box, you tend to be a little . . . off."

"Ah."

"But they are a loyal bunch."

"I can see that. And frankly, I'm not used to seeing it."

"You've been hanging around Challenge Command too long."

"I've been hanging around this ship too long."

"True. New Eden can't come soon enough."

"Do you think we'll actually make it?" she asked, and he could feel the uncertainty in her voice. "Do you think we'll survive the wormhole?"

"Sure. Don't you know? In all the greatest hero-conquers-all stories, you never kill off the dog. It's a sacrilege apparently. And look"—he stuck his finger into Frankie's cage who proceeded to lick his finger—"Frankie, here, is quite obviously thriving."

"Or was just very happy to see her master."

"You seem to like Tavian too." He hadn't meant to say it. And he felt like an idiot for being so obvious about.

"Sol," she said, her hand rising to touch his shoulder, "Tavian's . . . not you."

That set Solomon's eyebrows to rising and his thoughts to racing. For the first time, she had used Vida's old nickname for him. Vida had called him that ever since their university days together, after she had told him she had a thing for him but before he had a thing for her. Of course, by then it was all too late because she had started seeing Kasen Vokos, and the rest was history.

Solomon frowned a bit, not sure if Dextra was serious but hoping she was.

"When this is all over, I think you should take me on a proper date," she said coolly.

"Done," Solomon said without hesitation. He attempted to hide the foolish grin threatening to break out on his face with a subtle smile instead. "Well, if I'm still alive at that point."

"No promises, then." Dextra bit her lip, which drove him mad with desire.

"No promises." Solomon pressed her up against a supply cabinet and kissed her until she felt his promise anyway.

"We're agreed, then," Dextra said, when she could speak again.

"My God, woman. You are driving me crazy."

"The feeling is mutual." Dextra laughed and straightened her cap more tightly over her A-line shaped hair.

He let her go, then, and rolled away so he stood beside her, his back to the same cabinet, breathing hard. "Don't take this the wrong way, but I would take you right here on the floor of this laboratory if I thought I had the time for it."

She glanced sideways at him. "Time enough for that later, I should imagine . . ."

He wiped a hand down his face, and tried to

think of anything else. "If the wait doesn't kill me, you mean."

With a wide grin, she tilted her head toward the slider. "Speaking of that, shall we check to see if lover-boy has worked his magic as yet?"

He groaned but leaned over until he could see through the lab window. Tavian was pulling Reina into a maintenance closet, his mouth locked with hers, and his hands firmly gripping her ample hips. With a faint click, the slider closed behind them.

"We're clear." Solomon pulled Dextra toward the slider, desperately wishing he could grab something untoward on her but refraining while in his official capacity as savior of the SS *Challenge.* It was a rough life.

# THE ANGEL

Solomon glanced at the slider down the passage-way. "Let's quickly stop into Compartment 7F. We'll be able to pick up some protein bars before heading on to the Astro Lab."

"Sounds good to me," Dextra murmured. "I'm starving after that fight in the Olympia vivarium."

"Tavian was right. You are impressive," Solomon said, and he meant it. She smiled at him as he typed in the override code for the compartment. As the slider opened, five stern-faced Janus Security Corporation employees in standard grey uniforms greeted him. Not only that, but he spotted two Janus Corp guards unconscious or dead on the floor and a third tied up and gagged.

Solomon's mind raced with possible outcomes to this situation as they all stared openly at him with suspicion. He had no idea if they were loyal to Challenge Command or had their own agenda.

He thought it best not to make a scene by bolting down the passageway with Dextra in tow, but neither did he step into the compartment.

"The infamous Chief Solomon Reach, I presume?" said a black-haired woman who seemed vaguely familiar.

Then she trained her piercing, exotic eyes toward Dextra. "Hmm . . . and the daughter of XO Justice, I imagine."

Solomon waited. The JCorpers had them outnumbered. By the look of their stun guns and Lewies, they were outgunned too.

Janus himself, who Solomon always thought looked a bit like an older Kasen Vokos due to his Greek ancestry, pushed forward, cane in hand. "Reach, you're just the man we wanted to see, actually." He'd met Janus many times already, usually via holographic videoconferencing or occasionally in person.

The woman frowned at Janus, but eventually the crease in her forehead eased. She put two hands on the back of a nearby chair. "Have a seat, Chief and . . . Dextra, isn't it?"

"I have no time for a chat," Solomon said. "What do you want?"

"Let's put it this way," Janus said, his smile maddeningly enigmatic, "we may be in a position to be mutually beneficial to each other."

Solomon glanced at the others' faces. One was a man wearing spectacles, and his dark coloring made Solomon think he was some kind of islander. Perhaps the Caribbean or thereabouts? Behind him stood a man Solomon already knew: the SS *Challenge*'s Contract Manager, Marcel LeClerc, a Frenchman with a thin aristocratic nose, Old World Charm oozing out of every pore, and an agenda that usually didn't coincide with anyone else's. He'd be curious to know how this guy would view Challenge Command's betrayal of the Reachers. Would he find it beneficial to his own end game or a detriment?

Lastly, a woman stood apart from the others. Her short blonde hair and pale Scandinavian coloring made her stand out from the others. Or perhaps it was her ice-cold expression and thin-pressed lips. Whatever it was, more than anyone else, Solomon knew instinctively she was not to be underestimated.

Realizing he had little choice but to see where this would lead, Solomon finally stepped into the compartment. He couldn't bloody well stand out in the corridor all day in any case.

"Beneficial? And how's that, Janus?" Solomon asked, when he and Dextra made it in and he closed the slider behind her.

Finally LeClerc waved them over to the table. "Have a seat, Solomon. We have much to discuss." He pulled a chair out for Dextra. "I am called Marcel LeClerc. Pleasure to make your acquaintance." Dextra sat at the proffered chair while LeClerc sat next to her and took up her hand. "Enchanté, mademoiselle."

As each member of the JCorp crew sat, they introduced themselves in turn.

"Peter Cobb here," said the man with glasses, his Jamaican accent pleasing to hear. "Do mostly IT but starting to expand."

"Katya Ulyanov." The blonde woman's voice was sharp with impatience.

"And I'm Angel Flores." The dark-haired woman with stunning Asian-Hispanic features sat back in her chair and steepled her fingers as she studied Solomon.

"And they are?" Solomon asked, pointing to the various bodies on the ground.

"Not important." Janus's voice was gruff as he waved a hand at them dismissively. "Founder loyalists."

Solomon couldn't hide his surprise, but in his mind, this was the evidence he needed to be able to trust these people.

"Not all Founders are corrupt," Dextra said, glaring at Janus.

"That remains to be seen," Janus replied, his tone gruff. "The deal is simple, Solomon: we need your override codes so we can move freely about the ship and release some of our crewmen who are trapped in various locations due to the lockdown."

"I see." Solomon thought through that enlightening information. Could they be Founder loyalists as well? Were they attempting to acquire the access codes for some other nefarious purpose? "Why do you need further access? What is your end game?"

A flash of anger crossed Angel's face. "We have recently learned some of our crew are to be kicked off the ship along with large numbers of your crew. We assume you are aware of this."

Solomon nodded. So it wasn't just Reachers that Challenge Command was planning to oust.

"We find this . . ."

" . . . Unacceptable," Janus finished.

"So you are aware, then, of Challenge Command's betrayal," Solomon said, taking this as confirmation Janus Corp was more or less on his side.

Janus nodded. "Our goal is to protect our valuable assets."

"And what about the Reach Corp crew? Where do they fit into your agenda?"

"We are no fools." Angel leaned forward and laid her hands flat on the table. "We know the Reachers are irreplaceable on this ship and as future citizens of New Eden. We want you to remain on-board. We'll *need* your intelligence and expertise in the months ahead."

"Well, that's the first I've ever heard anyone utter those words," Solomon said.

"Challenge Command has gone too far, and we aim to level the playing field before they really get out of hand."

Solomon mulled that over and locked eyes with Angel. "So we agree on what exactly?"

"Give us unfettered ship access, and we'll protect your crew."

"And what exactly will you do with this access?"

"We want to free up several key players in our organization—some of which are just now prepping for cryo sleep—so we can begin readying for any eventuality."

Solomon raised an eyebrow.

"Any eventuality?" Dextra asked.

"Ms. Justice," LeClerc said with a patient smile, "with three thousand people waiting in the wings to take over the Reacher spots, we may not be able to put an end to this without a fight."

"That's not acceptable," Dextra countered. "We have obligations and procedures—"

"All of which Challenge Command has flatly ignored," Solomon finished.

Dextra glared at him.

"You've seen it with your own eyes," he said gently, willing her to understand sometimes you had to fight fire with fire, as much as he detested the idea. He was no warrior. He had no interest in fighting. And yet, how many times had Challenge Command pursued him? How many times was he forced to defend himself and his crew?

Solomon looked at each of the Janus Security Corporation crew members in turn, and then he settled his gaze on Angel: "I accept your offer with three caveats."

"And those are?" Angel asked, suspicion lacing her voice.

"I request that one of your JCorp guards accompany me to the Astro Lab."

"For what purpose?"

"Protection."

Angel paused, considering. "Done. The second?"

"Several of my crew are down in the Engineering Sector guarding . . ." He hesitated. Should he tell them he'd tied up Mads in the Cav Room? They'd eventually find out, and it'd probably be better if they heard it from him.

"Yes?" Angel prompted.

"The Cav Drive and . . . Director Graversen."

Angel crossed her legs. "How do you mean?"

"Graversen and I aren't exactly seeing eye to eye currently. He has been . . . neutralized."

"Dead?"

"No, just tied up and pissed off." Smiles crossed the faces of everyone in the room. It seemed no one was a particular friend of Solomon's old mentor. His own admiration was fading fast. "The Cav Drive is a critical element needing protection. While we control it, we control when we leave this godforsaken solar system."

"We had already planned to place security in the Engineering Sector for that exact reason," Angel assured him. "What is your last requirement?"

"I want you to send someone down to the Shuttle Sector to ensure Shuttle Bay 2 is operational with the bay hatch open."

The JCorpers glanced at each other, but did not immediately agree. Solomon crossed his arms and waited.

"Why?" Janus asked.

"It's best I don't reveal the details of my plan. What I can tell you is my end game: the SS *Challenge* will be launching within a couple of hours. Ready your crew and ensure all are safely aboard as soon as possible."

Murmurs among the JCorpers erupted.

Cobb shook his head. "That's not enough time. We have too many—"

"This is non-negotiable," Solomon interrupted. "It's the only way I can guarantee the Reachers' safety and avoid a bloodbath."

Janus and Angel whispered to each other, their gazes serious.

"I think we need to be aware of your movements for a variety of security reasons," Janus finally countered.

"It's not up for debate."

Janus didn't nod his acquiescence, but he also didn't push further for information. Angel whispered once more in his ear.

He glanced up at Solomon. "All right. We have a deal."

"Also, it's best only one of you holds the codes, and that individual should keep them in a heavily encrypted file. Agreed?"

Angel nodded. "I'll keep them."

"Fine. I will need to input them manually. I don't trust file transfer." Solomon stood and walked toward Angel. Peter gave up his seat so Solomon could sit next to her. She keyed through several screens on her DOT unit, and Solomon made sure she opened up an encrypted file. Afterward, she held out her arm toward him, and he began to input the codes along with their corresponding compartment numbers.

"Ensure you include the code for the cryo chamber," she added.

"Done." Solomon pulled back and released her arm.

"Where are your Reachers now?" Janus asked.

"You'll find the majority of them on Watch Deck 16. Please take precaution and don't attempt to engage with Challenge Command or their cronies for as long as possible. I'd like us all to get out of this without any blood being spilled."

"That's our preference as well," LeClerc assured him. "We'll station guards around them inconspicuously to alleviate suspicion. The original launch time table set forth by Challenge Command is still days away, yes?"

"I overheard the board say that they would need to

push up their time table by half a day. But they still have to take the time to switch out the crews, so that gives us some time."

"Let's get to it," Angel said.

Everyone began to rise from the table.

Solomon shook LeClerc's hand. "Thank you. What have you heard about what's happening elsewhere on the ship or even on the ground."

"Nothing good. Sporadic fights between Reachers and Founders are erupting ship-wide. The news is spreading about you. Challenge Command has been trying to track your whereabouts—we heard the chatter on the security feeds—but it's a lot of video footage to look at. You've been busy."

"And Earth?" Solomon almost didn't want to know.

"Wild reports of even more nukes dropping, but I don't know how accurate those are. And the Solix Sky LiftPort has been overrun with all the panicked people who were tipped off about the SS *Challenge*'s final flight."

"Damn it."

"The Paradisi Penitence, no?"

"I'll have to wait to entertain those thoughts when this is all over—one way or another. We all have a job to do today, so we better get to it."

"Katya, brief Lance Barrow on his new assignment," Angel said. "Tell him he's on protection detail for Chief Reach until we contact him further or when he releases him from duty."

Katya nodded once and sent off a message via her DOT. She glanced up at Solomon. "Chief Reach, wait here for Barrow."

LeClerc pulled Solomon aside as they waited. "How in the hell are you going to get this ship launched under the noses of Challenge Command?"

"As I said, that information is need to know. Let's just say, you probably wouldn't believe me if I told you."

LeClerc stroked his chin and leaned his head back slightly. "You never fail to surprise me, Chief. One of these days, I'm going to buy you a drink and weasel all your secrets out of you."

"Secrets? Oh, no, LeClerc, I'm merely an engineer. We don't generally do secrets. Today is rather . . . unusual."

"Regardless, I'm impressed you've made it thus far unscathed."

"Not quite." Solomon held up his bandaged hand, which had quite recently had a scalpel stuck through it by an angry ship's commander.

"Commander Edge?" LeClerc questioned.

"Indeed."

"That man has an insatiable thirst for blood . . . I told them from the beginning. He has no business being aboard this ship."

Solomon's smile was grim. "I couldn't agree more."

# THE BOY

"Barrow, how many technicians do you see through the window there?" Solomon crouched with Dextra and Corporal Lance Barrow behind a supply cabinet in the Astro Lab outside the control room for the airlock hatch.

"Two. One is monitoring Zander via the camera feeds trained on the nanosilc deployment panels, and the other tech is standing with her back to us inputting data at the wall screen, it looks like."

"Can you see if either of them have their eyes on the inner airlock hatch?"

"Nope, I think we're all clear in that direction—wait . . ." Barrow's eyebrows furrowed into a wide swath of black on his low forehead.

"What is it?" Dextra asked, alarm flickering in her eyes.

"Dammit," Barrow muttered, smacking the counter with the flat of his palm. "I see a guy inside the suit up compartment prepping to EVA."

"Not good," Solomon said. "He must be going out to assist the Marcks kid."

He locked eyes with Barrow after the guard crouched

1

down next to them again. "Can you neutralize the two techs if I focus on the guy suiting up?"

"Yes, no problem."

"You'll have to force them to open the outer airlock hatch for me when I give the signal while keeping them away from any communications devices where they could get word to Challenge Command. Doable?"

"Yes, sir."

"And me?" Dextra asked Solomon, the look in her eyes quite obviously a desire to be useful.

"Come with me. We may need to have you distract this guy." Solomon winked, and Dextra responded with a scowling smile, which somehow made her even more gorgeous than usual.

He led Dextra over toward the compartment adjoining the airlock. Scanning the control panel next to the slider, he realized the man had yet to flush the room of oxygen. He hadn't even donned his compression suit yet.

"There's still time," Solomon whispered to Dextra. "If you wave him over here, I can wait by the slider. When he comes out, I'll grab him."

"I've got a better idea. Instead of resorting to violence every chance you get, why don't I tell him he's needed urgently in the lab command module. Then Barrow can lock all three of them in there."

Solomon opened his mouth to respond, paused, and then flashed her a grin. "Because that would make far too much sense."

Dextra laughed softly. "I've got this. You stay out of sight."

With a smile, Solomon shuffled off to the back of the compartment behind a row of shelving. Once hidden, he gave her the thumbs-up, and she moved to stand in front of the glass slider.

With a wave of her hand, she got the man's attention. She motioned for him to approach, and the slider abruptly whirred open.

"Is there a problem?" The man's tone was gruff and low.

Dextra plastered a smile on her face. "We have a situation in the lab command module. You're needed in there."

"Are the comms down?"

"No, they are just busy in there. I know you're getting ready for an EVA, but they indicated this was critical."

The man grumbled, but strode through the slider and made his way toward the lab command module.

Solomon hoped Barrow would be able to handle him but didn't stop to worry about it. He jumped up and ran over to the slider leading toward the lab command module. With a quick scan of the slider's keypad, he keyed in an override code to lock it down.

"That should buy us some time."

"Think Barrow can handle all three of them?" Dextra asked.

"I hope so. Wait, I've got to message Vida and let her know we're a go." He pulled up Daniela Marcks's info in his contact list and shot off a quick message to Vida, who he hoped was still holding the docking commander in Conference Compartment 4C.

"You done?" Dextra asked.

"Yes, let's be quick about this. Help me prep."

They headed into the suit up compartment, and Solomon went straight for the compression suit. He made quick work of stripping out of the blue janitorial get up he donned earlier to hide his red Reacher uniform. Then he did a visual inspection of the compression suit. It wouldn't do to get everything in place only to find his suit had a puncture in it, however unlikely that scenario might be.

These suits were the most advanced models the space community had ever designed. Unlike the classic EVA suits of the previous decades, these suits contained nickel-titanium memory alloys, which shrunk them into form-fitting but flexible compression suits. He loved the new "shrinks," the nickname the crew used to describe the suits' shrink-wrap qualities. Or maybe it was that he loved spacewalking, and anything that helped him achieve more walk time was a good thing.

"Flip the expander switch for me?" Solomon asked Dextra, who nodded and rushed over to the suit monitor panel and turned it on. The suits were so effective at compression they had to use powered nanosilc technology to expand the suit enough for an astronaut to slip into it—a small price to pay for supreme mobility.

Once the suit was fully expanded, he began the process of shimmying into it, checking his uniform didn't get caught in the compression suit's tight weave.

"You're not going to take off your uniform first?" Dextra asked.

"I don't want to waste the time."

"Your mobility may be affected."

"I don't need to do intricate work, so it'll do for this EVA."

"All right."

After he was fully inside the shrink, he made some minor adjustments around the neck, and Dextra helped him slip into the arms and torso portions. He gave her the thumb's up, and she released the expander. The vacuum-like seal tightened around him, which was always a mildly uncomfortable experience. He checked the fit on all sides while Dextra unhooked the suit from the expander cable.

"You good?" she asked.

"Yeah. Can you find a full consumables module for me? I need to rummage around the tool modules for a pipe cutter."

"What? Why?"

"Don't ask."

Dextra glanced back at him, her expression wary. "You're not going to harm that boy."

"I don't plan on it, but I have to have a contingency plan."

She glared at him but said nothing further.

He picked up the most powerful pipe cutter he could find and secured it inside the tool module complete with a pistol grip tool and several other key repair and patching materials.

Dextra was already bringing over the consumables pack when he began piecing together modules using the module builder hanging from the bulkhead. Dextra helped him mount the pack onto his back, and then there was nothing for it but to get moving.

"All right, time for me to take a walk."

"You promise you won't hurt Zander?"

He gave her a tight-lipped smile. "How about I just say that the last thing I would ever want to do is harm that boy, and I will do my level best to avoid it."

"Not good enough." Her voice was low as she held out his helmet.

He took it and touched her cheek with his gloved hand. "I know it isn't. But my job is to save three thousand people—not one boy. He is our best chance."

"You may be right, but I still don't like it. He is innocent."

"Well, I wouldn't go that far. Didn't you hear about the time he—?"

"Solomon, you're getting distracted."

"You're my distraction." He slipped a light kiss onto her lips. A faint smile touched those lips after he pulled away, and it reminded him of why he needed to survive this spacewalk. He pulled on his helmet and locked it into place.

Dextra grabbed hold of either side of his helmet

and kissed the visor. "Take care of yourself."

Solomon gently touched her cheek again with his gloved fingers, and then she moved out of the airlock. He wasn't used to the feeling, but the room felt a little colder after she left. He locked himself in and glanced out of the airlock's tiny fenestella. He'd need to use his gold-plated visor to block the sun's rays before he headed out. He didn't bother with running the Gravitational Flux to switch the AGG to micro-gravity. He just hooked on his tether and strapped into a chair along the bulkhead before keying in the $O_2$ flush and airlock prep.

Solomon squeezed the pipe cutter attached to his belt, and mentally prepped to do whatever it took to force Docking Commander Marcks to start the ship's launch initiation. He figured he had maybe a 50–50 chance of success. He'd had better odds.

The airlock opened and Solomon unbuckled from his seat and touched off the bulkhead with his feet to start his trajectory out of the hatch. He couldn't see Zander from this angle, but he knew exactly where he was: the portside nose of the ship working on a nanosilc panel recently damaged by a micrometeoroid. It was a simple switch-out of the panel, which made it a perfect first job for the newest member of the Nanosilc Repair Team.

He had never admitted it to anyone, but incorporating nanosilc technology into the ship's design was Solomon's proudest achievement. Nanosilc was in and of itself an engineering marvel. An army of silicon-based robot-like nanobots only a few nano thick, nanosilc had multiple uses aboard Asteria-class ships.

First and foremost, once deployed, the fabric-like material created a shield on and around the ship's hull to protect against micrometeoroids. Its electromagnetic field aided in the hull's integrity and rigidity as well as funneled solar radiation toward the back of the ship where it was deflected further by nanosilc diffusion streamers trailing the ship for over a kilometer once they were underway.

Not only that, but the clever little things were going to get them through the Sideris Gate and through the wormhole, the Sideris Cavum. Once—or rather, if—the SS *Challenge* made it there in six months' time, Challenge Command would deploy the SE-CASM, another ridiculously advanced use of the nanosilc tech. The Solar Energy Collector portion of the SECASM was built to act as a solar collection array, which they'd make use of as they approached Jupiter. Once at the gate, they would deploy the second function of the SECASM: the one-kilometer diameter Ford-Svaiter Mirror.

Some genius back in the day theorized that giant mirrors would provide the missing piece for creating a man-made wormhole. It wasn't until nanosilc went into heavy use in the astro-engineering fields and Reach Corp started testing the material that it went from theory to production.

Solomon couldn't help smiling as he floated on toward the nanosilc panels. Nanosilc was the little engine that could.

Zander fiddled with his wrist unit, switched to a direct EVA-to-EVA comm channel, and waved him over. "Hey, man, what're you doing out here? I heard all about the shit you pulled earlier. What happened? Did they walk you or something?"

Solomon laughed, despite the seriousness of the situation. "Nah. I'm out here for a Sunday stroll."

"For reals? They let you out here with all that cha-os going on?"

"It was all a giant misunderstanding we finally cleared up. However, our time table for launch has been moved up exponentially, so they sent me out here to help you with your panel repair issue to get things rolling along."

"Wow. I haven't heard anything about a schedule change on the comms."

"I suspect that's either due to a spotty connection on your unit or the fact that everyone has been busy with the lockdown situation going on and hasn't had time to update you."

"What's the new ETA for launch?"

"Far too soon to be lollygagging out here. We need to hurry. What's your status on the repair?"

"Did you bring the tool I requested from the Astro Lab?"

"Yeah, got it here." Solomon unhooked the drill from his belt and handed it to Zander, hoping it was the one he wanted.

"Well, I've got the panel in, but I've been unable to lock it down since I stripped my good drill."

"Where's the damaged drill?"

"Ah, yeah, that bugger's probably made it to Ju-piter by now. I let it float. Didn't see much point in keeping it since we're heading out soon."

Solomon frowned. While the possibility was low that the drill would impact the station, ship or other smaller craft, it was still a safety hazard and not worth the risk. However, Solomon didn't chastise Marcks, because a brilliant plan had popped into his head. He silently thanked Zander for giving him the idea and simultane-ously hoped it wouldn't result in the kid's death.

Solomon worked alongside Zander until they accomplished the task of securely locking down the newly repaired nanosilc panel.

"All done. Good job, kid," Solomon said as the sunlight moved behind the hull of the ship. When they both raised their gold visors for better visibility, Zander flashed him a grin. "Reattach your tools and get things cleaned up. We'll head in shortly. In the meantime, I'll let the Astro Lab know we're finishing up."

"Yes, sir, Chief Reach. Thank you for the assistance."

That jabbed Solomon in the heart a bit. After all, he had nothing against this kid.

"You're welcome." Solomon also realized this was the perfect opportunity to disable Zander's comm unit. "I'm going to check out your comm unit. If for some reason it goes dead or wonky, our plan is to head right back into the airlock after I have a conversation with your mother to give her a status report on the repair. Stay tuned."

"We can wait until we get into the airlock if you want."

"For safety's sake, it's best we do it now in case we have an issue on the way back to the airlock."

"Understood."

Solomon moved around behind Zander and pretended to fiddle with the comm unit. "Your comm does appear to be showing an error. I'm going to remove it to see if re-seating it will fix the issue."

"Sounds good," Zander responded as he began to load up his pistol grip tool onto his tool belt.

Rather than waste an expensive piece of equipment they might need on the journey to New Eden, Solomon didn't float the comm unit. Instead, once he removed it, he faced away from the ship and station and slipped it into his pocket.

When he shifted back around, he tapped gently on the side of Zander's bubble helmet. Zander glanced up from organizing bolts.

"Lost your comm," Solomon mouthed as he gestured at the back of Zander's head and made the motion of floating.

"Gone?" Zander mouthed.

Solomon nodded.

Zander smiled and shrugged while Solomon pointed to his own comm unit, and then up at the Nautilus Command Bridge, indicating he wanted to make a call to Docking Commander Marcks. Zander nodded and went back to his work.

Solomon switched to a direct comm channel to connect with her. Glancing up toward the module where she worked, he could see her at her usual control panel. Vida Rosado stood behind her, holding something to the back of her head. Looked like Vida had escorted her into the Nautilus-11 Command Control Bridge and cleared the room as he had instructed.

This was it. Everything he had done thus far had culminated in this moment. Either she'd do the right thing and save the right people—including her son—or she'd choose Challenge Command's directive. Surely she wouldn't be that insane. Right?

"Marcks, this is Chief Reach on an encrypted channel."

"You bastard. What the hell are you doing? You need to call off your dog here, or I'll see you get walked."

"Look out your window," Solomon said. When she saw him, he gave her a little wave.

"Solomon, get your ass back on that ship. Get *my son* back on that ship." Her voice rose exponentially higher with every word.

"Take a closer look, Marcks. Look at what I've got in my hand."

He had already grabbed onto Zander's tether and held the compression pipe cutter he had brought with him up to the Spectra tether cord. It was cut-resistant, but nothing could withstand a Reach Corp-approved pipe cutter.

"What are you talking about, Reach? Wait! Stop—" She halted speaking when the realization sunk in. "Don't you dare touch my son, Reach."

"What happens next is up to you, Daniela. You're either going to save your son's life alongside the lives of three thousand Reachers, or you're going to make the wrong choice. I leave it to you. But I warn you: I have nothing to lose. You already know your son's life is not my priority."

"Take your hands off his tether. I'm going to call—"

"No, you're not, Marcks. If you call anyone, if you make anyone suspicious of what's going on here, I will cut this cord. I will cut your child loose, and make you watch him float off into the void."

"Zander!" she screamed.

"I've disabled Zander's comm unit, so don't even try. Besides, if you make him suspicious of me, he's likely to do something really stupid that'll get him killed."

"Dammit, Reach. What do you want?"

"I already told you. You need to make a choice right now. I know who you've got in Serica Sector. And I know what your vote was in that Joint Board Meeting. But now you can make the right choice. Now you can save your son. And you know as well as I do the Reachers have earned this ride."

"I can't help you. They'd leave me and my son behind if I helped you."

"I can save you both, Daniela, but first you have to help me."

"What the hell do you want, Reach?"

"Vida?" Solomon addressed his drive ops chief.

"Yes, Chief?" he heard her say faintly in the background.

"Has the Command Bridge been cleared of crew?"

"Yes, temporarily."

"Good. Your job here is done, Vida. You and Kasen evacuate to the SS *Challenge* Shuttle Sector immediately. You'll have one hour and no more."

"Yes, sir."

He watched as Vida's form moved away toward the back of the bridge, silently wishing her Godspeed.

"Don't even think of moving out of that chair, Marcks. I want you to start emergency undocking procedures for the SS *Challenge* right now."

"I don't—"

"No more excuses, Marcks. Do you want to live with your own son's death on your hands for the rest of your life?" With those words, he glanced at Zander who was staring at Solomon's face, obviously trying to figure out what he was saying to his mother as well as perplexed as to why he was holding onto his tether. Solomon had done his best to hold the pipe cutter behind the tether so Zander couldn't see it.

"What about everyone still aboard the Nautilus?" Marcks asked. "That's not enough time—"

"It's up to you, Daniela. If you think you can get aboard this ship before it takes off, then give it your best shot. After you key in the launch codes, you'll hit the station-wide evacuation emergency alarm. After that, I'll leave you to board in whatever way you see fit."

No way. I won't be left here to die."

"Your time is up, Marcks."

Solomon hadn't planned to go through with it, but he realized she was going to need some powerful motivation if he was going to get through to her. He opened up the metal shears and, without looking at Zander, clamped down on the boy's tether. He released the pipe cutters and let them float away, which wasn't the best idea, but they were the last of his worries at this point. He grabbed hold of Zander's tether before he lost him.

He heard Daniela screaming in his ear, mostly a mix of expletives and her son's name, but he focused on Zander's face, which was ashen and full of fear. The question in his expression nearly killed Solomon. He could even see him mouthing the word: why? Why? Why?

Hand-over-hand, Solomon yanked Zander closer. He could tell Zander was conflicted, both wanting to be as far away from his would-be killer as possible but needing that proximity to survive. Solomon didn't envy the kid's predicament. He'd be scared shitless too.

He pulled him in until they were nearly helmet-to-helmet. Solomon wrapped Zander's cord around his belt loop and secured it as best he could. And then he grabbed hold of Zander's helmet and looked him straight in the eye.

"I'm sorry," he mouthed. "I've got you."

Zander shook his head, disbelieving, but even so, he dug his gloved fingers in between Solomon's compression suit and his tool belt and held on.

"I'll do it, Solomon," Marcks shouted in his ear. "I'll do it!"

He glanced up at her, saw her shadowed arms flailing in anger through the fenestella.

"Just don't let go of him. Please don't let go."

"You understand now I'm dead serious, yes?" Solomon finally said in between her screams.

"Yes, all right, all right. I'll do it. It's going to take me a few minutes. Hold on to him."

"You need to focus on my instructions, Marcks. Lock it down with the emergency lockdown codes for the launch procedure. No one—not even you—will be able to override it."

"I don't have that code sequence—"

"Yes, you do, Marcks. I know the codes, and I'm going to watch you input them via remote DOT in my

HUD, so I can be assured you are not deviating from this plan. Only after that is completed to my satisfaction will I get your son back into the ship. Do we have an understanding?"

"Yes, Reach, we have a deal."

"You've made the right choice. Now open up your module remotely and share it with my suit's HUD. Suit number is"—he read off his armband—"4B52TTE84."

When she repeated the number back to him, her voice was shaky.

"That's correct."

A minute passed, and then Marcks's screen popped up in his helmet's HUD. One by one, he relayed the codes to her as she inputted them into her control module, a series of four that had to be keyed in at set intervals and in the right order.

"Set time to launch at one hour and no more," he prodded.

Solomon held up a hand to Zander and pointed toward the Astro Lab.

"Okay, it's done. Now let my son go."

"All right, Marcks, we're going to back away and head to the Astro Lab airlock. I suggest you sound the alarm, and then get to a compression suit. The hatches are locked down. Spacewalking is your only viable option. Good luck."

"I'm going to have you floated for this."

"You'll have to get aboard the *Challenge* before you can even attempt it, Marcks." Solomon grabbed Zander's belt, and mouthed, "Hold on to me." Then he switched his tether to retract mode and set the speed to high, which was fairly dangerous, considering he had Zander in tow. It jerked them aft toward the airlock hatch, and Zander held on tighter.

Solomon worried about Dextra and Barrow. By now, the Founders would likely have found them out.

And Kasen and Vida—would they make it aboard with so little lead-time?

As he dragged them along toward the hatch, Solomon heard the ring of warnings resound in his HUD as the docking commander's station-wide emergency alarm went off.

"Warning! Warning! All aboard the Nautilus-11 Space Station must board the SS *Challenge* immediately. The SS *Challenge* will launch in one hour. Secure the ship. Do not delay."

Solomon shook his head in disbelief. It seemed his insane plan was going to work.

# THE DIRECTOR

Solomon yanked Zander through the hatch and motioned him to strap into a grav seat along the wall. The boy glared at him but did as he was told. Solomon strapped into a seat along the opposite bulkhead, which seemed prudent.

Solomon punched the seldom-used inner grav switch. Under usual circumstances the technicians in the lab's command compartment would handle that for the astronauts. In this case, Solomon glanced up through the fenestella leading into the suit up compartment, and saw a lot of angry faces peering in at him. He knew it was inevitable, but it still came as a shock regardless. He hadn't thought past black-mailing Docking Commander Marcks, but he supposed it didn't matter what happened to him now. He had done his level best to keep his Reachers safe, and he had to get used to the idea he'd likely be out of commission for quite some time if not forever after this.

While he and Zander waited for the gravitation and oxygen levels to stabilize, Solomon studied the people outside the window. It looked to be a mix of blue-uniformed Founders and Janus Security Corp guards in their signature bland grey uniforms as always.

He was curious to know if Edge and Justice were milling around out there, too, waiting to pounce. He supposed some of Challenge Command and Joint Board members might even still be on the Nautilus. He had done what he could for them, but a pang of worry hit his stomach. He wondered again if Vida and Kasen were spacewalking right now even as he sat here waiting.

A loud alarm resounded in his ears telling him it was safe to remove his helmet. Zander ripped his off and threw it to the ground while Solomon carefully removed his and set it on the chair next to him.

"What was that all about, man? What the hell did I ever do to you?"

"I'm sorry, Zander. This wasn't about you. I don't have time to explain what's really going on. The main thing you need to worry about is your mother."

"What? I saw her up at her command module on Nautilus. Is she not there now? What happened?"

"Long story short, the SS *Challenge* is going to take off in less than an hour. Nothing can stop it now. An emergency protocol has been initiated, and we are leaving. Your mother is still on Nautilus, but I told her to drop everything and get over here. So you need to focus on your mother, and nothing else."

"Man, you better tell me what's going on. I have to report this. You could've killed me."

"It doesn't matter now. Look through the window."

Zander unbuckled himself from the seat, and stood to glance out the window at all the angry faces. "What are they all doing here?"

"They're here for me."

While they talked, Solomon moved toward the

suit expander panel and hooked his suit in. He flipped the switch and waited for the expander to do its magic. Once the suit was loosened, he wriggled out of it and stretched. Even in these flexible suits, spacewalking was still exhausting.

Somebody finally figured out how to override his emergency code on the airlock hatch, and they all came crashing into the room. Solomon found himself with five Tasers aimed right at his chest.

"You're under arrest Solomon Reach," a tall but bulky Founder guard burst out. Solomon raised his hands in the air, indicating he would surrender.

"All right, all right, you got me, but you better make sure you've got all your crew accounted for because this ship is leaving with or without them in less than an hour."

Three of them surged forward to surround Solomon, hands out with their Tasers at the ready. A fourth moved around Solomon to cuff him with a Lewie. He was not particularly gentle. Solomon grunted in pain, as the man nearly dislocated his shoulder.

Once they had him secured and two of the men stood on either side of him, the Founder security guard who looked to be in charge stepped forward.

"Did you force Docking Commander Marcks to put out the launch alarm and start the initiation sequence?"

"I did."

"Why?"

"You wouldn't believe me if I told you. Then again, maybe you're in on the game."

Several of the guards exchanged surprised and perplexed glances.

"In on what?"

"Don't you think you'd best make sure all your crew are accounted for? That should be your first priority. The launch sequence is in emergency override mode, and it's been locked down. Put your focus on your crew, and then I'll tell you what you need to know."

The man narrowed his heavy-lidded eyes at Solomon, studying his expression. Solomon kept his eyes on the man, willing him to believe his words. After all, it was the truth.

"Officer Bennett?"

The leader finally turned and whispered to one of the guards. The man nodded and headed out of the airlock. Bennett turned back to Solomon. "You'll cooperate if I comply?"

"I will."

"All right. Let's get him out of here." The guard turned to the boy. "Zander Marcks, I believe? Are you all right? We saw Reach cut your tether."

"Yeah, I'm okay. Though I have no freaking idea what is going on here."

"You will be informed later. In the meantime, you might get yourself checked out in the Med Bay to be on the safe side."

The guards made way for Zander, who glared at Solomon as he moved past them and out of the airlock.

"Remember what I told you about your mother, Zander," Solomon called out, but the kid had already disappeared into the crowd of guards out in the suit up compartment.

As they walked into the compartment outside lab command, Solomon heard a familiar voice ring out.

"Solomon! Are you all right? Is the boy safe?" It was Dextra. She sat in a chair surrounded by guards. Lance Barrow was nowhere to be found. They must have hauled him off to lockdown already.

Mads Graversen leaned over Dextra, both his hands braced on the chair's arm rests on either side of her. Solomon nodded to her and flashed her a half-smile, hoping it would settle her a bit. Her expression was fearful, and he hated that Mads Graversen had her within his grasp.

"Where is that bastard?" Graversen immediately stood and glanced around.

"Ah." Solomon watched Mads Graversen stride toward him, his fists clenched, his face already bruising from Solomon's earlier punch to his jaw. "Glad to see you are in good health, Director Graversen."

Mads didn't say a word. He just reeled back and let loose a solid jab knocking Solomon sideways and had blood spurting from his mouth. He leaned heavily onto the guy next to him, waiting for the stars in his vision to clear.

"Fucking happy to see you too, Graversen," he said, the blood in his mouth garbling his voice.

Mads gave him a smug smile. "I'm going to see to it personally that you take a nice long walk outside in the very near future, Reach." As ever, Mads's voice was as even as a lake of ice. "Right after you help me park this damned ship."

"Too late. Nothing will stop the sequence now. Your plan has failed." Solomon could hardly believe it himself. There was only one code that could stop the ship's launch sequence, and he'd be damned if he was going to spill that to anyone.

Mads leaned back to take another swing, but the guards next to him grabbed a hold of his arms and pulled him back. With his face smarting and his mouth bleeding, Solomon failed to come up with a clever comeback, so he just spat on the pristine flooring—and Mads's shoes for good measure.

Graversen stopped struggling, and Bennett nodded to his guards to release him. He meticulously straightened his jet-black uniform before turning to Bennett, his face now serene, his eyes showing no trace of his anger from a moment ago.

"Take Reach to Command Deck 19, Conference Compartment 1B, immediately."

"You don't want Reach in lockdown, Director Graversen?" Bennett asked.

"I want him where I can get to him." A final glance at Mads made his fists twitch. Given the opportunity, that man would most certainly send him out into the void.

Bennett didn't question Mads's orders. "Yes, sir," he said with a nod toward his security entourage, and began leading Solomon toward the Lab Sector's main passageway.

Solomon glanced at Dextra, and then found he couldn't keep his eyes from her. He was not entirely sure he would ever see her again. Memorizing her stained lips, her dark eyes, the endless curves of her small body before they led him out, he wanted only one thing: to take her straight to his quarters, peel that skin-tight uniform off her body, and make her scream in ecstasy. He didn't stop to consider he had no idea how to make a woman scream like that, but that wasn't the point.

Solomon hoped his gaze would be enough to tell her how he felt about her. She looked like she had tears in her eyes. Maybe she also realized this could be the end of the road for him. It was only a moment, and then one of the guards shoved Solomon out into the passageway.

Being paraded through the SS *Challenge* while everyone scurried around to prepare for the ship's launch was not Solomon's idea of a good time. Open stares greeted him at every juncture, but he was happy to see very few Reachers among the Founder crew. He hoped most were on the Watch Deck in relative safety. Then again, the hatches were on lockdown and the ship was taking off. It took him a moment to realize he really had saved his crew. There was no time now for Mads and his mad dogs in Challenge Command to replace the Reachers aboard the ship with the people they'd hidden in the space station's Serica Sector.

Along the way, he freely offered Bennett an explanation of what had transpired in the last twenty-four hours. He didn't pull any punches, and he didn't worry about hiding details, though he tried his best to keep Dextra and the rest of his crew out of it. It would be obvious based on security footage Dextra had been with him the whole time, but he didn't want to reveal the integral part she played in their successful mission. Best to make Challenge Command think he had kidnapped her against her will rather than implicate her. No sense in both of them going down for this.

He figured Alexandra Justice would attempt to keep her daughter out of trouble, but there was no telling what Commander Edge would do if he thought Dextra had useful information. He wondered where Edge and Justice were right now. Had they made it across to the ship? Were they still trying to find an available trafero to transport them across from the space station?

He rather hoped they wouldn't make it in time but figured it was an unlikely scenario. Besides, they would have need of Edge's skill set when they finally made it to the wormhole. They'd need his expertise to navigate the Sideris Gate and Cavum.

It certainly wasn't Solomon's realm of knowledge. Well, if he made it that far. They may shove him out the hatch for that long-threatened spacewalk. He wondered if it's what he would do to Graversen and Edge if the roles were reversed. He honestly didn't have an answer for that.

Bennett peppered Solomon with questions, and he answered as truthfully as he could.

The man narrowed his eyes again. "And you cut the boy's tether—why?"

"Docking Commander Marcks was less than enthusiastic about assisting me in my endeavors today," Solomon retorted dryly.

"Ah, I see. But to put that boy's life in danger . . ."

"I had no intention of harming Zander. He's a good kid. I wouldn't have cut his tether if I had any other choice. But I was tasked with saving the lives of three thousand of my crew. One life for three thousand was a chance I was willing to take. What would you choose?"

The man laughed grimly. "I don't know, man. I'm glad I didn't have to make that choice."

"Well, now you know what it's like to be me. At least in the last twenty-four hours, anyway. Frankly, I could use a damned drink. A stiff one."

"If you make it out of this alive, I'll buy you one."

# THE WALK

Vida hurried into the largest suit up compartment located in the Challenge Docking Sector. Several other people scrambled around the compartment in various stages of suiting up. Only so many suits remained. At this point, it was a free-for-all, each hoping to make it to the ship as soon as possible.

She ran over to an empty suit hanging on the wall and yanked it down, checking it over quickly for any immediate problems. She cursed the fact that Solomon still had her UiComm, but the suit's HUD would tell her the time and give her the ship's departure status. Her fingers trembled annoyingly. The last thing she wanted was to see the SS *Challenge* slipping from its dock while she watched it zoom away forever. She knew as well as Solomon did that the lockdown could not be overridden. She'd woken in a cold sweat from nightmares of that very scenario.

Vida hooked the suit up to the expander panel and pushed the expander button. While she waited, she grabbed a helmet and thruster module. Knowing she wouldn't be out there long, she left all the optional pack modules behind. She thought it best to go with the lightest module configuration possible.

"Vida!" she heard Kasen shout as he strode through the slider amid a crowd of panicked people.

A ball of anxiety leapt up her throat and threatened to strangle her.

"Kasen, what the hell are you doing here? You should be on the ship. You're supposed to be on the *Challenge*." She punched him in the arm while he leaned in to kiss her.

"So are you. Why are you still here?" He was still shouting.

"Never mind. Find a suit. We've got to get out of here now. How much time do we have left?"

He glanced at his UiComm HUD. "Twenty-five minutes."

"That's not enough time."

She saw another suit already hooked up to an expander, so she slammed down the button and told him to find a helmet and thruster. He rushed over to the storage rack and hooked his $O_2$ and thruster modules into the builder panel.

"My suit is prepped. I'm getting in," she said, her tone gruff. "Dammit, Kasen. It was foolish of you to come here."

"I can't believe it's taken you this long to get out. What the hell were you doing? I originally thought you boarded down at the lower hatch. But when no one could find you, I knew you had to be stuck over here."

"I was blackmailing Commander Marcks. You know, doing my job?"

"I should have been the one to do that."

"Let's not argue. Put your suit on and get moving."

They rushed through the prep and checks and hauled ass to the airlock, where several other people were preparing to open the hatch.

Kasen made eye contact with everyone in the airlock, which consisted of five men and three women.

All were strapped down to their seats.

"Fuck the grav," he said, daring anyone to disagree. Despite the looks of shock on a few of their faces, most nodded in agreement. "We don't have time for it. Strap in and hold tight. Head straight for Shuttle Bay 2 on the port side. I have confirmed it's still open."

Using the Gravitational Flux Chamber to switch from artificial gravity to micro-gravity would have taken another ten minutes they didn't have. With a final glare to make sure all of them were strapped down in their seats along the bulkheads, Kasen buckled himself in and hit the airlock's release button. As the hatch slowly opened, Kasen tapped on the comm unit on the back of his helmet, indicating to Vida they needed to connect comms.

He used his fingers to display the number she needed to call.

"Checking comms, over," Kasen said once they established a connection.

"Confirmed. Over."

"All right, we're going to use our thrusters and head over to Shuttle Bay 2."

"Good. I'll follow you, over," she replied.

Once the hatch had fully opened, everyone floated out, scattering out into the inky black between the station and ship. Vida checked her helmet's HUD. The ship-wide warning message flashed red in her vision, distracting her. She muted the alarm sound with a command.

The area between the docking module and the ship was a mass exodus of traferos and spacewalking astronauts heading to the Shuttle Sector. They'd have to watch for traffic. It would only take five minutes to thrust their way over to the correct bay for entry.

Kasen glanced back at Vida with a worried look in his eyes, which was not something she often saw.

"What is it?" she asked.

"My oxygen levels are low."

"Didn't you check the canister?"

"Uh, no. I was in a rush, remember?"

"How much do you have?"

"Not enough. Maybe it's busted. Didn't have time to do the proper checks."

"Let's move. No matter what happens. You keep your eyes on the goal. Get into the bay as soon as you can. Keep your breathing even and try not to talk."

"Yes, I know the protocol."

"Dammit, Kasen. Don't give me any trouble. You need to stay alive so I can beat the shit out of you when we make it back to the ship. Solomon ordered you to stay at the hatch."

"Yes, mother."

She glared at him and shoved him forward. Despite the urgency, Vida couldn't help glancing at Earth, knowing this would be the last time she'd ever see it on an EVA. She had contemplated that thought hundreds of times before, but now she was shaking all over. Because this truly was the last time. She thought of her grandmother and wished the old woman could see this.

She switched off her comms, not wanting Kasen to hear her sappy words.

"Wish I could take a picture for you, abue Malena. You would have loved the view." Somehow she knew her grandmother was looking up through the Earth-sky into the blanket of stars where she floated, wishing she was up here with her. "Only the best people are the ones who get left behind," she whispered.

Something slammed into her from behind and an arm came around to grab her. When she used her thruster to help her twist around, she came face to face with Commander Dickson Edge himself. She gasped as he grinned at her and yanked at the module pack strapped to her back. It took her a moment to register that he was trying to rip the thruster module out of its locked position, which made no sense whatsoever. As she struggled against him, trying to twist all the way around, it finally dawned on her his thruster must not be working so he was trying to steal hers.

"Over my dead body!" she shouted.

The sneer on his face made it clear that's exactly what he had in mind.

# THE GLASS

Solomon pounded his fist against the fenestella in Conference Compartment 1B, his knuckles turning pale with effort. He wanted to fall right through the glass and go out to her.

"No, Vida!" he yelled. "Turn around!" But she couldn't hear him, and nothing would stop Commander Edge from his trajectory. He slammed into Vida, pushing her off-course.

"Fight him, Vida. Fight." With both hands now pressed to the glass, he watched in agony as Vida struggled against Edge, who was attempting to rip her thruster right off her back.

"What the hell is he doing? Leave her alone, you bastard."

She fought hard, but he had her in a solid grip from behind. She tried to use the thruster to force him to release her, but he floated to the side to avoid her thruster's exhaust. They tumbled through space, drifting farther and farther away.

Solomon shouted at Kasen to turn around and help her, but he never wavered from his path, never looked back.

1

None of the other astronauts floating by stopped to help Vida. They hurried on, thrusting past her as if she meant nothing.

Commander Edge finally yanked the thruster from her module pack, and the force of it pushed them toward the trajectory of an oncoming trafero. Edge cruelly pushed against her with his feet, using her as a launch while he awkwardly held the thruster in his arms, but it backfired on him. Edge lost control of the thruster, and it slipped from his grasp.

Vida spiraled out of control, and Edge followed after her. She had no way to stop herself without her thruster. She slammed into the trafero's nose, and immediately began to tumble across the top, her arms flailing for any handholds she could find. But there was nothing, only a surface as smooth as glass. Commander Edge slid off the opposite side of the trafero and disappeared from Solomon's view.

"Grab a hold, Vida," Solomon whispered to nobody but himself. Watching her body skid across that cold metal with no ability to help her was agonizing. "Anything. A bolt, the tail wing . . ."

But then she slipped off the back, her body powerless to stop her momentum.

"Fuck it all," Solomon whispered as he watched her tumble backward. He glanced wildly around, looking for the compartment's comm unit.

Finally spotting it, he gave it a voice command. "Emergency contact, open comms."

"Emergency override code, please," came the unit's robot-like voice.

"Eight-nine-three-one," Solomon shouted, his voice breaking with the force of his words. "Vida, Vida, can you hear me?" He ignored the other voices on the open channel, the shouts, the chaos . . . he was waiting to hear the one voice that mattered.

"Solomon? Solomon, where are you?"

"I'm so sorry, Vida. I can't get to you."

"Kasen Vokos, if you can hear me, I command you to return for Vida. She is heading into deep space."

"No, Solomon! Don't ask him to do that. He's almost out of oxygen. He wouldn't make it."

"Vida? My God." Kasen's unmistakable accent burst through the comms. "What happened? I can't see you!"

"Kasen, it's too late. Edge took my thruster. But you've got to keep going."

"Fuck." Kasen's voice came out in a growl. "I only have a minute left of oxygen, Vida."

"I know. I know you want to help me, baby. But you can't. Live for me. Go now. There's no sense in losing both our lives."

"No—"

"I'm too far gone. I'll hate you forever if you don't go."

"Oh, God, Vida. Why'd you have to take so long?"

"Because I had a job to do. I needed to save your life. We all knew the risks. I'm going to die today knowing I saved the lives of three thousand people. Not many people can put that on their resume."

"Vida . . ." Solomon didn't know what else to say. What could he say to console her? To console Kasen? This whole disastrous plan was his idea. It was his idea to send her to Nautilus.

"I know, Sol. It's okay. It's the luck of the draw. Don't blame yourself. You've got to focus on surviving. I'm going to focus on taking in the sights. It's a lovely view out here. Say hi to the freaky aliens on New Eden for me, eh, Solomon?"

"Vida, I'm sorry. I wish I could stop this. I wish I could—"

"Get the Reachers to safety, Chief. They still need you. You're a good man, Solomon Reach, but you've got to let me go."

"I love you, Vida. Thank you for saving all of our lives."

"You're the one who did that, Sol. I only came along for the ride. Tell Tavian . . . to ask out that girl in the Paradise Bar. He'll know which one I mean."

"Dammit, Vida. I wish I could save you."

"I know. But it'll be rather nice to go out a hero. Now let me say my goodbyes to Kasen and my grandmother. I love you. Godspeed you on your way to Paradise."

Solomon slammed his head against the glass as the comms went dead. Soon, Vida Rosado, his best friend and his best crewmate would be dead, and all she would have left in this galaxy to mourn her were the stars.

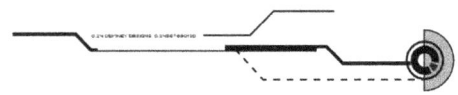

Mads Graversen burst into the conference room, shouting obscenities, his usually cool demeanor already shattering into a near madness.

"How? How do we stop it, Reach? Stop it, or I'll kill you."

"I already told you." Solomon didn't turn. He kept his fist to the glass, struggling with an overwhelming desire to kill this man. "You're far too late."

Mads didn't even approach Solomon. He strode directly to the fenestella and stood next to him, his eyes wildly scanning the windows. Solomon glanced back toward Nautilus and gasped as hundreds of people from the Serica group stormed into Nautilus-11's Command Bridge, not far from where Daniela Marcks's had initiated the emergency launch sequence.

Solomon felt a shudder beneath his feet, and he

felt his heart shudder along with it. The SS *Challenge* was finally pulling away from the station.

Chaos erupted on the Command Bridge. Hundreds of people pounded against the windows, their mouths open in soundless screams, as they watched the ship undock and move away.

Graversen must have eventually spotted his wife, because his whole expression changed. His body went rigid, his hand went to the glass, and he stared open-mouthed. Solomon had long since lost sight of both Edge and Vida. They floated off in opposite directions, and he was grateful at least that Vida wouldn't have to lay eyes on her murderer.

"Too late to save your wife, Mads."

Mads turned to him. And the look in his eyes made Solomon wince and lean back. It was the torture he felt only a moment ago for Vida. It was what he still felt and could not shake.

"Would you be able to do that, Solomon?" Mads asked him without turning from the window. "Could you walk away from the woman you love, knowing with certainty you were leaving her to her death?"

Solomon grabbed him by the collar and pointed toward the void. "I am! Right now. Vida Rosada is out there and she is going to die today because Commander Edge ripped the thruster right off her back. What kind of monsters are you people?"

"I'm not a monster. I was trying to save Jessia's life."

Solomon shoved him back and paced the room. "At the expense of everyone else. Vida was innocent. She didn't deserve to die for your selfishness."

"Jessia begged me to leave her. She said at least one of us should live."

"She's a smart woman."

"She was my responsibility."

"You were responsible for a lot more than one woman. What of the three thousand Reachers you'd be sentencing to death in a dying world? Reachers who built this ship for you and everyone here?"

"You don't think I considered the consequences of that choice every day?"

"I think you considered it but not objectively."

"Ah, yes. Solomon, the wise one. The logical engineer who always makes the right decisions."

"I did what you taught me, remember?"

Mads scoffed at that. "You never listened to a word I said."

"The moment I chose to save my crew I knew I was simultaneously condemning the Serica group to die. It was Challenge Command—you—who forced me to make that decision. You think I want their deaths on my conscience? Do you think I want Vida Rosado's death on my head?

Mads's mouth drew into an ever harder line, his eyes never wavering from his wife.

"Cold logic was what you taught me back at MIT, and I employed it well. Reachers are far more useful alive than dead. We have skill sets unlike any in the world. We'll be the ones building your new cities and running your utilities. We'll be the productive citizens your Serica group could never be."

"This isn't a business deal involving money and politics. Lives are at stake."

"How did you convince Justice and Edge to go along with this?"

Mads was quiet for a moment. Then he finally spoke. "It was Edge's son in exchange for the Reachers."

"Let me ask you something, Mads. If you had to do it all over again, would you have made the same choice?"

Mads considered his question, and then he finally looked Solomon in the eye.

"Yes. I would."

"I suppose we were always meant to be enemies, then. Because I would choose to protect the Reachers again and again."

"At any cost?"

"No. And that's where we're different. You were contractually obligated to honor our agreement. And I had an obligation to ensure my crew retained that right."

"And what of the obligation I have toward my wife?"

"Remember what you said to me back at the hospital when you turned me away from my dying sister? No? I'll remind you. 'One girl versus the lives of so many others. Is it even a choice?'"

The expression on Mads's face turned to the pure rage of a man who's had his words thrown back in his face. He did not respond, only turned on his heel and strode out of the conference room without looking back.

Solomon finally picked out Mads's wife in the massive crowd. She pressed her hand to the glass and stood ramrod still amid the screams and cries Solomon knew were erupting around her. He raised his hand to the glass himself, as if he could reach through it to touch her hand.

She was beautiful. He shook his head at the thought. *Was.* As if she were already dead. As if he had walked her straight out into the void and let her go as he had Vida. Just the thought of Vida pricked his eyes with tears, and he let them course down his face unchecked. He hadn't wept the day he walked away from his sister Nisolda lying so still in her hospital bed. Was he a monster back then? Or was he the monster now? He did not move to wipe the tears from his face as he stared at the woman pressing her own hand to the Nautilus's glass. She stared at him, as did all the others surrounding her that he had condemned to die.

With an agonizing pain in the center of his chest, he realized it had all begun this way. It seemed he was always looking out through a pane of glass at those he could not save: Vida, Nisolda, the innocents who would die aboard the Nautilus, a dying Earth. And all their deaths lay on his head. He fell to his knees, unable to look any longer. He wept for them, and left no tears for himself.

# THE UPRISING

"Solomon," Dextra shouted from behind him. He turned around immediately, hoping she wasn't surrounded by angry Taser-wielding Founder crew or worse: Mads Graversen again.

Solomon's shoulders dropped with relief. Dextra was surrounded but this time it was loyal JCorp Security Guards, including the intense Scandinavian-looking woman Katya from his earlier impromptu meeting. She and her team scanned the area and quickly spread out looking for enemies, but upon realizing the room was clear, they parted to let Dextra through to Solomon.

Without hesitation, she rushed over to him and moved directly into his embrace, whispering, "Did Vida and Kasen make it back to the ship?"

Still reeling from the news himself, his emotions caught somewhere between his chest and his throat, he could only shake his head and say, "Kasen made it."

"Vida?"

Solomon shook his head and blew out a breath, trying not to picture Vida spinning forever surrounded by an endless black void.

1

He glanced up at Katya. "What is your plan now?"

"That's up to you, Chief Reach."

"Commander Edge is dead," Solomon said, unable to keep the anger from his voice.

She gave one curt nod to acknowledge she was aware of this recent development and studied his expression. "Do you want to take his place?"

Solomon's jaw dropped. "What do you mean, take his place?"

There was bound to be a hierarchy for these kinds of things. Maybe Mads Graversen or Alexandra Justice or even Docking Commander Marcks, if she had made it aboard.

"Do you want to be the new commander of the SS *Challenge*, Chief Reach?"

He stared at her with no idea what to say. He was still trying to grasp that he had just lost his best crewmate and the ship lost its commander.

"I don't think so," he stammered out, glancing down at Dextra. He half-expected her to start spouting the rules against such a thing, but she only looked up at him expectantly. "There's bound to be a set protocol—"

"Good. Then that means the job is yours," Katya stated flatly.

"Now hang on," Dextra started in, "this has to go through the Joint Procedural—"

Ah, now there was his Dextra. Rather than annoying him, it made him want to kiss her and gather her even closer into his arms.

"Time is past for rules and procedures." Katya's tone was clipped.

Solomon stared at Katya, thinking hard. With Mads or Alexandra in charge of the ship, he'd surely find himself out on a long spacewalk in short order. And now that he'd saved his crew, he probably needed to consider how he might save himself.

But to take over command of the entire ship, which was no less than a mutiny of the highest order? Did he have the balls to do that? On the flip side, he was qualified in many regards. He knew this ship backward and forward; he had security clearance; he had the loyalty of at least half, if not more, of the combined crews.

"Solomon?" Dextra whispered.

He waited for her to give him all the reasons why he should surrender himself to Challenge Command.

"I think you should take it."

"What? You're serious?" He couldn't hide the surprise from his face.

"Katya's right."

"Frankly, I'm well aware that if your mother or Graversen gain control, they'll either throw me in lockdown or walk me. Neither sounds appealing. And given the circumstances, I'm probably the most qualified to take the position since I'm so familiar with the systems aboard this ship."

Dextra held his gaze, mulling over his words, it seemed. After an interminable moment, she finally nodded. "Take it." Her mouth curled up into a smile. "But just remember: I don't like it."

He flashed her a crooked grin. "I'd be disappointed if you did."

Solomon glanced around at the rest of the crew surrounding Katya, taking stock. A JCorp team of five stood alert, ready for anything. A stern-faced dark-haired woman he'd never seen before kept her un-blinking stare on Solomon, watching his every move. Two men of Middle-Eastern descent stood to the right, hands at their Lewies. And another woman with long blonde hair methodically tapped a shockstick against her leg. One guard with an ugly red scar across his forehead stood slightly apart from the others and kept his eyes and Taser trained toward the group's rear out in the corridor.

"All of you would accept my leadership? Janus Corp and the Reachers have always had a good relationship, if strained at times. But this is something altogether different."

Slow nods came from everyone except Scarface in the back. He had his eyes on something out in the corridor. At that moment, Angel, Janus, and Peter strode through the open slider.

"Are you ready to take control of the SS *Challenge*, Chief Reach?" Angel asked, her tone even.

"This was your idea, wasn't it?" Solomon countered.

The barest smile hinted at her answer.

He nodded in acknowledgement. "Thank you for your assistance today."

"The day isn't over yet," she replied.

"True. There's one thing I have to ask first, Angel."

She waited with no visible signs of impatience for him to finish.

"Is all of JCorp loyal to you? Because I recently had an uncomfortable run-in with several of your crew in the Olympia Vivarium."

"We have a faction that still remains loyal to Challenge Command. We are currently in the process of weeding them out."

"And by weeding out, you mean . . .?" Dextra's leading question was clear in its intention.

"We'll take care of it, Ms. Justice. We have our own internal rules and procedures," she finished dryly.

The faint scowl on Dextra's face required no interpretation.

"I'll assume, then, that as we storm the Command Bridge, the majority of JCorpers involved—if not all—will be loyal to our cause?" Solomon asked.

"Perhaps," Angel replied noncommittally.

"Ah."

"Do you need a weapon?" Janus asked Solomon.

"Yes."

Janus handed him a Taser. "We all know you can handle yourself in a fight. At this point, your combat skills in the Olympia Vivarium are already legendary."

Solomon hooked the gun into his belt loop. "How do you even know anything about that?"

Janus grinned. "Gossip travels fast and security cameras don't lie."

Solomon nodded. "So, what's the situation out there?"

"Katya report," Angel snapped.

"We have security details stationed near the bridge, the private mess hall, the officers quarters entrance, Cargo Hold 7, and Watch Deck 16. They are at the ready."

"Neutralizing Director Graversen and XO Justice is key—"

"No," Dextra interrupted with gritted teeth. "Don't you dare."

Solomon touched Dextra's arm, and held her gaze. "Have you seen your mother since you arrived on the Command Deck?"

"I have. Why?"

"What's her state of mind?"

"She's . . . extremely angry and upset."

"And she knows Commander Edge is unrecoverable?"

"She does."

"And how did she take the news?"

"Not well." Dextra glanced away. "I think they were lovers, though they kept it from me."

"Is she able to think clearly?"

Dextra shook her head and looked up at him.

"I don't think so. Not right now."

Solomon glanced toward the fenestella and the rapidly disappearing space station—and Vida.

"So your mother is currently volatile and unpredictable," Angel interrupted.

"Yes, but you're not to harm her."

Angel's lip compressed into a tight line, and she looked to Solomon, almost as if she was deferring to him as commander of the ship already. It didn't seem to soften the woman's obvious stance in the slightest, however.

Solomon met Angel's strong gaze with the same intensity. "XO Justice is not to be harmed."

Angel nodded her agreement.

"And Director Graversen?"

Solomon hesitated. "Your best bet is to throw him in lockdown. We may need him later. But use whatever means necessary to take him down," Solomon added.

"Where are Graversen and Justice now?" Solomon asked.

"We've been monitoring their movements. XO Justice is on the Command Bridge, and Mads Graversen is . . . holed up in a conference room, saying goodbye to his wife."

"Do you have any idea who else among Founder crew are loyal to Challenge Command?" Solomon asked Angel.

"No, I don't. Impossible to know who had family in Serica Sector."

Solomon looked out of the fenestella again, picturing again all the people slamming their fists against the glass, wanting desperately to board the ship and live. No matter how far the SS *Challenge* made it from the Nautilus-11 Space Station, he knew no distance would make him forget their faces—or the part he played in their deaths.

"All right." Janus held up a hand to get everyone's attention. "So this is how we're going to play it: Katya, your team will take the lead. You'll lay down a flash bang, and head in. Solomon, Peter, and Angel will follow. I'll cover your six. Let's move out."

Solomon turned to Dextra. "Stay here. You'll be safer."

"No way. I'll stay in the back, but I want to be there to ensure my mother's safety."

He shook his head. "And what about yours? It's going to be chaos in there."

"I'll stay far behind all of you."

Solomon eventually nodded. He studied her face. "I know you're not okay with a mutiny aboard an Asteria-class ship, but will you back me up on this?"

"If you promise me not to do anything like this ever again," she said, unable to help the smile that crossed her face.

"That I can definitely promise." He swept her up into one final embrace before following a scowling Angel out of the slider and into the corridor.

It wasn't far to the Command Bridge. A few short corridors and a lobby to get through. They marched single file. Twice they met with Founder Command Crew members, who eyed them quizzically but let them pass, which led Solomon to believe they were innocent of Challenge Command's betrayal.

Before long, they all stood, Tasers and batons at the ready, behind the slider leading directly onto the bridge.

"Manual override, Solomon?" Katya asked.

He nodded, and the group parted as he made his way up to the slider's code panel. He glanced back to check everyone's readiness. Once he opened the slider, it would begin. Katya stood at the front, and Scarface held the flash bang ready to deploy. Everyone else had filed in behind them. Katya nodded, and

Solomon punched in the code, his body tense with adrenaline.

The flash bang was already flying through the slider by the time Solomon looked up. He closed his eyes to avoid the bright flash, but he couldn't evade the deafening bang penetrating his eardrums. Katya and Scarface took center, while the rest of her team rushed in, the black and blonde-haired women taking the left and the two men fanning out on the right.

Shouts erupted around the room, and from his peripheral, Solomon saw the command crew getting up from their scan and telemetry stations to analyze the threat. Graversen and Justice had obviously posted extra security guards around the bridge as well. Some were starting to fight, while others held up their hands in surrender.

"Justice," Solomon shouted, "don't move." He focused his Taser directly on XO Justice who stood in the center of the bridge still shaking her head to clear the noise and light.

She locked eyes with him. The first thing out of her mouth was, "Damn you, Reach. Damn you to hell."

"It's over, Alexandra."

"You have no authority here, Solomon. You killed Dickson. The only place you're going is lockdown. I am now commander of this ship." She glanced wildly around at the members of Katya's team, shouting, "All of you put your weapons down!"

"An unofficial vote has left you out of the running, Alexandra," Solomon said, his voice firm.

"Mother," he heard Dextra's voice from behind him, "you have to surrender."

"Dextra, stay out of this." Alexandra's voice was cold, as if she no longer considered Dextra her daughter.

"No." Dextra's tone was just as firm. "You and the

joint board betrayed everyone aboard this ship. Solomon Reach is now going to take commandership of the SS *Challenge*."

"Like hell he is."

"Like hell he is," Mads Graversen echoed, as he strode into the room, his Taser trained on Solomon. Mads pulled the trigger, but Solomon spun out of the way. The shock hit Alexandra instead. She fell back into Scarface's arms, and then all hell broke loose. Hand-to-hand combat erupted throughout the bridge, as Dextra pulled her mother toward the back, away from the melee.

Mads and Solomon faced each other and charged. He could feel Graversen's rage over the loss of his wife as he slammed into him. But Solomon was angry too. If it weren't for Challenge Command's betrayal, Vida wouldn't be dying today.

Solomon put all his anger into his right hook, and Mads fell back against the telemetry panel. But he shook it off and charged at Solomon again, this time with the guttural shout of a man who has nothing left to lose. They tumbled to the floor.

Mads got his hands around Solomon's neck, squeezing as hard as he could. Solomon attempted to break his grip, clawing at the fingers pressing against his carotid arteries, but he was losing his strength as he struggled to get oxygen into his lungs. The seconds ticked by. Through the cacophony of shouts, he heard Dextra scream his name, felt the jerk of movement as she tried to pull Mads off of him. But in Graversen's eyes he saw his death. Blood rage burned like an uncontrollable fire there. Mads could not stop—even if he wanted to. The need for revenge was too great.

Solomon's vision blurred until all he saw were Graversen's eyes. Fear surged into adrenaline, pumping strength into his hands. He had to do something. Anything. He wasn't going to die today. He had fought too long and too hard. Solomon slipped his hands through Mads's arms and reached up to grab the sides of his head. There was only one way to stamp out that rage in Graversen's eyes. Solomon pressed his thumbs into Mads's eye sockets, eliciting a roar of pain from him. Suddenly the pressure against Solomon's neck slackened and Mads's hands pulled back.

Solomon sucked in a ragged breath and coughed violently. By the time he realized he could breathe again, Mads had nearly recovered, blinking wildly and reaching down to grab his neck again. But Solomon was already throwing a punch directly into Mads's throat. Solomon should have leveled it against his temple to get a knockout, but his own level of rage was rising. It did knock Graversen partially off of him, so he slid out from under him and slowly rose to his feet, waiting a moment for his head to clear of the dizziness.

He faced Mads once again, both of them now on their feet in the center of the bridge behind the commander's chair. Dextra stood behind Mads, holding out a stun gun toward Solomon, but he shook his head and waved her back further. No, he wanted to finish this, with his own two hands.

The fights around the room were quieting down, but Solomon didn't glance away from Graversen. He leaned in to feign a punch to the right, but Mads rushed him, sacrificing the protection of distance for pure offense. Solomon was ready for him. He twisted to the side and positioned himself for the hardest punch he could muster. Mads's head snapped back and to the side as Solomon's fist slammed into his temple. Graversen's eyes were closed before he hit the floor.

Dextra was already moving toward Solomon, walking right in between his balled up fists to press her body to his. The hard steel of his anger softened until his fists uncurled to press her closer.

"Are you all right?" he whispered as the room quieted. He glanced around at everyone. Challenge Command crew were either sitting up against a wall nursing wounds or being held by the JCorpers with Lewies.

Dextra leaned back to look at him. "Are you?"

He looked down at Mads Graversen, whose head was lolled to one side. And then he looked back into Dextra's soft eyes. When he thought about the choice Mads had made, to save his wife above all else, he suddenly understood. And then he thought about Vida's sacrifice for Kasen, for all of them. And he understood that too. He thought about a choice they had all made decades ago to only build eleven ships, to save just 110,000 people out of 11 billion. And he understood. But most of all, he understood that the Paradisi Penitence would never let him go.

"I'll survive," was all he could whisper back, but she heard in his tone what he meant when he said it.

"Command Crew of the SS *Challenge,* Challenge Command and the Joint Board betrayed Reach Corp and did not honor our contracted agreement. In addition, Commander Edge murdered Drive Ops Chief Vida Rosado while attempting to make it aboard this ship. Therefore, we are taking back the ship in the wake of Edge's death. Having been lead designer of this ship, it has been determined that I am uniquely qualified for the commandership of the SS *Challenge.* Janus Security Corp has agreed to back this decision and provide security for a peaceful transition if needed."

"If any of you cannot submit to my authority, you will need to step down from your positions immediately. Speak now if you want to step down." Solomon looked at every one of them in turn, slowly examining their expressions. None spoke up or stepped forward.

"All right, then. Welcome to the new leadership, everyone," Solomon said, as he propped himself up against a desk, attempting to recover. "I promise it won't always be this exciting."

"Don't make promises you can't keep, Solomon," came Dextra's reply from somewhere behind him.

Solomon laughed, which somehow turned into a coughing fit. He waved a hand at Dextra by way of introduction as he looked over the whole sorry group in various stages of nursing their wounds.

"And meet your new advisory and ethics board in its entirety: the incomparable Dextra Justice."

# THE PARADISE

"Your schnauzer is adorable, Tavian," Dextra said. "You're going to let me visit her once in a while, right?"

"I'd have to distract Reina first. But for you, I'd do anything." Tavian laughed a little too loudly at his own joke and took another shot.

Solomon noticed Tavian was already deep into his whiskey and looking a little glassy-eyed when he and Dextra sat down at his table. The bar was overcrowded with Founder and Reacher crews, likely for the same reason they were: to drink off last week's tense standoff between Challenge Command and the Reachers.

As he glanced around, he didn't see much intermingling between Founder and Reacher crew in the bar tonight, but he hoped tensions would ease as the days passed. He wasn't naïve enough to believe that there weren't pockets of Founder crew still loyal to Mads and Alexandra—and even the blessedly deceased Commander Edge—but he planned to keep his ears and eyes open for dissension.

As soon as Kasen and Brooker arrived at the Par-

1

adise Bar, they'd begin their whiskey toast in honor of Vida. Solomon would much rather have had Vida join them in a toast to victory over their Founder overlords, but she was floating into the void forever. It was so strange for her not to be there with them. Stranger still, to have Dextra Justice join their weekly get together at the Paradise Bar on Deck 17.

Solomon glanced over at her. She was laughing at one of Tavian's lame jokes about his dog. She seemed so comfortable and at ease among the Reachers. He was grateful she wasn't on his crew. If she had been, she wouldn't have been there to burst in on Edge's torture chamber and save his life. And he was sure she had saved him, because it was unlikely he would have made it out of that room alive.

But now Edge was gone and Mads and Alexandra still languished in lockdown. The crew and passengers of the SS *Challenge* had all survived the madness of the Founders' betrayal and were on their way to the Sideris Gate . . . all save one.

"So . . . what's the deal with Frankie, Tav?" Solomon asked.

"Frankie was a gift from my girlfriend. She said I had to get her aboard the SS *Challenge*, or she would break up with me."

Dextra smiled and touched Tavian's arm. "Did you break up with your girlfriend before you shipped out for the last time?"

Tavian's jaw tensed, and he looked down into his shot glass, swirling the liquid gold around and around.

Dextra frowned at Solomon. He shrugged in response, not actually knowing much about Tavian's love life beyond the outlandish stories of his legendary conquests among his Reacher crew.

An awkward silence ensued until Solomon asked, "Was she rejected for medical reasons?"

"No, she was all set to come with me. She had nearly passed all the tests they gave her. No, I . . . Well, I was on leave a couple years ago. I took her out on the town back at Georgia Tech. Went to a party at somebody's apartment. She looked like a goddess that night, I swear," Tavian said, in an almost pleading way, as if they didn't believe him.

Dextra nodded, encouraging him to continue. Solomon wasn't so sure he wanted to hear it.

"We drank a lot that night. Stumbled out of the party sometime past 2 a.m. laughing and talking too loudly. And then one of those roving terrorist gangs jumped us in an alleyway. The leader—had gang signs tattooed all over his bald head—he stabbed me in the stomach right off." Tavian lifted up his shirt to reveal an old scar carved into his otherwise unblemished skin.

"Francesca screamed over and over. I watched as they . . ." He couldn't finish, so he downed his shot instead.

Dextra pressed her hand to his forearm again. "They hurt her."

"They made me watch. And when they had finished . . . They slit her throat."

"I'm so sorry, Tavian," Dextra whispered, even though the noise in the bar was deafening by this point.

"I had no idea you went through that, Tavian. It wasn't in your file," Solomon said, not knowing what else he could say.

"I never told anyone. If I had, I'm sure those Founder bastards would have made it a reason to kick me off the *Challenge*."

"You renamed your dog, didn't you?" Solomon said.

Tavian nodded.

Dextra's smile was sad. "Frankie for Francesca."

Tavian's smile didn't reach his eyes, and he ran a hand roughly through his hair. "Anyway, I've done gone and had too much to drink, and Brooker and Kasen aren't even here yet."

"Yes, where are those two?" Solomon asked, glancing around the bar. He spotted Brooker meandering toward them, chatting with friends along the way. Unfortunately, he saw Kasen heading straight toward their table from the opposite direction, and the look on his face didn't bode well.

A deep scowl plastered on his face and a beer in his hand, Kasen strode with purpose and Solomon could tell he was already drunk since he could barely walk a straight line. Another patron accidently bumped into Kasen, who swung around to punch the guy out. Solomon stood up immediately and caught Kasen's fist in his palm before any damage was done.

Kasen continued his swing, pushing against Solomon's hand. His breath came heavily and his balance was off.

"Steady on," Solomon said.

"You bastard," Kasen yelled into his face.

Everyone in the bar went dead silent as they watched how this would play out.

"Vida's death is on your head."

"I know it." Solomon nodded. "I know—"

"She trusted you. *I* trusted you." Kasen's voice was hard as iron, and he wiped the remnants of beer and spittle from his mouth as he stared Solomon down.

"If I could trade her life for mine, I would do it."

"Kasen," Tavian said, rising unsteadily to his feet, "Let's you and I head to Deck 16. We can drink some more and—"

"No!" Kasen shouted. He shoved Solomon's chair aside, knocking it to the ground. Tavian came around the table to stand closer to Kasen while Brooker walked up behind him and made a movement to restrain him. But Solomon shook his head, motioning them both back.

"Kasen, I am your commander aboard this ship." Solomon kept his voice as low and even as he could. "Beyond this night, you must control your anger in a way you've never had to do before. I know Vida was always there to bring you back from the edge, and you've lost that—you've lost her. I know more than anyone else here how profound your loss is because I feel that same loss."

"You have no idea how I feel." Kasen's words were clipped with rage.

Solomon felt his own anger rising. "I do, because I loved her too. Always have, always will." And he meant it. It wasn't that long ago he had missed his chance with her back at university. But then he glanced at Dextra and remembered that life would go on because it had to. And because he had someone in his life worth living for.

"She told me. Told me you had a thing for her. Well, now it's all too late, isn't it?"

"Kasen, you want to take a shot at me? Then do it." Solomon stood, legs apart, waiting.

"Solomon, no," Dextra said, touching his arm, but he pressed her behind his back when he saw Kasen was going to take him up on his offer. He barely had the time to get Dextra behind him before Kasen's right hook landed a solid punch to his eye.

Solomon shook his head to clear the spinning lights in his vision, and squinted out at Kasen. The look in his eyes was one of belligerent and raging grief, and he was winding up for another shot. Solomon might have let him keep going but Tavian and Brooker weren't having any of that. They grabbed Kasen by the arms while he erupted into a slew of obscenities that would have made Vida slap him upside the head.

Dextra came around to examine his eye, but he stayed her hand as she reached up to his face.

"I'd let you keep going, Kasen, but this ship needs a functioning commander to get her through that wormhole."

"Coward!" Kasen shouted, straining against Brooker and Tavian. "I could kill you."

"Tavian and Brooker, take him back to his berth and make sure he sleeps this off."

"Boss, you gotta throw him in lockdown." Tavian spoke quietly, since all eyes were on them.

Solomon didn't respond. It wasn't like Tavian to defy his orders, but he understood. Solomon needed to assert his authority so that everyone looking on would see him as a strong leader willing and able to carry out justice. But there were other kinds of justice that had nothing to do with saving face.

Solomon just shook his head at Tavian and motioned them off. Kasen never let up on the obscenities as they walked him out, but his shouts were lost now in all the talking that erupted in every corner of the bar.

"Solomon, what the hell were you thinking?" Dextra was there again at his side, touching at his eyelid to inspect the damage. He waved her away, so he could pick up the chair Kasen had knocked over.

"It may sound strange, but the pain feels good."

"What on Earth are you talking about?" She shook her head in disgust. "You should have had him go straight to the lockdown. Protocol dictates it."

"Feels like a just punishment, you know? Like I gave Kasen a little bit more control of a situation that he has no control over."

"No, I don't."

Solomon wrinkled his nose, and groaned as his eye smarted. "I know how he feels, because I watched it all. I saw Commander Edge go after Vida from the safety of that Command conference room. And I couldn't do anything to stop it. That feeling . . . well, it's worse than getting punched in the face. Do you see?"

"Sometimes you just make no sense to me, Solomon."

"I know, but maybe when I take you on a real date, you can uncover all my secrets and figure me out."

She raised an eyebrow. "A date?"

"Anything against that in your eight-thousand page protocol manual?"

She rolled her eyes at him. "It isn't eight thousand pages, Commander Reach."

"Oh, so now it's commander again, is it?" He smiled and pulled her to him, kissing her right there in front of everyone. He closed his eyes, and listened to all the gasps swirling around him. "My name is Solomon Reach, Miss Justice," he murmured in her ear as he pulled back to look at the reddening glow on her pale cheeks. "And I'm pretty sure that just by existing, I render your rule book obsolete."

She was about to protest, but he clanked together their shot glasses loudly and jumped up on top of his chair.

"Crew of the SS *Challenge*, may I have your attention? I would like to ask you to raise your glasses in a toast to one of our fallen: Drive Ops Chief Vida Rosado."

Around the bar, crew members stood up and held their glasses high, including Dextra beside him. He smiled at her, and tears welled in her eyes.

"Vida lost her life in order to save all of us. I will tell you the truth—a truth I saw with my own eyes: it was Commander Dickson Edge who took her life in an attempt to save his own.

"But Vida would not want her death to divide us. Founder or Reacher crew made no matter to Vida. She died for all of you. So we honor her sacrifice today and always. Life will always be her legacy. To Vida!"

# THE GATE

"Solomon?"

"Hmm . . .?"

"Do it again."

Solomon, his heart still pounding from their recent exertions, opened one eye and squinted over at Dextra lying naked next to him in the semi-darkness.

"You better be good, or I'll drag you into the infamous G-Room and make love to you on the ceiling."

"Yes, please . . ." She tucked in her chin and looked up at him with those impossibly dark eyes that had always made him weak all over. "Come to think of it, you haven't taken me in there yet."

With a laugh, he pulled her beneath him and ran his hand from her thigh to her lips.

"You know the G-Room is off limits to anyone not involved in the human reproduction experiments, right?"

She grinned impishly and didn't say a word.

1

"Ah, I see. Since when are you a rule breaker, Mizz *Justice*?"

"Since I met you."

"No longer living up to your name, then," he teased, planting a playful kiss on her forehead and sliding over to lie closer to her.

"Ha ha," she said, her tone mocking. "Think I haven't heard that one before?"

He studied her face. "Is that why?"

"Why what?" She shivered and pulled the sheet up to hug her body.

"Why you went into the procedural group when the crews were mobilizing."

"No, it was my mother."

"What do you mean?" Solomon reached for her under the sheet, and rested his hand on her hip.

"My father was the one with the irreproachable honesty and ethics. I admired that most about him. Everyone did. But my mother was . . . well, you've seen her."

Solomon nodded. "Swayed by the lure of power more than anyone I've ever met—and that's saying something."

Dextra sighed and glanced away. "Yes, which is why I'm glad she's still in lockdown, so she can't be swayed by anyone else. But in any case, her lack of ethics made me all the more interested in the subject. Besides, I needed to make myself useful on this ship, or they would have kicked me out long ago."

"A good thing too. Who else would keep me on the straight and narrow?"

"Who, indeed?" She kissed his shoulder as she snuggled closer.

"At this juncture, I feel it necessary to point out I didn't turn into a criminal until your bosses went rogue."

"Excuses, excuses." Her laugh was soft, and the

smell of her lilac-scented hair filled his senses with memories of earth and flower gardens. As he threaded his fingers through her glossy black hair, he wondered if they had lilacs on the new planet.

Dextra turned his face toward her, toward the meager light afforded by his bedside table lamp.

"Solomon?" Concern etched deep into her face, as she ran gentle fingers across his cheek. "Why won't you have Kasen put in lockdown?"

Solomon sighed. "Not this again. Dextra, I told you. I owe him. He's lost the love of his life. And I was the only reason Vida was over on the Nautilus-11. Her death was my fault."

"That was six months ago, and he's still as volatile as ever. He isn't getting better. He has it out for you, which makes him a danger to everyone aboard this ship. And you're wrong, you know. Challenge Command was the only reason Vida Rosado was over there. Because *they* were the ones who breached protocol."

"It isn't that simple. I broke protocol, too—or don't you remember?"

"Sometimes the rules have to be broken in order to set things to rights—even if I don't like it. Chief Solomon Reach taught me that."

"It's Commander now, you know . . ." he murmured into her hair as he ran a hand over her bare stomach.

"You were still a chief back then, Commander."

He couldn't stop the smile from forming on his lips. "It always comes back to the greater good, doesn't it?"

She contemplated this pearl of wisdom, and then broke into a grin.

"The greater good dictates that you do that again."

"What?"

"That thing you did with your tongue earlier."

"Ah, yes. Pretty sure *that* one isn't in your rule book."

"The rules don't apply when I'm off duty."

That was all the invitation he needed. "This time, I'm starting from the top," he whispered into her ear, the touch of his tongue on her neck eliciting a gasp from her lips. He had to admit that for an awkward engineer, he was getting rather good at this.

Solomon's UiComm buzzed loudly. He let out a profound sigh and rolled his eyes at an exasperated Dextra.

"Ignore them," she said, biting at his chest. "It can wait."

He shook his head, knowing already what the call was about.

"Yes," he responded.

"Commander, the SS *Challenge* will be docking at Sideris Station in approximately one hour."

"All right, all right. Heading to the Command Bridge now."

"You owe me one, Commander Reach," Dextra whispered.

"I owe you my life, Mizz Justice." He leaned back down to kiss her one last time.

"Damn right you do."

"How about I make it up to you right now?"

"Yes?" she asked, brightening.

"Want to see Jupiter up close and personal with me?"

Her bright smile took a nosedive. "Depends."

Solomon raised an eyebrow. "On what?"

"Do you use that line on all the girls?"

He burst out with a loud laugh. "Definitely not. But now that you mention it . . . it is a very good line."

"Docking sequence initiated, Zeiss at Sideris Station on stand-by?" Solomon asked the Command Group at large, as he and Dextra walked side by side onto the SS *Challenge*'s Command Bridge. Everyone was at their stations, save for the noticeably absent Docking Commander Daniela Marcks, who had not made it aboard the ship in time.

During the six months of travel time between Nautilus-11 Space Station and Sideris Station, which orbited Jupiter from within Jupiter-Sun Lagrange Point 4, Solomon had tried to talk to her son, Zander Marcks, several times. But the boy had wanted nothing to do with him. Solomon didn't blame him. He, alone, was directly responsible for the loss of the boy's mother.

"Yes, Commander. We're ready for docking. Zeiss on the other hand . . ." The new docking commander, Fen Rhodes, flashed him a look of frustration and ran his hand up his ruddy face to rub his bloodshot eyes. Rhodes, a notoriously irritable American from somewhere out west, got along with only one person: XO Alexandra Justice. There was much speculation they had a relationship, but Solomon doubted it. Edge had always been her target: in the bed or on the Command Bridge, she had always sought his power.

"Is she or is she not ready for us?" Solomon pressed.

"Oh, she's ready all right. Rolling out the red carpet." The man had been stroking his dirty blond goatee and suddenly flung up his hands in disbelief. "Said she's been ready for three days and gave me an earful on proper docking procedure."

"Yes, well, that's protocol." Solomon smirked at Dextra.

Rhodes didn't respond; he whirled around in his chair, mumbled obscenities to himself, and got on with his work.

"Dextra, come take a look with me?" Solomon

asked, his voice softened by the very recent memory of her silky skin as she lay next to him in the dark.

She smiled as they descended down into the main brains of the operation, where they happened to have the best view in the house. The fenestellas here on the bridge were broad and substantially higher than those throughout the rest of the ship. There was also a great deal more radiation protection inside the glass.

Set up near one of them was a state-of-the-art telescope. The command crew had had it trained on Jupiter of late, considering how close they were to Sideris Station now.

"Here, take a look," Solomon said, motioning Dextra forward. "Jupiter is about two years out from where we are now in Sun-Jupiter L4."

"Wow," Dextra whispered with a gasp. He knew what she was seeing without having to look: the breathtaking view of a jaw-dropping Jupiter, its moons orbiting in a silent dance around its magnificent body for millennia.

"I know Jupiter's not full at this angle—maybe eighty percent at most—but at least you get to see the Great Red Spot."

She glanced up at him, wonder making her eyes nearly glow. "Thank you for showing me this."

Solomon grinned. "Did Jupiter win me a date?"

Dextra smirked and punched his arm. "No, but the moon Io did. She's gorgeous!"

"Excellent. I'll take you somewhere fancy. Would a new galaxy suit?"

She feigned a bored look. "Well enough, I suppose."

"You're tough to impress."

"I'm not going to make it easy for you, Commander."

He walked her over to the fenestella revealing a full view of the rapidly looming Sideris Station, which was attached to a massive asteroid. He hadn't been out to this remote station since before the ten other Asteria-class ships had left for the Andromeda galaxy. It had held up well thanks to Alarica Zeiss's iron-fisted management.

Reach Corp had built Sideris Station in stages, with the process taking several painstaking years of design and construction. They first lassoed the well-known 243 Ida Trojan asteroid along with its moon Dactyl and hauled them to a relatively uncluttered area of L4, the forward-most Lagrange Point in the Jupiter-Sun System.

They mined the iron from Dactyl and began hollowing out asteroid Ida to make room for some of the station's inner facilities as well as the quadrant 1 bay leading into the asteroid and toward the Sideris Gate, a concentric Ford-Svaiter mirror array at the far end of the asteroid's quadrant 2.

From this vantage point of two-dozen kilometers out from the station, they could see the various towers constructed into the Ida's surface, most of them research facilities built for Founder astrophysicists to study the Sideris Cavum among other things. Those Founders were a galaxy away now. Only the station's eccentric commander remained.

"You've met Commander Alarica Zeiss?" Dextra asked.

"Yes, a few times. She runs a tight ship, so to speak. You'll meet her soon. Best advice? Try not to piss her off."

"Self-sufficient, then?"

"That's one way of putting it."

"You lot have everything in order?" an annoyed Alarica Zeiss said after the Sideris Station's Main Hatch slid open.

Solomon smiled. "Commander."

The commander tucked her jet-black bobbed hair behind her ear and attempted a smile. It didn't work out. She had been out here for two years on her own with minimal systems running and rare communication to and from Nautilus-11. She had probably forgotten how to smile.

"This better be your entire boarding party." Zeiss glanced sternly at Dextra, and the four other Founder crew members who stood behind them, waiting to enter. "I don't want a bunch of idiots running about making messes on my station."

He was itching to remind her they would shortly be leaving this station—and the galaxy for that matter—forever, and it wouldn't matter, but he kept his mouth shut.

"Yes, indeed. Any issues with the station we need to be aware of before we open the gate, Commander Zeiss?"

"Does it look like it?" She scrunched up her face, and slid her boxy glasses up the bridge of her nose with her middle finger and stuck her thumb in the air indicating the spotless corridor behind her. She narrowed her eyes at him. "I don't recognize any of you. Where is Commander Edge, eh?"

"We had some issues at the undocking. Commander Edge is dead."

She took in this information without flinching. "Didn't like that bastard anyway."

Solomon couldn't help his smile. "We have that in common."

She took one more long moment to look him over, and then waved them on to follow her.

"You better not be tracking any Earth microbes onto my station floors. Wipe your boots on the mat."

Solomon glanced down, already knowing what it would say: "Touch me. I want to feel dirty."

He exchanged a stifled laugh with Dextra and followed Zeiss deeper into the station. Sideris had a darker feel to it than its counterpart, Nautilus-11, due to the mined iron making up the majority of its bulkheads and floors. That rough-hewn aesthetic was carried into the furniture of the living quarters and mess hall, which made the station the perfect environment for Zeiss but not so much for the rest of the space population who inevitably craved a more Earth-like feel. Rarely had anyone volunteered for a rotation out here, even to perform the fascinating experiments needed to develop the wormhole. Of the hundreds employed here over the years, almost all were assigned begrudgingly.

"James, Hanna, and Feo here will go over the cargo logistics with you. As I understand it, we'll be picking up some raw materials from you for our temporary housing needs on the new planet, correct?"

"Yes, that's correct. Once done, we can leave. I've shut down the majority of the station already."

"Excellent. And do you have baggage of your own we can attend to for you?"

Zeiss gave him the evil eye. "One bag. I'll handle it."

"Understood."

"Hey, where has the drive ops chief been?" Zeiss asked, glancing back at Solomon. "She get thrown in lockdown for mouthing up to Challenge Command? Been trying to message her for days."

He was hoping not to think about Vida on the day when he'd be leaving her for all time. He had almost succeeded.

When he couldn't answer, Dextra didn't sugarcoat it. "Commander Edge killed her."

This did shock Zeiss, who, for the first time since

Solomon had met her, failed to find a clever come-back. She stared off through a fenestella across a lounge filled with empty iron chairs.

When Zeiss did finally speak, her only words were: "She was the only tolerable person in the Solar System. It's a good thing Edge is already dead."

# THE JUMP

"Have you said your goodbyes?" Dextra waved a hand toward the back corner of the Command Bridge, where the window still looked back on Earth, now a mere speck of light from their vantage point in Jupiter's orbit.

They awaited final word from Docking Commander Rhodes that the quantum computer aboard the SS *Challenge* had successfully calculated the exit point through the Sideris Cavum. Their destination was just outside the orbit of Tenebra, the third planet out in the Paradisi Planetary System.

Solomon shook his head.

She squeezed his arm, and whispered, "Go."

He didn't want to, but he got up from his commander chair feeling suddenly like a fraud. How could they have made him commander when he had so much blood on his hands?

When he looked out the fenestella, the glimpse of Earth—a tiny but bright pinprick of light from this distance—made him think first of his sister, Nisolda. Could she still be alive after all these years? He hoped she was no longer in any pain, that the doctors had found a cure, that she could live a little while longer out in the last of the sunshine before the world went dark.

Tears touched his eyes, and he rubbed them away viciously. "I'm sorry, Nisolda. I'm sorry I couldn't save you."

Vida's smiling face came to him, then. Her punching Kasen's arm after he spouted out a ridiculous joke. Her teasing Tavian about his love life. Her calling him Sol when he wouldn't let anyone else get away with that. What would he do without her? She was the one who saved him—saved them all. And he left her there to die, to float off into the darkness without even an attempt to save her life. He could have done it. He had the code to stop it.

His conscience argued that entering the abort code would open the door to Challenge Command attempting to get the Serica group aboard again. He had no choice. He touched the glass with his palm. Cold seeped into his skin, making him shiver. No, there was always a choice. He forced himself to picture her clearly in his mind, to picture the children, the grandmothers, the old men crying out against him as the SS *Challenge* pulled away from them and left them to die. As *he* left them to die. He pictured Mads Graversen's wife, and he felt the tears in her eyes stream down his own cheeks.

"Please forgive me because I cannot forgive myself."

Dextra touched his shoulder. "It's time."

All the noises on the bridge faded back in: Rhodes's grating voice calling out commands, the chatter among the crew, the ever-present buzz of the HVAC systems within the bulkheads surrounding them.

He nodded, and rubbed the moisture from his eyes. As they walked back, she squeezed his arm.

"Tell me about what's going to happen step by step. I'm not going to lie. I'm terrified."

He nodded and tried to offer her an encouraging smile, knowing she was also attempting to take his mind off Vida and his sister.

"All right. Strap in and make sure you're secured." He did the same, and nodded to Navigator Jonasa Keyes and Docking Commander Rhodes.

"Commander Reach, Ada has nearly completed her calculations," Navigator Keyes said.

"ETA?"

"T minus five minutes."

He checked the overhead HUD screen lighting up the Bridge's main fenestella. All looked well.

Solomon switched his comms to all-ship. Most of the skeleton crew had been strapped into chairs in specialized compartments in the Operation Sector already. Everyone else—around seven thousand crew and passengers—had been secured in the cryo chambers long ago. He cleared his throat to make the transit announcement.

"This is Commander Solomon Reach with the final announcement to all skeleton crew members of the SS *Challenge*. Sideris Cavum transit begins in 5 minutes. Ensure you are strapped in and secure in your seats. It is an honor and a privilege to lead you through Sideris Gate and on to the Andromeda galaxy. Our first stop will be the planet Tenebra, and then we will head on to our new home: the planet New Eden. Godspeed to us all."

"Solomon, who is Ada . . .?" Dextra asked.

"The crew's nickname for the quantum computer we have aboard. Named for—"

"Ada Lovelace, the first computer programmer." Dextra looked pleased.

"Yes. So, once Ada's calculations are done, we'll accept her recommendation for an exit destination, and Keyes will lock those numbers in. After that, the ship will take off for the asteroid, traveling at speed to ensure we both enter and exit the gate with enough time to make it through. The transit time via the Cavum is only twelve minutes."

Dextra studied his face. "What happens if we don't make it through the gate?"

"Are you sure you want to know?"

She seemed to hesitate, and then nodded.

"T minus three minutes to launch, Commander," Keyes said.

"Final systems check," Solomon called out loudly.

A series of shouts erupted at short intervals from every crew member in the room as they all indicated they were a go for launch.

"Deploy SECASM, Rhodes."

"Deploying SECASM, Commander."

"The SECASM aboard our ship houses a mirror array," he explained to Dextra, "which you will see deploying out in front of our nose shortly. That mirror will lock onto the two static mirrors attached at the far end of the asteroid. That will deploy enough negative energy to allow the ship space to travel through the gate's force field."

In seconds, the view out of the fenestella was solely taken up with the SECASM's nanosilc mirror, which began to balloon out in front of them, taking shape.

"And if that doesn't happen?"

"The wormhole won't open, and we'll slam into the gate, shattering the mirrors."

"But we're going to make it, because you've built us a strong ship."

He smiled, but pride in his accomplishment eluded him.

"We'll make it because we must," was all he could muster. His promise sounded hollow even to own his ears. What did he know? Certainly, the precision of the design was on his head, but beyond the ship lay the vacuum of space and the unknowable. So many things could go wrong. Things he could never dream up in a thousand years.

"T minus one minute to launch, sir," Rhodes said.

"How long until SECASM is fully deployed?" Solomon asked Rhodes.

"We're cutting it close, sir," he replied, wiping sweat off his forehead.

"How long, Rhodes?" Solomon repeated.

"Sixty more seconds."

"Will our launch impede the SECASM's full deployment?" he questioned the docking commander.

"I'm not certain, sir."

"Launch initiating in ten . . . nine . . ." Keyes yelled out, her pale, tense fingers hovering above her keyboard, waiting for any eventuality.

Solomon flipped open the abort switch on the panel in front of him. He glanced at Dextra, who was gripping her armrests with white knuckles.

"It's going to be all right," he reassured her.

". . . Five . . . four . . ."

Dextra's breathing quickened but she tried to smile.

"Keyes and Rhodes, prepare for launch abort sequence if needed."

"Yes, sir," Rhodes said, as Keyes continued her countdown.

"Three . . . two . . . one. Launch has commenced."

A shudder coursed throughout the bridge. Solomon felt the ship's Cav Drive engage at seventy-five percent power.

"Ada is operating optimally, sir," Docking Commander Rhodes said.

"Keyes, final word on launch?" Solomon had his finger hovering over the red abort key, waiting.

"Hold please, sir," Keyes said.

For several agonizing seconds they all waited as

they watched the SECASM begin to form the concentric ring array. The center ring opened up, and suddenly they had a myopic view ahead toward the Sideris Gate. The massive sliding door behind the gate was already fully opened, and they had already entered the asteroid, their destination loomed large in the fenestella.

"Keyes, respond now."

"I'm sorry, sir, we have passed the safe abort stage."

"Report, Keyes," Solomon nearly shouted as he abandoned the abort key and held tight to his chair.

"Entering quadrant 2," Rhodes said.

Another second of interminable waiting, and then Keyes uttered the words they had all been waiting for.

"SECASM fully deployed. Wormhole expansion has commenced."

And indeed, the wormhole field began to morph its shape, its colors shifting wildly between the mirrors. They caught glimpses of the Sideris Cavum sphere expanding beyond the gate outside of the asteroid. Stars from inside shown out like pinpricks of light, as they rushed ever closer.

Seconds later, the lights flashed brilliantly, and the SS *Challenge* left the Milky Way galaxy behind. The Sideris Gate sucked them up into what felt to Solomon like a madness, a waking dream. His body shook in places he never knew existed. The only words in his mind as they screamed through space-time were "don't blink, don't blink, don't blink."

And he didn't. He grabbed hold of Dextra's hand across the divide and watched worlds and suns pass by in light so brilliant it blinded him. Whole galaxies whirled past, seemingly expanding and contracting in refracted light as he gazed in both awe and amazement. Time was passing in front of his eyes, years, centuries . . . it was unfathomable as they moved like gods through the gas clouds of new stars and passed supernovas burning in the distance.

The shaking moved into his teeth, jangling his head so it felt like it would burst. He wanted to ask Dextra if she was okay, but he found he couldn't form words. Somehow their hands had broken apart, and they were holding onto their own chairs once more.

Beyond the brightness and the swirling greens and pinks and oranges of new star formations, Solomon gasped at the shape of something he could not comprehend. It was a flash of grey speeding toward them like a train on a track. What was it?

"My God . . ." he whispered only to himself as it passed by. Another ship!

The SS *Challenge* shuddered violently, and warning alarms sounded everywhere.

"We've had a collision," the feeble voice of the navigator rang out. "Ada course correcting. Sixty seconds to cavum exit!"

He didn't understand what he had seen. The ship was there, and then it wasn't. It looked identical to the SS *Challenge*, but how was that even possible? Could the Founders have sent another ship back through? Was it a mirage, a trick of the eye? And yet they had hit something. Something had gone wrong. Solomon glanced wildly at the HUD, trying to make sense of the numbers Ada was spitting out.

The ship veered toward the edge of the wormhole. If they hit the threshold, the ship would disintegrate.

"Course correct, course correct!" Solomon heard himself shouting through the maddening alarms.

"Ada correcting," Keyes shouted back, as she struggled to keep her fingers from shaking off her keyboard.

With quantum precision, Ada began to turn the SS *Challenge* toward the center of the cavum. But it was as if he could feel Ada fighting gravity and the negative energy within the wormhole. The ship shook from the immense forces.

And then Ada's calculations failed to hold their course. The ship convulsed, and Solomon felt a nauseating centrifugal G-force threatening to rip him to pieces as the massive ship began to spin.

"Five seconds to exit!" Keyes yelled out, as the ship spun out of control, and the SECASM began to warp and collapse.

The stars began to take on a familiar, solid shapes, and the passing galaxies disappeared.

"Exit achieved. Programming Ada to decrease speed."

The ship's spinning slowed to a stop and her shudderings quieted. Solomon gazed out into the view of billions stars in a galaxy he had never seen before: Andromeda.

He glanced at Dextra, but her head lolled against her chest. As he unstrapped himself from his chair, he shouted out orders to the crew.

"Keyes and Rhodes, complete a full crew and systems check immediately. Report any anomalies. Report also on the extent of the SECASM damage."

"Yes, Commander," came a chorus of replies.

Solomon ripped the straps away from his body, and knelt at Dextra's side, gently shaking her shoulder to try and rouse her.

"Dextra, wake up."

She jerked awake, and shrank back, not immediately understanding her surroundings.

"What happened? Did we make it?"

"Yes, we're through. You must have passed out partway through."

"Yes, I—I saw something. I swear I saw—"

"A ship."

"Yes, you too? How could it be?"

"I don't know anything yet. We're in the middle

of a systems check. Will you be all right?"

Dextra ran a hand over her face and ripped off her uniform cap so she could clutch at her head. "That was hell."

"Yes, it was." He contracted and relaxed his neck muscles, trying to release the effects of the forces on his body. He felt impossibly tired.

"Commander, extensive damage to the SECASM. Full nanosilc repair team required."

"Are you able to retract the SECASM manually?"

"Unknown at this time, sir. Recommend space-walk team be assembled before any attempts to retract."

"Understood. Bridge crew check complete? Is everyone all right in here?"

Several voices rang out that they had survived the transit, though a little worse for wear.

"Keyes, turn this ship around and line up fifty kilometers from the cavum's exit. I want a more thorough systems check before we go anywhere."

"Fifty kilometers from exit, confirmed."

Solomon made the rounds to check in with each of the bridge crew as well as make a general ship-wide announcement to the skeleton crew and med bay crew scheduled to be awake during the journey requesting any damages or injuries be reported immediately. He hoped they made it all through safely.

"Commander Reach, we have an . . . anomaly."

Solomon looked up from one of the modules to find a group had gathered at the main fenestella.

"What is it?" he asked as he strode over.

"You'll have to see this for yourself," Dextra did not take her eyes off whatever lay outside.

When he saw it, he wondered if it, too, were a mirage, like the strange ship in the cavum.

"Impossible," he whispered.

But there it was: a space station, not unlike Sideris

Station in what was now the next galaxy over.

"It is, but we can all see it," Rhodes said. "Like we all saw that other ship."

"It could have been a mirage," Solomon said. "Strange things can happen with negative energy. Even Ada here doesn't have it all figured out."

"But that doesn't explain this space station," Keyes said, shaking her head. "There is no way in hell the Founders could have built a station out here in two years. It would take that long just to transport materials out this far."

Solomon ran a hand down his face, trying to think. "Rhodes, try to make contact with that station."

"Yes, sir," came his reply, and everyone on the bridge waited in silence as Rhodes worked the comms on his module.

"Sir?" Rhodes turned and his expression was unreadable.

"Rhodes?" Solomon said, feeling uneasy.

"The time," was all he would say.

Solomon frowned and looked at the HUD. Nothing seemed amiss at first glance.

"What about it? The time is right. Only about twelve minutes has passed."

"I pinged the station and they responded."

"Put it up on the main HUD, Rhodes."

The message read simply: "Communication acknowledged. State your business in Paradisi Planetary System immediately."

"Look at the time stamp on the message, sir," Rhodes said quietly.

"What do you—?" Solomon did a double take. The year read 2244, not 2094. He frowned again and glanced at Dextra whose face mirrored the churning confusion settling in the pit of his stomach.

"Ada must have gotten damaged or the transit screwed up her data streams," Dextra said.

"Hmm . . ." Solomon rubbed at the back of his neck, thinking. "Keyes, is Ada throwing out any errors?"

"No, none that I can see."

"Double check it."

"Ada's data is accurate, sir."

"A timeslip?" Solomon ventured, not believing the words coming out of his mouth.

"That's scientifically impossible . . ." Dextra murmured. "Isn't it?"

"We're in Andromeda galaxy where time could move sideways for all we know . . ., Solomon whispered to her as he watched the fear flickering across her face. He pulled her to him but couldn't take his eyes off the space station that looked way too similar to Sideris Station, right down to the asteroid it was attached to.

"I have a bad feeling about this," Solomon whispered to Dextra, unable to help voicing his own fear. "A very bad feeling."

# JANUA MUTINY

Book 2 in the
Paradisi Exodus Series
is Available Now!

# More Stories in the Paradisi Chronicles Universe

You can also check out these other fantastic books and stories set in the Paradisi Chronicles Universe. Each story reveals more details about 200 years of history in the Paradisi Chronicles. The universe is yours to explore!

## David Bruns

* "A Touch of Deceit," *Chronicle Worlds: Paradisi*

## Andy Bunch

* *Saber and Science, Tenebra Triangle Series,* Book One

## Claire Davon

* "Solar Crossroads," *Chronicle Worlds: Paradisi*

## Lindsay Edmunds

"Happiness," *Chronicle Worlds: Paradisi*

## Tristan Hunter

* "The Fall of Seren," *Chronicle Worlds: Paradisi*
* *Sideris Gate: Paradisi Exodus*, Book One
* *Janua Mutiny: Paradisi Exodus*, Book Two
* "PlanetFall," Short Story

## Joseph Robert Lewis

* "Truth is Stranger," *Chronicle Worlds: Paradisi*

## Louisa Locke

* "Aelwyd: Home," *Chronicle Worlds: Paradisi*
* *Between Mountain and Sea: Caelestis Series*, Book One
*Under Two Moons: Caelestis Series* Book Two
*Through Ddaera's Touch: Caelestis Series*, Book Three
*The Stars are Red Tonight: Canistro Series,* Book One

## S. J. Mayesky

"Unbreakable," *Chronicle Worlds: Paradisi*

## Roselyn McFarland

*Light the Way: Love's Light*, Book One

## Andy McKell

* *Faces of Janus,* Book One
* *Janus Final Flight*, Book Two
* *Janus Challenge,* Book Three
* *Janus Arrival*, Book Four

## Bill Patterson

"God's Sandbox: A Paradisi Short"
*Live Wire: A Paradisi Novella*
* *Eye of the Needle: A Paradisi Short*
* *Nuking the Noomies: A Paradisi Short*

## Felix Savage

"Down and Out in Caprinet"
*Chronicle Worlds: Paradisi*

## Auburn Seal

*First Watch: A Watcher Bay Adventure*

## Jeff Seymour

"Cold, Angels, Paradise"
*Chronicle Worlds: Paradisi*

## Sarah Woodbury

*Erase Me Not*

## Rey Wright

*The Stars are Red Tonight*: *Canistro Series*, Book One

\* "Aderyn Tanllynd," in *Chronicle Worlds: Paradisi*

Go to ParadisiChronicles.wordpress.com to find details on these works. Those with asterisks (\*) are of special interest to those of you who have read my series because they focus on Reachers or events relevant to Reach Corp.

# ABOUT THE AUTHOR

Tristan Hunter is the pen name of *USA Today* and *Wall Street Journal* Bestselling Author Cheri Lasota. is an author, editor, and designer. Tristan helped found the Paradisi Chronicles, a massive open-source Sci-Fi universe set on the fictional planet, New Eden. Her *Paradisi Exodus* series focuses on the early years of the human exodus from Earth to the new planet.

## Thank You!

If you enjoyed reading *Sideris Gate*, Tristan would love for you to review the book. Thank you for reading.

## TristanHunter.com

# ACKNOWLEDGEMENTS

To Paradisi Chronicles Authors Bill Patterson and Andy McKell for your generosity and advice.

To the Paradisi Chronicles founding members:

Ashley Angelly, Andy Bunch, Louisa Locke, Roslyn McFarland, Auburn Seal, and Sarah Woodbury. It is an honor to be in your company!

www.ingramcontent.com/pod-product-compliance
Lightning Source LLC
Chambersburg PA
CBHW060532180626
46817CB00002B/533